FOREWORD

PUNK SHOWS IN EL PASO WERE always magical for me. As an awkward and always out of place high school freshman It was liberating, truly, to be with people who didn't feel as though they had to follow the conventions of fashion or music, people who had somehow escaped the pressure to conform or fit in. And to see kids my age or younger (like Cedric Bixler-Zavala, who at all of fifteen or sixteen years old was fronting the phenomenal Phantasmagoria) realizing their creative power—starting bands, writing songs, playing shows, founding labels, and booking tours—changed what I thought was possible in my own life.

It was at these shows (very often at the peripatetic Sound Seas, which sometimes would come together in a warehouse on Texas Avenue and other times would be found adjacent to an auto repair shop on east Montana Street. Once it was in Joey's living room, and the last time I saw a show at Sound Seas it was in Northeast El Paso on Dyer Street) that I got to know the people who would be friends for life, many of us banding together to write, record, and ultimately tour our music, bringing our version of El Paso punk rock to as many places as would have us. We played living rooms, basements, bars, and clubs in El Paso and across North America, from Auburn, Alabama, to Calgary, Canada and many a place in between.

I am fortunate to have grown up here and also to have seen so much of the rest of the country. It makes me realize how special the music is that came out of this place. Especially in the pre-internet era, when the influences were found in the bands that made the effort to come here and the records we bought at the Headstand. El Paso and Juárez, so close to each other but so distant from the usual centers of power (political, cultural, economic, or otherwise), produced a sound and style that I've never found anywhere else. Something extraordinary was able to grow and bloom and make the world a better place for it.

Beto O'Rourke

ELPAS★

ELPASO★

A PUNK STORY

BENJAMIN VILLEGAS

TRANSLATED FROM THE SPANISH BY JAY NODEN

FOREWORD BY BETO O'ROURKE

DEEP VELLUM PUBLISHING

DALLAS, TEXAS

Deep Vellum Publishing
3000 Commerce St., Dallas, Texas 75226
deepvellum.org · @deepvellum

Deep Vellum is a 501c3 nonprofit literary arts organization
founded in 2013 with the mission to bring
the world into conversation through literature.

Support for this publication has been provided in part by the City of Dallas
Office of Arts and Culture's ArtsActivate program:

ISBNs: 978-1-64605-061-1 (paperback) | 978-1-64605-062-8 (ebook)

LIBRARY OF CONGRESS CONTROL NUMBER: 2021934797

Cover Design by Benjamin Villegas
Interior Layout and Typesetting by KGT

PRINTED IN THE UNITED STATES OF AMERICA

To Lupe and Teresa

Punk is not really a style of music. It was more like a state of mind.

—Mike Watt

ELPAS★

A PUNK STORY

INTRO

MY RELATIONSHIP WITH LITERATURE HAS ALWAYS been a strange one. At school, as I grew up, books became worryingly scant on illustrations. At the tender age of three or four, drawings were strewn across all the pages of the stories I used to read, but with each passing academic year the space for writing gained ground over the visuals. I remember, in year five, opening a book and finding the bodies of text had finally sent the pictures into exile. The illustrations had gone, and they weren't coming back. This was hard for me to accept. Disappointing, you might say. "The pictures have all gone," I thought to myself and decided to resort to my dad's comics to keep up my dose of illustrated literature. From that moment on, I began to live by a mantra that, for some reason, stood the test of time: "I don't read novels. I don't like them. I don't know how to read them." I'm sorry to say, you're actually reading a book written by someone who was coming out with this kind of nonsense until well into his thirties!

Lucky for my brain, music biographies soon appeared, and I fell in love with magazines and their format. I liked reading, there was no doubt about it, but wading through fiction was a nightmare for me. I found it a whole lot easier to "listen" to a writer explaining how a particular guitar had reached the top of the sales lists. The interviews that backed up the prose and their techniques for gathering information were astounding. Before I knew what was happening, I'd begun to idolize the music biographer Michael Azerrad, whose book *Come as You Are: The Story of Nirvana* became a bestseller.

It made life kind of tricky for me, not having read any of the books that were the source of so many conversations with people I respected and with whom I enjoyed having a sense of connection. What bothered me most was the prospect that I was never going to read them, as I didn't know how. I felt like I was suffering from a kind of incurable literary disorder, which had left me unable to consume fiction. I became a hardened film buff and expanded my profile as a comic fan with French classics and the best comics from the American underground. Tarantino, Moebius, and Daniel Clowes were my dealers, and their drug was shot straight into my veins, satisfying my need for fiction.

I had to wait for love to turn up, as the most predictable end to any story, before my illness was cured and before it was too late. I fell head over heels for a journalist who was studying comparative literature and who explained to me and my eleven-year-old self that there is life beyond bestsellers, curing my phobia of unillustrated books. I discovered that there was a kind of novel that was perfect for me. That it was simply a question of finding it and that, to find it, I had to read novels. From then on, that journalist became my fiction dealer of choice. I will never be able to thank her enough for curing my incurable idiocy disorder. I now delight in reading novels.

Cordoba. May. Year 2014. Something is happening. Two books have collided. A violent, head-on crash that will be sending shockwaves through me forever. On one side of the ring and weighing in at sixty-four pages, my first experience as an author: *Smells like Post-Teen Spirit*. Applause. In the other corner, weighing in at 560 pages, the champion of the music literature heavyweights: *Our Band Could Be*

Your Life: Scenes from the American Indie Underground, 1981–1991 by Michael Azerrad. The stadium is going wild. The bell rings and my book is knocked flat in the first round. Fight over.

In the middle of the promotion campaign for my first attempt, Marga, Antonio, and Pedro aired the possibility of writing a second book, which could be accompanied by a CD—a book-album, they said. They had published one once, and their experience as editors had been a positive one. I liked the idea. I was immersed in reading Azerrad's American indie chronicle when Daniel Álvarez and ELPASO turned up on the scene, and I knew immediately that the book-album had to be a music biography. The genre that kept me afloat in my years of literary abstinence.

Daniel had formed part of a Chicano proto-grunge group in the Texan city of El Paso in the late eighties. He told me that, without actually being one of the musicians, he felt like a full-fledged band member. He started off playing the drums and was also the official photographer-designer-driver of ELPASO, which was the name of the band. ELPASO, a band from El Paso, Texas. The guy had left the United States in 1990 and had been living for twenty years in Andalusia. The Andalusian Chicano. When I met him, his mom had just died and one of his sisters, Rosa, had come to visit him in Spain to patch things up with her brother. Daniel hadn't been to the matriarch's funeral, and his sister wanted to see him and finally put an end to this estrangement, which had kept them apart for so long. Rosa turned up in Cordoba with a suitcase that Daniel had left in his bedroom twenty-four years before. When he opened it, he came face-to-face with his Texas past. It was like in those scenes from *Pulp Fiction* when Marcellus Wallace's briefcase bathes the face of whoever opens it in a golden glow.

In that suitcase were old flyers, shirts, stickers, a heap of photos, and homemade videos of the band; letters that he and Ricardo (the ELPASO singer and guitarist) had exchanged during their time at university; and, especially, a few tapes containing the only two recordings the band had made between 1985 and 1990: an EP with Spanish versions of Hüsker Dü, Minutemen, Mission of Burma, and The Judy's, which they self-released in 1988, and the album that ELPASO recorded in 1990, which was never released. Daniel had been in charge of designing the album art and to do so had gathered together all the graphic and audiovisual material on the Texan four-piece band for the release of what would have been their first LP.

With Daniel as a point of reference, I began investigating this band that had never done anything anyone would remember. A group of losers singing punk rock in Spanish in a border town in the south of the United States, far from the happening scenes of Los Angeles and Austin. As I discovered more and more things about the history of ELPASO, I found more and more parallels with my own frustrated career as a rock musician. The heady excitement of a first rehearsal or the arduous task of finding a definitive name for the project was, in some ways, the same in the early eighties in Texas as it was in the late nineties in suburban Barcelona. The musical chronicle of ELPASO was just like mine and that of so many other bands that crashed and burned before they had the chance to shine.

To delve deeper into the context they emerged from, I traveled twice to Texas (March 2015 and May 2016) and, with the help of Jordi, Eloi, and Lou, I was able to interview a great number of people who helped fuel the punk movement in El Paso between 1979 and 1994. The city, the scene, and the people I came to know made me see things from a different perspective. ELPASO was no longer a band of losers and instead became a cursed band of visionaries whose unfortunate fate was to be kept inside the cave. I realized that without this kind of band, popular music as we know it today would not exist. To enjoy the part at the top of a pyramid, you need a vast base to support it. I realized how critical it was for me to tell this story.

History's greatest and most legendary bands do not even account for one percent of the total bands that are put together every day in every far-flung corner of the earth. That's why I decided to write the biography of a band that no one knows, because in their songs, their hardships, and their lack of glamour are the foundations of the incredible history of rock 'n' roll.

"Welcome to the Caverns of Sonora. Welcome to the underground experience."

First Movement
(1979–1985)

I-10, HEADING FOR TEXAS

WHAT THE HELL IS THE AMERICAN DREAM? Fiction and popular culture tell us the US is a place full of opportunities, a land of freedom, and that attaining the American dream is relatively straightforward: it's enough to want it and work hard. For the Álvarez family, originally from Guadalajara, Mexico, it began when they crossed the border in the 1940s. First Emiliano for work (through the Mexican Farm Labor Program) and then Rosario, illegally. Work, stability, and progress—that was their American dream.

Most workers who traveled to the US would do so, essentially, to work in the fields, the kind of work that *gringos* refused to do because it was too hard and precarious. Typical. Only a few lucky ones would travel there to work on the railways. That was the case for Emiliano. Ambitious and charismatic, Daniel's father was able to make friends and learn quickly. Shortly after arriving in California he was already an important member of the team and immediately began to rise in the ranks to positions of greater responsibility. In 1946, Rosario and Emiliano got married in a small church in Los Angeles. Days before their second anniversary Gustavo was born, the first US citizen of the Álvarez clan.

The fifties brought with them Gustavo's two younger sisters and his father's definitive job move. The construction of Interstate 10, which would connect the south of the United States, meant the

Álvarez family were settled in the US once and for good. Emiliano began to work on the highway, and the family moved to Oxnard, California, where Daniel Álvarez was born in 1962.

The age difference with his brother and sisters was thirteen, eleven, and ten years, so Danny got thoroughly spoiled at home. His older siblings would take him to the movies, concerts, and burger joints, his outgoing and sociable nature taking shape in a prosperous and happy family environment.

In 1965, the clan moved to Phoenix, following the route of the interstate, and lived there until 1968. They then went on to Tucson, Houston, San Antonio, and finally El Paso in 1979. Five houses and five schools in fourteen years.

Daniel's childhood was spent switching from one friend to another. He learned to fit in quickly. His siblings, one by one, stopped off en route, each at a different university. He went from being "the kid brother always hanging around with the older kids" to seeing them only on set dates. Gustavo was in the habit of writing more often than the girls, and whenever he came home, he brought with him an album he'd discovered that his little brother just had to have. This cassette collection began with the Beatles' *Sgt. Pepper's Lonely Hearts Club Band* and was blown to pieces with *Ramones,* the debut album by the band of the same name, the group that introduced the youngest Álvarez to the world of punk.

The generation gap between Daniel and his parents became more apparent and problematic each time one of his siblings left home for university. As a child, it would drive Daniel into a fit of rage when Emiliano would get mistaken for his grandfather. "He's not my grandfather! He's my dad!!" he'd shout in protest. But on turning seventeen and having recently settled in El Paso, the differences between them made Emiliano look more like his great-grandfather. Daniel was always of the belief that fate and I-10 took them to El Paso for a reason. Even though it took him seventeen years to work it out.

TOO MEXICAN FOR THE AMERICANS, TOO AMERICAN FOR THE MEXICANS

EVERYONE SAW CONSTANCE EVANS AS A black sheep. She had been to Ciudad Juárez a thousand times as a kid. Her father worked for a company that sold flour, and his clients were all on the other side of the border. In the fifties, Juárez was a magical place. For Constance it was like being in Las Vegas. After growing up, she often crossed the border. She would spend the night listening to live music and in bed with whichever lucky guy she happened to pick up. Connie was a kind of American version of Brigitte Bardot. In one of her nights of debauchery she met Felipe, a good-looking kid with a perfect hairpiece who had also been to see *Los Reyes del Twist*.

Felipe Salazar was a cook from Mexico City who had gone to Juárez to work in a bar run by one of his uncles. He'd been on the border for just three days. As a child he had discovered American culture through the music of Elvis Presley, and on a previous visit to see his cousins in Juárez, he saw Bobby Fuller at a club in El Paso. Texan music fascinated him, and he promised himself that one day he would cross the line and become an American.

Thanks to Buddy Holly he discovered Ritchie Valens and got interested in rock in Spanish, switching from the likes of Johnny Cash and Chuck Berry to Mexican classics like *Los Griegos'* first album.

Before he knew what was happening, a drunken Connie sidled

up to him and said, in English, something along the lines of: "I would fuck you right now." The eyes of the guy next to him nearly popped out of their sockets. Felipe looked at him and asked, "She just told me she wanted to fuck me, right?" The guy burst out laughing and answered, "Right now, my brother! She wants to do it right now!" His English wasn't great, but, hell, there are some things you don't need to speak the same language for.

They spent the night in the back room of Felipe's uncle's bar. A few months later they were married and had moved to El Paso. He began working in the Jalisco Café, and she whiled away the time spending the money she'd inherited from her parents. Those were truly crazy months, in which Connie seemed to shed her reputation as a black sheep. Without giving it much thought, they had Ricardo. His name was given in homage to Ricardo "Ritchie" Valens, and it could be said that the baby was the fruit of the love they felt for each other. Until then at least.

Immediately after Ricardo was born the fights began between the couple, two people who, although parents to the same child, had really only just met and whose relationship was based on spontaneity, depravity, and wild sex.

She soon began to go out alone again and have her own fun. One night he got home to find a couple of guys in bed while Ricardo was sleeping. He threw them out, screaming bloody murder down the sights of a double-barrelled shotgun. Constance Evans and Felipe Salazar never said another word to each other. On March 6, 1965, Connie left the marital home and was never seen again.

Felipe and the little Ricardo moved to El Segundo Barrio. "Your mom's left, kid, and I don't think we'll be seeing her again."

✳

Ricardo grew up with the feeling of not quite fitting in, the son of a chef who rejected his Mexican roots and an American mom who'd abandoned him when he was little more than two years old. Unlike everyone else in the neighborhood, he didn't speak fluent Spanish and lacked the roots that would help him understand where he came from. His grandparents on his mother's side were dead, and it had been years since his Mexican family had spoken to his father. Too Mexican for the Americans and too American for the Mexicans.

The record collection Ricardo's father had amassed was what brought the two together. Felipe would often take his son to concerts and encouraged him to play the guitar. They often shared books and had long conversations about the history of rock and who would headline the perfect gig. His father, still a classic rocker, kept himself up to date musically and always put money aside to buy albums that would get the young Ricardo bouncing up and down. The repertoire of the family disco began to expand with the Beatles, Led Zeppelin, and Black Sabbath.

The arrival of new wave and punk brought more bands into their lives, and music by Television, Talking Heads, and Ramones sang out from the record player one after the other. For Felipe, it was vital to keep his connection with live music, and he often asked Debbie, a friend from work, to make cassette recordings of those albums for his son, Ricardo. At that time, in El Paso, there was a local band who were starting to dominate the scene called Teenage Popeye, formed by Mike Nosenzo (vocals and guitar), Pierce McDowell (bass), and John Evans (drums). The trio were just as good as the bands from New York. They sounded fresh, they were excellent musicians, and their lyrics hit you right in the gut, making you shake like a rag doll.

"Teenage Popeye are one of those bands you become a fan of the first time you hear them, Felipe. Your kid's gonna love 'em. I think they're playing with the Talking Heads next week, you can't miss it!"

Father and son drove to Las Cruces to see Nosenzo's band open for Talking Heads at the university ballroom. Debbie was right: by the end of the night they were devoted fans.

On December 23, 2011, Teenage Popeye teamed up with other legendary bands from the punk scene to put on a show in El Paso at the Tricky Falls concert hall. During the show, Mike Nosenzo leapt from the stage, flashing his red T-shirt bearing the face of Che, a pair of Converse sneakers, and the bald spot that gave away the thirty years since he first appeared in the city. In the middle of the set, Nosenzo came onstage wearing a kind of ball of light on his head, which he'd made himself, making him look like a human light bulb. The image was awesome. In fact when I saw the videos on YouTube, Mike fascinated me. You could say that in a way I also became a fan, through the internet, after hearing them for the first time. I'll second that theory of yours, Debbie.

Shortly after playing with Talking Heads, Teenage Popeye performed again in El Paso. And it wasn't your average show; they were opening for the Ramones. Unluckily for the Salazars, Felipe was working a double shift that week. He was going to clock off too late and wouldn't get to the gig on time. He had to decide whether to let his teenage son go to a punk concert by himself. Ricardo wasn't the most popular kid in school, and the few friends he had didn't share his music tastes, but he knew that neither that nor his dad's double shift would make him miss his favorite band. "Come on, Dad! You're always telling me you used to go to gigs by yourself . . . I have to see them live!" The boy's insistence reminded him of that concert of *Los Reyes del Twist*, the day he met Constance, the night that turned his life on its head. He looked at his son and saw himself, took a deep breath, and said, "What the hell! Just you go and enjoy those *cabrones*, Ritchie!"

WELCOME TO YSLETA HIGH SCHOOL

THE FAIREY SWORDFISH WAS THE LEAST cool torpedo bomber in the British Royal Air Force during the Second World War. These were biplanes that flew at little over 140 miles per hour. Somewhere on the internet there's a list of the ten fastest cars in the world, and the slowest of these is a Ferrari whose top speed is no less than 225 miles per hour. This is a car in which you could travel the 430 miles that separate El Paso and Phoenix in just two hours, and not the six and a half you had to spend doing the same journey in the eighties.

Despite its technological obsolescence, the Swordfish was made famous by its contribution to the sinking of the *Bismarck* battleship off the French coast in 1941. A squadron of sluggish biplanes bombing an eight-hundred-foot Nazi battleship. And they sank it . . . boy, did they sink it. Daniel felt a bit like the *Bismarck*, bombed by the other students. A squadron of acne-faced, wonky-toothed, and hard-nosed boys and girls who had destroyed his rudder and left him drifting, like the Swordfish had done to the *Bismarck*. He wished he would just sink once and for all.

The teacher, Mr. Milam, addressed one of his students: "Salazar! Can you lift your head from your notebook and join the class?" Sniggers. "Er, yes, sir . . . what sir?" At that moment the teacher removed his glasses and with the index finger and thumb of his left hand squeezed the bridge of his nose. He took a deep breath, "I was saying that since you and the new boy are both wearing sweaters with biplanes on them, you could move over and let him sit next to you, don't you think? And we might be able to hear him speak."

That was how Daniel met Ricardo Salazar. They had both been bought the same horrible, mottled gray biplane sweater, with olive green sleeves and the enormous silhouette of the Fairey Swordfish on the chest. "You can sit down now. Welcome to Ysleta High School, Mr. Álvarez."

※

It was true that Ricardo had been wanting to see the Ramones live for ages. He had been blown away by the album *Road to Ruin*, which the band from Queens had released in 1978. Songs like "I Wanna Be Sedated" or "I Just Want to Have Something to Do" made him feel like someone understood him, as if he were less alone in the world. The use of the first person in the lyrics, the total directness of the message, and the speed and sound they produced turned Ricardo into a young aspiring punk rocker. He dreamed of being the Latin version of Joey Ramone, albeit a slightly shorter and chubbier one.

Debbie, his father's work friend, had supplied him with the New Yorkers' previous albums in inverse chronological order. First, *Rocket to Russia*, then, *Leave Home,* and lastly the band's namesake album, *Ramones,* to finish off. He felt like his head was about to explode; this was the perfect music style. What people were calling "punk" brought together everything he wanted to experience, and now he had the chance of seeing them live. He'd be able to study them close up and observe Marky, a newcomer to the band, as he pounded away at the drums.

That night there was a special atmosphere in the Old Buffalo in El Paso. As if the very air itself knew that something big was about to happen. Ricardo had gone to the club by himself. None of his friends had wanted to pay for a ticket to see the Ramones, so he had to persuade his father to let him go alone to a punk show. With the room still half empty and the lights on, Ricardo recognized the kid who was relentlessly pummeling the sound guy with questions. It was Daniel Álvarez, the new kid, the weirdo who had turned up at school wearing the same biplane sweater as him. They had been sitting at the same desk for months and hadn't said a word to each other, and there they were, maybe the only two Ysleta students at the concert.

Ricardo was plagued by doubts in situations like this. "What should I say to him? Should I treat him like a friend or play it cool? He'll think I don't have any friends!" When he turned to look at Daniel again, he'd disappeared among the people in the first rows, and just as he was about to go over, the locals, Teenage Popeye, started to play, as the Ramones' opening act. The concert had begun.

*

"Hey! Aren't you Ricardo?" shouted Daniel as he pushed his way through the crowd. "Yeah, how's it going? Are you here for the concert?" asked Ricardo. "What do you think, man? Of course!" The two boys looked at each other knowingly and burst into laughter. From their accelerated speech, it was clear that the Ramones had blown their minds. "Hey, man, that Marky is one sick drummer!" "Yeah, man, that was unbelievable! And did you see Teenage Popeye? I liked them more than the Ramones! And they're from El Paso!" Daniel was fascinated that a local group could be so good. The Ramones were the stars of the show, but Mike Nosenzo's band were no letdown.

Combative lyrics, powerful music, and an attitude to match were just some of the virtues of a band that had a very promising career ahead of it. Ricardo told Daniel that he'd seen them before and that he and his father had become instant fans. They gave each other another knowing glance, as if they'd realized they'd both met someone who would change their lives.

I have to confess, I've never enjoyed the Ramones live. I think their last concert in Barcelona was in 1993, and at that time I was eleven years old and hadn't the faintest idea who they were. I hadn't seen Teenage Popeye, either, but in March 2015 when I interviewed Mike Nosenzo at his home in Dallas, he played us an acoustic version of "Enemy of the State" that I fell in love with. That song was over thirty years old and had been written to be played with an electric guitar, a powerful drum pattern, and some clever arrangements, but I found the naked version that Mike played us in his living room deafening, fresh, and direct. When he began to sing, all of us there entered into a mini trance, carried off by the melody, the lyrics, and the space cakes he'd given us on our arrival. As I watched him play, I imagined myself thirty years before, watching him play with the rest of the band and jumping and dancing like a man possessed. I'm sure if I'd been there in '79, I would have been more impressed by Teenage Popeye than the Ramones, too.

"What are you doing now? I can't go home feeling this high. What do you think if we go get a few beers and head for the mountains? I've got my car here." Ricardo hesitated for an instant, but Daniel's offer was pretty tempting. In fact his adrenaline levels were through the roof and there was no way he was going to be able to sleep, so, "Why not?"

Despite their differences, the connection between the pair was palpable, and by the end of the evening they were finishing each other's sentences. They talked about the Beatles, Black Sabbath, and their favorite comic artists. Daniel talked about how he'd lived in so many different cities, while Ricardo told Daniel about how hard it was for him to have spent all his life in El Paso. They fantasized about changing the "fucked-up world" and proposed putting together a band like Teenage Popeye and one day opening for a group like the Ramones.

There's something magical about a sunrise in El Paso with a healthy dose of alcohol running through your bloodstream. Daniel suddenly reached for his notebook and pen and scribbled out a contract, under which the two signatories would one day have to form a band and change things. With the first rays of sunlight reflecting off the tins of Lite beer and without either of the boys able to look anywhere with much clarity, Daniel took a deep breath and put his arm on Ricardo's shoulder, making the young Salazar feel completely at ease. "You know something, Ritchie, I'm glad I went to that concert."

No. 19 $2.25
$2.50 in Canada

LOVE
AND
ROCKETS

FANTAGRAPHICS BOOKS

ROCK Shorts
FANZINE 2

PREVARES & RICARDO   EL PASO, TX

LOS
MURALISTAS
DEL
BARRIO

MUSIC:
TEENAGE
POPEYE
RAMONES
BLACK FLAG
AND
TSOL
RATHSKELLER

ROCK & LOVETS

"**NO, IT'S JUST THE OPPOSITE. ROBERT** Crumb illustrates the stories and Pekar writes them based on his own life. No super powers or any of that shit . . . I know you love him, me too in a way . . . You know . . . I have total respect for Stan Lee . . . Whatever! What I'm trying to say is that we could make a team, Ritchie. Think about it, you love writing, and although you won't let me read a single one of your stories . . . I'm sure they're fucking awesome, man! I could illustrate them . . . You don't need to be talking about yourself, but you could base the stories on your experience, the borderlands, I don't know . . ." There was the hint of a sigh from the other end of the line. "Fuck, Daniel, *American Splendor* is incredible . . . I'm not sure we can do something that cool, honestly . . ."

This was a standard conversation for Daniel and Ricardo. The former was all enthusiasm, a car salesman in full throttle with total faith in his friend's talent. As a seasoned doubter, however, Ricardo had only misgivings when it came to talking about anything that involved him. It's true that Daniel had never read anything written by Ricardo, but he didn't think he needed to. Ricardo's eloquence and unique vision of life and the world were enough for Daniel to know that he had the potential to be a great artist.

Like that guy from the NBA, Marty Blake, the scout who took Lenny Wilkens to the top and who, in 1970, chose the Mexican

Manuel Raga in the first round of the draft, 166 points behind the number one (Bob Lanier) and 164 behind the legendary Pete Maravich. For the laymen among us, this would be like entering a human in the basketball Olympus of the gods, and that human was a Mexican, perhaps the best Mexican basketball player of all time. The point is that Marty Blake didn't need much time to see that gift in Manuel Raga. You could say that the gift of both Marty Blake and Daniel Álvarez was the ability to see the gifts of others.

For the rest of the school year the two were inseparable. They listened to music together and played basketball (quite badly). They spent the winter evenings at Ricardo's place reading comics and talking about girls. They cried, laughed, and got drunk. They went into the desert to shoot tin cans and told each other their secrets. In the spring, they drove to Phoenix to see a conference semifinal between the Suns and the Lakers. Magic Johnson was extraordinary. The Suns won the match by twenty points, but lost the series four to one. They created dozens of comic strips with outrageous characters, inspired by the people around them: Mr. Milam, Sue (the cook), Debbie (Felipe's punky friend), Mr. Kennel (their algebra teacher), or Patrik Lauwens (the Belgian exchange student).

In the summer they graduated from high school and bought a couple of tickets for the Black Sabbath concert at El Paso County Coliseum. For Ricardo it was one of the best years of his life. He'd met his soul mate, someone he could spend time with without feeling overwhelmed, and he was starting to feel motivated.

✳

The guitar of Tony Iommi announced the beginning of "Iron Man," and Ronnie James Dio repeated the title of the song, his distorted voice soaring across the Coliseum. As it traveled it grew in size, becoming more robust thanks to the cries from the crowd, like a rolling snowball getting bigger and bigger. The avalanche ended in an explosion of the song's main guitar riff, the bass and the drums coming in together.

"You're going?! What the fuck are you telling me, man? The whole fucking year you've been telling me what we're gonna do and what we won't have to do anymore and now you're saying you're running off to Austin?! Go to hell, Danny . . . Fuck you, man." Ricardo pushed Daniel off him and started pushing his way through the crowd. Daniel grabbed him by the wrist and spoke into his ear. "Come on, Ritchie, we'll still be able to do stuff, man, and I'll come back all the time. We'll work out a way to keep doing our thing . . . I've got a plan!"

The crowd was screaming out the verses that Dio was singing. They were even humming the melodies that were blasting from Iommi's guitar, like it was some kind of mass exorcism. Black Sabbath were on tour presenting their first album without Ozzy, *Heaven and Hell*, and, despite the (hateful) reviews, the band sounded fantastic.

"Plan? What plan? Screw you, Danny!" How long have you waited to tell me that you're leaving? A month? Two? And on top of that you tell me in the middle of a Black Sabbath concert. You've completely screwed up my whole fucking night, you asshole!" shouted Ricardo as he threw his concert ticket at him. At that precise moment people starting applauding and screaming like mad, as if they were celebrating Ricardo's reaction, as if they wanted to give him an ovation for what he'd said. Daniel looked at the stage and noticed that the British band had finished the first half of the show. When he turned back to his friend, Ricardo was trying to push his way through the seething mass and, looking at the ceiling of the Coliseum, he said: "Ritchie, man, they haven't done the fucking encore yet."

Ricardo felt he'd been let down, like when his mother had left him. Abandoned once again. This was the feeling that had made him so doubtful and untrusting. His ghosts were back, reminding him that all that talk about the comics and the goddamn pats on the back were nothing but the fruit of teenage zeal and drinking too much Lite beer.

For Daniel, however, the distance wasn't a problem: he'd come up with a plan. Ricardo would send the scripts by mail and he would illustrate them and respond with a copy of the original. This way they could both photocopy the strips and hand them out at the same time. The distance didn't have to be a problem. "Shit, we have to be able to do it!" he shouted as Ricardo walked away, "I'll always be coming back to the city, we can write, call each other up! You're my best friend, Ritchie, I'm not about to walk off and leave you."

✳

During the first two years of college it was difficult to keep up a steady production rate. Daniel, who was studying art at UT, found it hard to find time between homework and exams. Ricardo had more free time studying literature at UTEP, but was so into the Spanish literature classes given by one of the teachers, Ben Sáenz, that he spent most of his time outside of class reading the translated works of authors like García Márquez or Julio Cortázar. Nevertheless, they were diligent in finding time to call each other and kept up a regular correspondence. In their letters they told each other things they found difficult to put into words. Their writing was how the two boys maintained their friendship. They loved each other, they understood each other, and neither of them found anyone of much interest to them at university. The odd girl had come onto the scene, but nothing of any great importance.

In November 1982, Gustavo Álvarez (Daniel's big brother) sent an envelope to his brother from Oxnard, California. On the envelope he put something like, "I think you're going to love this, little bro . . . Let me know what you think!" The package contained the first issue of *Love & Rockets*, the comic created by the Hernandez brothers. Gustavo knew Mario, the eldest of the three authors, and as soon as he read the first copy, he knew that he had to send it to Daniel. That magazine was made for his little brother.

Mario, Jaime, and Gilbert Hernandez had self-published the comic a year before, and the publisher Fantagraphics Books was now showing an interest in republishing it with a color cover. That comic was the encouragement that Daniel and Ricardo needed to set their fanzine in motion. The authors of *Love & Rockets* were children of Mexicans like them, and were also into punk and believed in the possibilities of telling stories through comic strips. If the Hernandez brothers could do it, so could they.

It's worth noting here that that issue of *Love & Rockets* marked a before and after in the history of alternative comics in the United States. The magazine would reach phenomenal levels of popularity and continue to be published until well into 1996. The Hernandez brothers would come back to the series in early 2000 while at the same time publishing their own stories: *Locas* (Jaime Hernandez) and *Palomar* (Gilbert "Beto" Hernandez).

October 4, 1982

Hey Ritchie!

Sorry I haven't replied sooner, man. I've had a few problems getting focused these last few weeks. It's been a pretty
shitty start to the year, but anyway . . . Have you listened
to The Judy's yet? Man, I can't get the tune from "Guyana
Punch" out of my head, it is truly one sick song! I'm waiting for them to play in Austin to see them live, it'd be cool
if you could make it.

I'm still flipping out over *Damaged* by Black Flag but this
thing of The Judy's has really blown me away. It would
be awesome to mix the vibe of their melodies with Flag's
intensity and attitude. If we ever put a band together that's
what we'll do: melodies and attitude!

About what you said to me last time:

1) I'm very seriously thinking about finishing my degree
in El Paso. I've got to work out how to do it, but if I can't,
maybe I'll take a sabbatical year there. I'm onto it.

2) With Edna things are coming to an end. She often hangs
out with the hipsters from last year and so we see each

other a lot less . . . It's pretty fucked up, but anyway . . . I've spent more of my time painting and doing other stuff. You should see the collages I'm doing now! I'm really hooked on *Fallout* and all the cool shit that Winston Smith does; my buddy in San Francisco is an endless source of ideas. I feel like my head's gonna explode!

3) About the TSOL concert at Rathskeller, I'm not worried it was a few months ago: do a feature and we'll stick it in the first issue of the fanzine!

4) *ROCK & LOVETS*: I love it! I have an idea for a logo that I've drawn below. I love the idea of using the same style as the actual magazine, making it more of an obvious homage. If you like it, let me know and I'll get a mock-up ready of the front and back covers to get started with the fanzines.

I miss you man. I hope I can get down to the border soon. If I hear The Judy's are playing in Austin I'll call you up and we'll get you up here right away. My roommate spends his whole life with his girlfriend, so no problem there. Give your dad a hug from me.

Daniel

November 9, 1982

It would be awesome if we could study together at UTEP, man. We can totally get into the fanzine.

You've got to bring a heap of music from up there, I can't wait to listen to The Judy's. I'm going crazy over Mission of Burma, they've got a really interesting sound and the way they play is just amazing. They've released an EP called *Signals, Calls, and Marches* and it's far out Danny, the first song is just about the best thing I've ever heard! They remind me a little of Television, but I'm much more into them . . . Whatever you do, make sure you give them a listen!

Oh and I'm sorry about Edna, man. I'm looking at when I can get away up to Austin. I might have a few weeks free in February. Stay in contact, brother.

P.S.: My old man says he'd love to see you and that *Damaged* by Black Flag is not bad at all; he says you're learning to listen to decent music!

Take care.

Ricardo

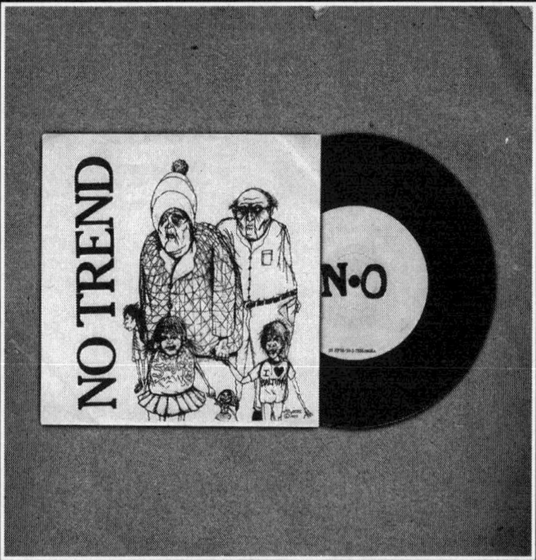
NO TREND
N•O

NO TREND. NO SCENE.
NO MOVEMENT.

IS THERE ANYTHING BETTER THAN UNWRAPPING a freshly purchased vinyl? Smelling it, touching it. I'll never forget the feeling of opening my first record. It was back in '95 and I'd just discovered Nirvana. Kurt Cobain had been dead about a year when the acoustic version of "All Apologies" changed something in my brain forever. Tired of turning over the sixty-minute TDK cassette on which someone had recorded *Unplugged in New York* for me, I decided to save my miserable weekly wages to get enough money together to buy Nirvana's albums on compact disc. Holding coats while everyone had fun at the fairground, watching everyone else eating Whoppers at Burger King, or asking to borrow the latest issues of *Spider-Man* was all worth it when I pulled off the plastic from Nirvana's *Nevermind*, took out the booklet, and ran my fingers over the image of the underwater baby reaching for the dollar on a fish hook. What an album cover! A few years later, a good friend gave me a secondhand vinyl copy of the same album, with no plastic and pretty battered round the edges . . . But, my God, the cover looked good at that size! That day I made a promise to myself that I'd try to get vinyl copies of my favorite albums because, as everyone knows, a good cover looks so much better on a twelve-inch.

My **TOP FIVE** album covers from the eighties:

1. *Metal Circus* by HÜSKER DÜ (SST Records. 1983)
2. *Slip It In* by BLACK FLAG (SST Records. 1984)
3. *Signals, Calls, and Marches* by MISSION OF BURMA (Ace of Hearts. 1981)
4. *Surfer Rosa* by PIXIES (4AD. 1988)
5. *Teen Love* by NO TREND (Self-released. 1983)

Black ink on white. What looks like an old woman with a three-quarter-length jacket and a bobble hat is holding the hands of her grandchildren, or children . . . who knows what that's about. The little girl, in turn, is holding on to her doll by the hand and is wearing a Smurfs sweater, while one of the other sprogs is wearing a T-shirt that says "I ♥ BALTIMORE." An old bald man wearing glasses is following behind. On the left and in vertical type is NO TREND, the name of the band from Maryland. The cover is both attractive and disconcerting. The seven-inch title (which doesn't appear on the cover) is *Teen Love* and the track list comprises "Mass Sterilization Caused by Venereal Disease," "Cancer," and the album's namesake song, "Teen Love." These four kids from Ashton self-released a first version of the album in March 1983 and an expanded twelve-inch version about a year later. Self-release. Do-it-yourself music.

The original formation of NO TREND was active between 1982 and 1984. Four guys making alternative music and trying to get away from the increasingly rigid arrangements of hardcore and punk. Doing their own recordings and making their own albums. The influence of Dischord, Minor Threat, and the whole Washington, DC, scene was clear in NO TREND. After all, they grew up little more than half an hour from the US capital. Underground. Alternative.

Before putting the band together, Jeff (lead vocalist) would go round slapping stickers that read, "No trend. No scene. No movement." on all the Coca-Cola machines in Georgetown. In July 1983, NO TREND would play in an old Coca-Cola factory in El Paso known as the Koke House, at 2728 East Yandell. Folks from the underground music scene had set it up and kitted it out by themselves. The concert would be for all ages. Start. Create. Believe.

That night, on June 24, 1983, Ricardo held NO TREND's seven-inch in his hands, with that bizarre family drawn in black ink on the cover. He and Daniel were back together jumping up and down in the front row, after Daniel had made the decision not to go back to Austin. The two had talked with Frank Price, the group's guitarist, about the underground scene in the States. About the differences between the country's north and south. Frank told them they were opening for Suicidal Tendencies in August. They agreed that *Land Speed Record* by Hüsker Dü was an interesting album and that *Murmur* was going to give R.E.M. a whole new status for an alternative band. Daniel had the theory that something big was going to happen and that, sooner or later, everything that was bubbling under the surface of American music would erupt, blazing a new and more popular trail. There were just a few bands at that point, but they were growing exponentially, and R.E.M. was a clear example of how far they could go.

Ricardo gave the NO TREND guitarist a couple of copies of the first issue of *Rock & Lovets*, the fanzine that he and Danny had just published. "Awesome! It looks cool. I'll look at in in the van on the way to Arizona. Thanks for the fanzines and for coming to see us, it's been a great show. El Paso kicks ass!"

✳

At the end of 1983, the two friends were studying together again, this time at the University of Texas at El Paso. Ricardo went on studying literature, and Daniel was going to finish the art degree he'd left halfway through in Austin. At this point, the local scene was starting to look pretty interesting. A handful of venues were offering their stages to exciting bands and putting on some impressive concerts. Aside from the Koke House, there was also the highly recommendable Rathskeller, a small club close to the crossroads of North Mesa and East Robinson Avenue, where seriously cool bands would play, like the Dirty Rotten Imbeciles, TSOL, Jerry's Kidz, or Ragged Bags.

The shows that needed somewhere bigger were often put on in the Sancho Bros. Ballroom, a concert hall in the Lakeside Center on Alameda Street. In March of that year Victims and Civilians had played there, two bands that were getting really big on the local scene; the former closer to new wave and the latter a PUNK band in capital letters. For Daniel and Ricardo, there were a few more mythical places on Dyer Street: the Hamburger Hut (5720) and Headstand, the record store at 4409. Burgers and albums, the perfect combination.

Everyone I interviewed in El Paso spoke extremely highly of Headstand, the music store. It was able to adapt to the different music trends that were bursting onto the scene at the time and ended up employing guys that were part of that musical effervescence. On a rainy afternoon in May 2016, Jordi and I went down to the store with the idea of taking some photos of the façade. Lou, our official translator for both trips, was out of action for the day, so I tried my luck inflicting my broken English on Stan to tell him about my project: a couple of guys from Barcelona heading across the Atlantic for El Paso, intent on documenting a punk scene that was already in full swing before they were even born.

Stan just looked at me, his eyes sparkling with enthusiasm, and nodded, firing me a tremendously gratifying "cool" when I'd finished my piece. He looked at my chest and saw I was wearing a T-shirt with the ELPASO (the band) logo, along with the phrase "A punk story." "Wow! You have to send me that logo. We could make some T-shirts and sell them here in the store. It'll give your project some publicity and, what the hell, they're awesome!" He wrote down his email on a card and encouraged me to push on with my adventure.

As I write these lines, I'm thinking how cool it must be for all those kids eagerly getting into their music and coming across someone like Stan. And I still haven't emailed him the logo. Fuck.

Black Flag slams home 'hardcore'

By Joe Jeppson
Times staff writer

While Black Flag plays, an audience member flies during the "hardcore" band's performance Monday night at the Sambo Brothers Ballroom.

in my opinion

FUCKING WITH HENRY ROLLINS

THE WHITE SHIRTS OF THE GUYS in front were soaked in
blood. You know the ones, the typical couple of brick shithouses who
couldn't give a fuck about you at gigs, guys who you're sure have been
carefully selected and paid to go to the same gig as you, just to get
in front of you right from the first minute. It must have happened
to you at some stage. It really gets you pissed. These muscle heads
wore those typical shirts with the sleeves cut off and some cheesy
detail written in marker: an A for anarchy or a shameful version of the
Dead Kennedys logo. And you might not believe it but these punks
do actually wash their clothes, and their hand-scrawled symbols fade
to a barely visible light gray. To start with there were just a few drops.
But when Ricardo realized he could get back at those big fuckers, he
began to spit blood like a man possessed, it was disgusting but funny.
"We're getting blood all over those fuckers that are always in front of
us, awesome!"

Flying elbows at a concert were the order of the day and, fuck if
it wasn't the Big Boys playing, the kings of Texan punk! During "We
Got Your Money," everyone screamed, "You'll never understand /
And to all you frat boys," and Daniel jumped up, his arms soaring into the air as he landed an elbow right in Ricardo's mouth. He
split both his lips. When you're howling Big Boys songs and you've
no idea what's going on, there's no such thing as pain. In the heat of

the moment nothing hurts. So it wasn't until those guys' backs were stained red that they noticed what had happened.

What do a few scratches matter when Tim Kerr is grinding his guitar in your face? They had driven more than nine hundred miles to see these guys at the On Broadway Theatre in San Francisco!! Who cares about a few busted lips when Randy Turner is giving you the finger? For Daniel and Ricardo, none of that mattered. We're talking about the guitarist and singer of the Big Boys, two legends of punk. When you've got these kinds of guys in front of you, you don't give a shit about anything else. You have to realize that back then there was a kind of camaraderie in the audience, sort of like, "We're just a bunch of guys at a gig, so fuck it!" So when these two meatheads saw that Ricardo was spitting blood at them, they just laughed their asses off. They ended the night licking their wounds over beers with these two bruisers and their bloody shirts.

✳

Nineteen eighty-four was an incredible year, the concerts came one after the other, and in a single week Daniel and Ricardo managed to see three massive bands: the Dead Kennedys at the Sancho Bros. Ballroom and the Minutemen and the Dickies at the Koke House.

Red Zone and the Rhythm Pigs were the bands chosen to support Jello Biafra, two legendary groups on the scene, both from El Paso, whom they would see many more times live. That night, however, would live on with them thanks to the unbelievable performance the Dead Kennedys gave in the city. The boys from San Francisco came to the border at one of the best moments of their career, the period between the albums *Plastic Surgery Disasters* and *Frankenchrist*. The group was like a musical monster truck, its gargantuan wheels crushing everything in its path. And Jello Biafra, who'd turned up with a bandage wrapped around his leg, was behind the wheel. The concert really was one to remember, and Daniel dived into the crowd for the first time, pushed, he claims, by Biafra himself as he teetered on the edge of the stage in front of a stormy sea of punk rockers all screaming and spitting out the band's lyrics.

Anyone who'd lived through such an intense period of music would have enjoyed telling such an anecdote, but for Daniel Álvarez, the best was yet to come. It was in the Koke House, in El Paso, during the encores of a Minutemen show, the night when D. Boon, the band's giant front man, tested the strength of a stage set up by the boys from the city with their own hands. Weighing in at over one hundred kilograms, Boon jumped like a madman throughout the concert, easily enough to leave the floorboards in tatters, but by some minor miracle the structure held up and the Minutemen played their show without incident.

Mike Watt (bassist) and George Hurley (drummer) also gave it their all, and Daniel recalls, at the climax of their performance of "Jesus and Tequila," tearing off his Red Zone T-shirt and throwing it at the drum kit. It landed right on the head of George Hurley, who carried on playing like nothing had happened. When the song was over he took the T-shirt off his face, used it to dry his sweat, and put it on to launch into "History Lesson," the song they wrapped up the concert with. The trio from San Pedro finished the night performing acoustic versions outside the Koke House. Those who were there remember it as a magical moment. That night, a bare-chested Daniel told George Hurley that is was him who threw the T-shirt but that he could keep it. They talked together about Steve'O'cide, the local artist who had designed all the merchandising for Red Zone, and how much they both admired the artwork of Raymond Pettibon.

Most likely, after that conversation, the members of Minutemen loaded their material into the van and took I-10 to get out of El Paso. A year later, in December 1985, that same highway would witness a traffic accident that would claim the life of D. Boon. The front man's death was a stinging blow for the American underground scene and made any memories anyone had of him all the more mythical.

It was during that time that Daniel and Ricardo became Rhythm Pigs groupies. They were fascinated at how these three guys from their city could combine technique, speed, and an ear for awesome music to blast out the most exquisite punk tunes, like "I Can Fly," "Baal," or "Military Fairy." Ricardo dreamed of fusing Greg Adams's guitar playing and Ed Ivey's voice in his own songs. The feeling they created reminded them of when they'd seen Teenage Popeye for the first time opening for the Ramones, the night they met. The day that started it all.

That year's gig schedule, however, was still missing one of its major dates, the day everyone had circled in red:

November 13, 1984
The day Black Flag would set El Paso on fire

There was Henry Rollins, lit by a single spotlight. His sweaty, scraggly locks, straight out of the Ramones' barbershop, covering his eyes while he read from Henry Miller. He wore his classic jogging shorts and black mesh T-shirt. When he'd finished reciting the passage, he closed the book and the band exploded with "Nervous Breakdown." Greg Ginn on guitar, Bill Stevenson (the drummer for Descendents), and Kira Roessler on bass. For many, this was Black Flag's most glorious lineup.

One hit came after the other. It was like listening to a "best of" album: "Slip It In," "Black Coffee," or "Six Pack" sent the young (and not so young) punk rockers gathered for another night at the Sancho Bros. Ballroom into a frenzy. Yet another unforgettable night, I imagine. Ricardo and Daniel had managed to push themselves to the front. Ricardo, right below Rollins, couldn't take his eyes off the band's bass player, Kira. He claims that, on that night, he fell in love with her forever. Daniel, however, has his eyes fixed on Ginn and company. As a massive fan of Descendents, having Bill Stevenson so close, hammering at the drums, was an almost mystical experience.

Despite their thunderous performance, you could tell there was a certain distance between the musicians and their point man. Rollins screamed and roared down the microphone like a wild beast, but he seemed to be alone on the stage, as if the music wasn't really with him. He shook his black mane and, with every bang of his head, beads of sweat would fly through the air, reflecting the light from the spotlights, the resulting image resembling some kind of psychedelic exorcism. Ninety percent of Henry Rollins's sweat ended up on Ricardo, whose face gave away an obvious satisfaction, as if this was exactly the experience he was looking for. The effects of the acid he'd shared with Daniel were also helping, but witnessing that performance by this four-piece band from Los Angeles was to be one of the turning points of his youth.

"I want you to touch my filth. I want you to feel my filth. I want you to look into my eyes. I want you to look through my eyes," whispered Rollins as he glared threateningly at the kids in the front row. They finished "Rat's Eyes," went straight into "My War," and the whole place went insane. This was clearly the grand finale of a mind-blowing night. Everyone began to push each other and shout, while in the middle of the chaos stood Ricardo. Entranced, apparently oblivious to the madness. As if everything was being played in slow motion. He simply stood there smiling, feeling Henry Rollins's sweat fall onto his face.

Kira Roessler unplugged her Rickenbacker and turned off the amp, exchanging a smile with Bill Stevenson. The drummer got up from his kit and put an arm around the bassist, and they left the stage while the front man went on preaching to the crowd. He seemed really pissed. Greg Ginn basically disappeared, looking like this had nothing to do with him, wearing the smart shirt and dark pleated trousers you might find on someone fresh out of college and looking for a job.

Daniel approached Ricardo, who was still standing motionless in the middle of the dance floor, nodding his head at everything Black Flag's lead singer was saying. The ballroom steadily emptied; people formed groups to talk about the show. Daniel, in a state of ecstasy, couldn't stop hugging and shaking his friend, "Holy fuck, Ritchie! We've got to put a band together right now!" Just as Ricardo was about to answer, a hand squeezed both his cheeks at the same time, turning his face away from his friend. A slim, attractive girl planted a kiss right on his lips and looked him in the eyes, "Remember me? We've got some unfinished business to attend to . . ." Ricardo looked at his friend while the girl dragged him away by his left arm. Daniel smiled and strummed an imaginary guitar, "Think about the band, motherfucker!" Ricardo winked at his friend and disappeared into the crowd waiting to get out of the Sancho Bros. Ballroom. Black Flag had set fire to something more than just the city.

"Fucking with Henry Rollins" is a feature article written by Ricardo Salazar for issue No. 3 of the fanzine Rock & Lovets:

It was all set up by a friend of mine. He can't stop following this girl around with a Boston accent who's always hanging out with the photographer. We call her "the photographer" because you normally find her taking pictures of anything and everything that crosses her path. She carries her camera over her shoulder like a handbag and looks like she spends hours in the dark room.

The girl with the Boston accent threw a party in September in her shared house, and my friend said we should go, assuring me I'd get it on with the photographer. It seems the time he was supposed to spend scoring Miss Massachusetts my fine friend had dedicated to talking to the photographer about me, to the point that the girl was desperate to meet me. I was single and pretty horny so I thought, why not?

At the party I saw what a fine job my buddy had done, and the photographer forgot about her camera and we were drinking and talking and the space between us was getting smaller and smaller, until I felt her tits touching my right arm and my lethargic dick came to attention. A combination of nerves and too much booze sent it back to sleep and I realized I wasn't going to get the night of wild sex I'd been promised. So I decided to get the fuck out of there, making it clear that this wasn't over, and dragged my own Cyrano de Bergerac away from the girl with the Boston accent.

I didn't see the photographer again until yesterday, and I've only got a few clear images of last night:

- Daniel and me dropping some acid before the Black Flag concert
- Black Flag kicking everyone's ass
- Me secretly falling in love with Kira Roessler

- Getting covered in Henry Rollins's sweat
- The photographer grabbing me and taking me off to her Plymouth Valiant
- Me, the photographer, and Henry Rollins fucking in the back of the Plymouth

The truth is it was amazing. She really wanted to fuck me and I was desperate to fuck anyone, so things were already looking up. And Henry Rollins's pheromones did the rest. My T-shirt was soaked in the sweat of the Black Flag front man and, holy shit, have you seen that guy? I'm sure that his goddamn pheromones are as pumped as he is, and as soon as they caught sight of the photographer's mammaries they shot from the pores of my skin straight into her brain, convincing her that it was Henry inside her and not me.

We didn't get totally naked, but I like to take my shirt off and she liked it when I took hers off. I did the classic and fumbled with her bra strap, trying hopelessly to undo it until she whispered a gentle "let me do it" and my erection got a thousand times harder. She put her arms behind her back with unbelievable grace and then grabbed my head at the same time as I launched myself at her breasts.

That was about it for the preliminaries, that and some awkward oral sex lying on the back seat. A Plymouth Valiant is not the most comfortable place on Earth. Then we were back where we began, only this time without pants, and she starts to mount me like a wild Amazon, a sublime movement of her hips taking me to levels of pleasure I'd never felt before and which almost had me coming scarcely after we'd gotten going.

I tried to distract myself and lifted my head to look somewhere else so I could hold on a little longer and just at that moment, the acid took the reins and Henry Rollins himself appeared on the back seat of the car. He turned and started bawling at me, telling me to do his pheromones justice. "This girl thinks you're me, so act like a man!" For some strange reason, Henry Rollins sounded like Clint Eastwood and talked like his character in *The Gauntlet*, with the same mean voice.

I admit that I looked at my arms, and between the sweat and faint light inside the car I began to see muscles that aren't there, I even imagined seeing some of Rollins's tattoos on my biceps. I got my confidence back, took hold of Guadalupe, and saved face with an unforgettable performance. She screamed with pleasure and fell on top of me, her head resting on my right shoulder while she laughed and gasped for air. I looked toward the front of the car and saw Henry looking back at me with pride, giving me a wink and a thumbs up—good work, kid. Thanks, Henry, see you soon, I hope.

THE FIRST REHEARSAL

TO REHEARSE, RICARDO MANAGED TO GET his dad to let them set up in the garage. Daniel had gotten hold of a sorry-looking drum kit, and all they needed was an electric guitar. Ricardo had only ever played a nylon-stringed acoustic guitar that, apparently, had belonged to his grandfather on his father's side. They still hadn't saved enough money to buy a Gibson Flying V like the one used by Bob Mould from Hüsker Dü, so they had to be imaginative.

Debbie, Felipe's friend from work, let them use her white Fender Stratocaster on the condition that they picked it up from her house and took it back after every rehearsal. The friends had to decide where and when they would rehearse, tell Debbie, and stop by her house on the corner of Yandell and Montana. When they finished, they drove the guitar back to her place, alive and well. And that's how they got their first rehearsal off the ground.

In the garage, they went over and over a slowed down version of "Blitzkrieg Bop" by the Ramones. Daniel showed a surprising knack for playing the drums, with a good sense of rhythm and impressive coordination for someone just starting out. Ricardo was no stranger to the guitar, but he had to get used to the Fender and its narrow neck. He had big hands and beefy fingers and found it hard to get them into the right places for chord-playing. "Motherfucker! My fingers don't fit, man . . . what the fuck. Listen, I'm gonna start with the main riff and you come in."

They spent an hour repeating the main riff for "Whole Lotta Love" by Led Zeppelin. To their ears it sounded like it'd been sent straight down the stairway from heaven. Ricardo's father, Felipe, came up to the small door that connected the kitchen with the garage, leaned his left shoulder against the door frame, took out a Monterrey from his shirt pocket, and lit up. "What do you think, Pheel? How does it sound?" Felipe nodded and gave them a thumbs up and Daniel smiled and looked at Ricardo. They were one step closer to being rock stars.

For me, there is an unrivaled feeling you get from a first rehearsal, musically. Maybe you could compare it to your first orgasm or first kiss. It's true that you then have another "first kiss" with your second girlfriend (and that could be kiss number 152), but it still can't compare with the very first. I remember my first rehearsal as something awkward, beautiful, and anarchic.

It's the late nineties. We've just turned sixteen, and after much discussion we've settled on a name for our first band. We were called Nameless, and Lady Luck had seen to it we could have a free space for the first of countless rehearsals. Our operations base was a dressing room with a shower attached to it in the small carpentry workshop of the drummer's dad, in an ugly industrial park on the outskirts of Barcelona, where we grew up. The outskirts of the outskirts. One guitarist, a drummer, and a bass player (me), who had known each other their whole lives. We were going to make what we thought might well turn out to be the greatest album in rock history. From the guitar came a basic riff in E. The sound produced by the small amp was abominable and made the snares vibrate. The drummer thumped out a simple hi-hat-kick drum-snare, and I just followed the rhythm, switching between the open E on the fourth string and the same chord on the seventh fret of the third string. One damn chord. The whole time. No changes. But then, something happened. Suddenly the three of us were playing as one, and I could imagine us doing that in *Wembley* fucking *Stadium*. We looked at each other and laughed like idiots, egging one another on with our eyes. I can assure you it was one of the most incredible experiences of my life, and I totally get it when Daniel says that in his first rehearsal with Ricardo, he truly believed the pair would reach the top. The feeling they had in that garage conjured up a hugely successful career filled with monumental songs that flashed before his eyes.

In my case, the first rehearsal went on with that riff in E for almost an hour, and the blisters that appeared on my fingertips the next day restricted what I could do in our second rehearsal, in which, surprise surprise, we spent another hour playing the same riff in E.

For Ricardo and Daniel, the high they got from their first rehearsal made them seriously consider a name for the band. This might sound like a simple task, but, in reality, it's surprisingly taxing. They made lists with made-up words, marked random words on pages from the Spanish dictionary, and noted down the names of their favorite comic book characters. This plunged them into a spiral of paranoia and contradictions that ended with a short list of five possibilities:

- Sweet Border
- Orion
- Fort Bliss Kids

- White Desert
- Existential Void

They put their hearts and souls into creating logos and illustrations with these names and shelved their *Rock & Lovets* fanzine. Five years had passed since they had met at that fateful Ramones gig, and that night in 1979 they were already fantasizing about having their own band, so it seemed OK to set aside the typewriter, scissors, and photocopier and move on to strings and drumsticks instead. They would always contend that their fanzine was the germ for their band and decided that they would explain this each time they were asked. And I can confirm this, as Daniel Álvarez repeatedly told me that the *Rock & Lovets* fanzine was a fundamental part of the band's history. He believes that, at that time, setting up a group, organizing a concert, or creating a fanzine was all part of the punk culture. In fact, it was partly because of the fanzine that they saw so many concerts, interviewed bands, did collages, and wrote stories. It was intellectually demanding and much less endogamous than a band. One thing led to the other, although it was the band that the two friends really fantasized about. Nineteen eighty-four was about to come to an end, and they made a list of resolutions for what was going to be a great year:

Aims for 1985
- Get a bass player
- Settle on a name
- Write songs
- Buy a guitar
- Play a gig

As well as a list of names and resolutions, they created another with five covers they would include in their live shows:

Covers
- "Guyana Punch" by The Judy's
- "Rise Above" by Black Flag
- "Sheena Is a Punk Rocker" by Ramones
- "Never Talking to You Again" by Hüsker Dü
- "Venus" by Television

December 1984 was the beginning of what would turn out to be an obsessive routine for Daniel and Ricardo. From Monday to Thursday they would leave campus together to go straight to Debbie's place, pick up the guitar, drive down to Segundo Barrio, and eat while they rehearsed in the garage. Fridays they went to concerts, and the weekends were for writing songs with Ricardo's acoustic guitar. If they were going to go through with this, they needed to play and play and play.

THE "HANSON BROTHERS"

WHEN WILL'S FIST MADE CONTACT WITH the lower jaw of the Mirrors' front man, Jimmy, that was clearly the end of the concert. The punch, which had been amplified by the main mic, silenced the crowd and the other band members. Except DD, who was the least talkative guy in the world and had hardly said a word for years. "That's the last time you hold back on me with that opening beat, you son of a bitch!" Will shook his right hand in the air, as if he needed to get the mobility back after such an act of hostility. "Get your things DD, we're off." With the group's lead singer lying flat in the middle of the stage, the sparse audience in a state of shock, and the Shure 55s giving off feedback, the Davis brothers began to gather their instruments together. As if their repertoire had come to an end, as if they'd played their encores. But the fact was that these two thickset Texans, with their hair combed back and wearing maroon sequined blazers, were dismantling the stage with the lights still turned out and half the song list yet to play.

Will, the band's drummer, was now taking apart the Slingerland Buddy Rich his grandmother had given him in the seventies piece by piece. He was blowing on his bruised knuckles while shaking his head and muttering an endless barrage of insults aimed at Jimmy "Mirror": "Fucking smug asshole, who the fuck do you think you are? If we say we're coming in on the second fucking bar, then we come in on the second fucking bar . . ." He blew on his knuckles again. "Fuck you,

Los Angeles! I'm going back to goddamn Texas. The Mirrors can go to hell, along with my season tickets for the Lakers!" They both left Roxanne's Bar with the material, loaded the car, and drove the forty miles that separate Pomona from Los Angeles. DD was waiting in the passenger seat of the 1965 Lincoln Continental Sedan he'd inherited from his grandpa Jacob, while his brother went into the apartment they'd rented at Wilton and Santa Monica Boulevard. He brought down a few suitcases and a six-pack of Budweiser, and they began their drive back to Texas.

※

DD was the nickname of David Davis, Will Davis's kid brother. They had both been born in Brenham, Texas, but grew up between Austin and Denison. Their mother, Maureen, was a waitress with a weakness for cigarettes, Jack Daniels, and unfaithful men. The daughter of a modest couple who were much loved in the community, she gained a reputation as a submissive romantic in her high school days. She graduated but didn't go to college. She began serving coffee in the business of a family friend, and that's where she met first Will's father and later DD's. With two children from two different fathers and the savings she'd managed to scrape together, she headed for Austin and then on to Denison, the home city of President Eisenhower, on the border with Oklahoma.

The two children went back to Brenham to spend their summers with their grandparents. Maureen's mother was a die-hard music lover and self-taught musician. She gave them their first instruments, a bass for DD and drum kit for Will. "You two were born to be the rhythm section. The rhythm section is everything. A good bass line makes any song better!" she told them. And they spent their afternoons improvising with Lorraine on the piano, the best way to avoid thinking about their mother's dark episodes of depression. Music made life less difficult for them.

In 1977 *Slap Shot* was released, a film directed by George Roy Hill. In this sports comedy, Paul Newman plays Reggie Dunlop, the coach of the Charlestown Chiefs, a calamitous minor league ice-hockey team. His players include three brothers, the Hansons, long-haired, with thick-rimmed glasses and breath that you wouldn't want to feel on the back of your neck. At that time, DD and Will often wore Black Sabbath T-shirts, black tortoiseshell glasses, and hair down to their shoulders.

They didn't have many friends and got themselves into trouble on a regular basis. They were thrown out of school for tearing apart the wrestling team. Six bruisers covered in blood and humiliated by two short-sighted freaks. The eldest Davis was locked up for three days after breaking the nose of an enormous truck driver on the San Antonio-Kansas highway who'd stopped to eat at the diner where Maureen worked. Apparently, the guy didn't like his coffee and spilled it on the floor while at the same time insulting Will's mother. Gripped by an uncontrollable rage, Will leapt onto the bar and threw himself at the truck driver, smashing his head right into the middle of his face and destroying his nose. It took five or six guys to peel him away, while his brother flicked through the *Herald* without batting an eyelid. It was incidents like this that earned them the nickname they became known by in the city: the Hanson Brothers.

✳

They parked the Lincoln at door number 3 of the Dunes Motel complex in Blythe, California. They were a few miles from the Colorado River, the natural border between California and Arizona, and they still had a good drive ahead of them before reaching Texas. They dropped everything from their pockets onto one of the beds in the room: car keys, three bass picks, less than a hundred dollars in bills and coins, a half-smoked pack of Kool menthol cigarettes, and a piece of paper with the phone number of Bill Gray, an old friend of Will's. "We're screwed, DD. I'm gonna call Bill, see if he can give us a hand in El Paso. We've got just enough money to get there and eat something along the way . . . Back in a minute."

DD went to the bedroom door with his brother and watched him walk down to reception. Leaning against the doorframe he could see Will talking on the phone through one of the windows of the booth. He seemed pretty relaxed, nodding his head and smoking that menthol shit he'd got himself hooked on in LA. He saw him hang up and most likely curse the lead singer of the Mirrors and God knows who else. He watched as his big brother said something to the receptionist and finally looked up at DD, as he came out of reception and starting walking toward him. A couple of glances from his brother was enough for DD to realize that Bill would help them out, but that Will was going to have to pay for it. "The fucking drums . . . I'm gonna have to sell my fucking drums that Grandma gave me, goddammit!" They emptied the car, putting the instruments and everything else into the bedroom, ate the Value Pack they'd bought at McDonald's, and got some sleep.

The next morning they loaded the Lincoln again and drove the six hundred miles to El Paso in one hit, picking up Bill close to San Jacinto Plaza. Bill had worked for the Davis's grandfather in Brenham before moving to West Texas. He was a small, affable man who often got mistaken for the actor John Hillerman. He had a broad forehead and dark hair, slicked back just like Higgins, the character Hillerman played in the series *Magnum, P.I.* He was little over thirty years old but looked twice his age. He got into the car and greeted Will and DD. In his high-pitched voice, he gave directions to the pawn shop so they could sell the old Slingerland Buddy Rich, cymbals and all, for the $650 they would need to rent the apartment. A drum kit for a house might sound like a good swap to most people, but for Will, making that decision was a hard blow that took a long time to recover from. "Do either of you two know how to cook burgers?" asked Bill while showing them a flyer. "At the Hamburger Hut they're looking for a cook, the manager's a friend of mine, I could talk with him . . ." Will took the flyer and looked at his brother, who looked back approvingly. "When do I start?" said the eldest Davis. "Tomorrow, for sure. Get down there before nine and I'll let them know now. Good luck, Will. Anything you need, just give me a call."

The next day, Will Davis arrived at the Hamburger Hut on Alameda Avenue, put on an apron, and got down to cooking hamburgers with the idea of earning enough money to buy a new drum kit and get back to Southeast Texas in less than three months. It was the second Monday in January, 1985, and by April he wanted to be back in Houston trying out as the drummer for one of the city's bands.

1985

NINETEEN EIGHTY-FIVE BEGINS WITH THE same routines that 1984 ended with: university—rehearsals—go to gigs—write—university—rehearsals—go to gigs—write and so on. Daniel and Ricardo are trying to take their project seriously, and the band becomes the definitive backbone of their lives. The relationship is strong. It began suddenly and intensely, they got through a three-year separation while at college, and they're now spending most of their time together. They talk about groups, songs, and concerts, their conversations as impenetrable as Fort Knox. Just a few lucky people are able to scale the walls and get inside their bubble. As a rule, these are people who also go to concerts and who, in one way or another, prove themselves sufficiently knowledgeable to keep Daniel and Ricardo's attention. One of these is Grant, a younger guy who has been playing the drums for some time. In fact, they are seriously considering giving him the drumsticks and moving Danny to bass.

They don't have any mutual friends. Grant and the other music lovers they spend their time with are friends from school and not from the punk scene. People they exchange information and have a beer with but nothing more. Daniel, who has a gift for socializing, forms relationships with other students in his major and often goes to the parties they organize. There is no written rule that stops them from forming relationships with people from outside the band, but the two of them definitely feel that the band comes first and that nothing else should affect or interrupt their shared music project.

Ricardo follows this rule to the letter. Daniel less so. Quite a lot less.

Early on in the year they manage to get to grips with a few of the covers, and two of their own songs have enough power to be classified as "playable live." The name remains a mystery, and a new, niggling concern is that they want the band to have that "something" that defines them, that makes them stand out from the rest and, what the hell, that makes them unique!

The previous year they'd been to the concert that the Hickoids played in El Paso as part of their "Texas 2-R 84" tour. This Texan group from Austin had a distinctive mix of sounds, and their shows were transformed into full-fledged demonstrations of power, attitude, and technique. That night in 1984, with the excuse of the fanzine, they talked with the Hickoids' front man, Jeff Smith. He told them that the Texan flavor of his music was not at all forced: they were from Texas and, at the end of the day, giving their songs a Southern touch was genuinely what defined them. It was a group that rejected the rigidness of some sectors of hardcore and became a leading example of cowpunk, together with the Meat Puppets from Arizona.

A year later, Daniel and Ricardo would remember the words of Jeff Smith. They had to find that "something" that would genuinely define them too: "Fuck man, we've gotta do like the Hickoids and give our music our own touch!"

They were always remarkably open when it came to music. The song "Guyana Punch" from The Judy's was, undoubtedly, the cover they enjoyed playing most. The Judy's were a new wave group from Pearland that formed part of the punk circuit but had a truly distinctive personality, not to mention some awesome songs. Daniel had discovered them while at college in Austin and had told Ricardo about them, knowing they might appeal to his eclectic tastes. Television and Talking Heads were two groups Ricardo often listened to with his father, and there were three other groups from this new wave that had climbed to the top of their list of favorites: The Judy's, Devo, and One Second Zero (who used to be the Victims from El Paso—they had changed their name and released a single with two songs on it: "Money Talked" / "Spring Heel'd Jack").

Their joint list of favorite groups in 1985 was, therefore, divided into three styles:

Punk / Hardcore
1. Hüsker Dü from Saint Paul (Minnesota)
2. Rhythm Pigs from El Paso (Texas)
3. Minutemen from San Pedro (California)
4. Black Flag from Hermosa Beach (California)
5. Big Boys from Austin (Texas)

New Wave
1. Devo from Kent (Ohio)
2. The Judy's from Pearland (Texas)
3. One Second Zero from El Paso (Texas)
4. Television from New York
5. Talking Heads from New York

Pop Rock
1. Mission of Burma from Boston (Massachusetts)
2. Beat Happening from Olympia (Washington)
3. Daniel Johnston from Austin (Texas)

4. Sonic Youth from New York
5. R.E.M. from Athens (Georgia)

Nineteen eighty-five is the year of *Bad Moon Rising* by Sonic Youth, of *Dinosaur* by Dinosaur (before including the "Jr." in its name), Descendents' release *I Don't Want to Grow Up,* and SST Records' releases *New Day Rising* (Hüsker Dü), *Up on the Sun* (Meat Puppets), *Loose Nut* (Black Flag), and the compilation *My First Bells* by Minutemen. Daniel Álvarez gets a call from one of his best friends in Austin, who tells him that MTV are broadcasting a special on the music scene in the Texan capital. The program *The Cutting Edge* in Austin would surely go down in history for recording Daniel Johnston's magnificent live performance of "I Live My Broken Dreams." In our interviews, Daniel Álvarez always insists that the rawness of that song, which combines Johnston's peculiar voice with some awkward guitar strumming, is the most punk thing he's ever seen on television. Beautiful, intense, and inspiring. If you haven't seen it, you should.

That same year, Ronald Reagan's second term in the White House begins, Mikhail Gorbachev is elected president of the USSR, and James Cameron releases the first part of *Terminator.* In the short history of Ricardo and Daniel's new band, 1985 stands out for three key moments: the definitive choice of a name for the group, Ricardo's trip to Mexico, and the formation of the band's first lineup.

The Definitive Name

Daniel and Ricardo often help each other out with schoolwork. Daniel, an art student, excels in his graphic design classes and often runs his ideas past Ricardo, who turns out to be a first-rate sounding board. One of the tasks they have to do is create a packet of souvenirs for a fictitious tourism campaign in El Paso, Texas. To do this, Daniel designs a logo composed of two parts:

- The text "ELPASO," with spaces between the words and in black, using the typeface Futura Extra Bold, the empty space in the "O" filled with a star (the "Lone Star").
- Graphically the Texan and Mexican flags are fused inside of a circle outlined in black with a height three times that of the text.

They print the logo on gray T-shirts and create stickers and post-cards with it printed over the top of arty photos of the city. Daniel defends his project as a series of products aimed at young people, arguing that he wanted to get away from the hackneyed aesthetics of the tourism sector. He passes with top marks, and his teacher even suggests he try to put the idea into practice.

That same afternoon, during rehearsals, Felipe goes into the garage and smokes a cigarette while listening to his son and Daniel distorting and speeding up "Never Talking to You Again" by Hüsker Dü. Through the smoke of his own cigarette, he sees a large card-board box slowly moving toward him with the vibrations produced by the syncopated drumming of the bass drum and crouches down to pick up one of the printed T-shirts. He looks at it, smiles, and slings it over his right shoulder, just as the waiters do every day with their tea towels in the Jalisco Café. He waits patiently for them to finish their song and with the cigarette bouncing between his lips he says: "ELPASO! What a great name for the group! And I see you already got the merchandising for your first concert . . . ELPASO, a band from El Paso, nice idea. I'll keep this one." He crosses back through the garage door, and his silhouette vanishes in the darkness of the kitchen. The boys look at each other and smile, silently confirming that they are indeed ELPASO, a band from El Paso, Texas.

The Trip to Mexico

Due to circumstance, Ricardo Salazar had never left Texas and grew up as one half of a small, two-member family. His father managed to get by with his broken English when he arrived in the US, the language he used to talk with Constance, Ritchie's mother, unless he was cursing her, which he normally did in Spanish. When she left, Ricardo and his father developed an unusual linguistic relationship. The boy understood the language of his grandparents on his father's side but didn't want to speak it. It was quite normal to see them having an argument over the shopping in the supermarket, each in his own preferred language. Felipe would often reproach his son for reading the Latin American authors he was studying in English. "You should be ashamed . . . Reading books by Carlos Fuentes like a *gringo* when you could do it in the language it was written in!" he would exclaim. The boy, however, was angry at Felipe for never talking to him about his family and where he came from. Despite his rebellious attitude toward his father's mother tongue, Ricardo had an irrational curiosity to learn about his Mexican roots. This peculiar language-family relationship changed radically in April 1985, when, out of the blue, Felipe decided to take his twenty-three-year-old son to Mexico to meet his family.

The trip was something that Ricardo kept to himself. He told little about what happened there to his friend Daniel, but it was clear that meeting his family was to change him forever. He came back to the border eager to expand his knowledge of Mexican culture and, for the first time, it was him who persuaded Daniel of something that would have a dramatic impact on the band. He sat down with his friend and told him of his desire to sing all of ELPASO's songs in Spanish. In fact, he was convinced that they should translate all the covers they did of their favorite groups into Spanish. "That's our secret weapon, man. We're Mexican, that's what distinguishes us from the rest. We're a Chicano punk band, so we should sing in the language of our ancestors." For Daniel, who had a natural gift for marketing, this was an absurd idea. So much so that it was brilliant. They could become the only US punk band that sang in Spanish. That would be their selling point, and a pretty good one at that. The idea just needed a little fine-tuning.

Ricardo's Chicano activism grew exponentially, along with his awareness of class and a keen eye for detecting and denouncing social injustice. While musically he was increasingly eclectic, open, and wary of what punk demanded, intellectually he began an ascent into anarchism that would lead him to read Noam Chomsky and develop a keen interest in the situation undocumented immigrants were facing in the United States. Whatever happened on that journey, it awoke the Mexican that Ricardo carried inside him and somehow stirred up something in Daniel's consciousness too. They took up their notebook and, with Felipe's help, began to rewrite their songs and translate the lyrics of Hüsker Dü, Minutemen, and company. They had a name and they had a personality. They just needed a bass player.

The First Lineup

The Salazar home is always empty in the mornings. Felipe is up early to go to work, and Ricardo has breakfast with Daniel at UTEP. One morning is the same as the next. Predictable. But there always comes a day when that monotony needs to be broken, and, one morning, Ricardo suggests to Daniel that they go to the garage and have a go at writing a song. Daniel is up for it. When they park the car outside the house, the boys hear strange noises coming from the garage and look at each other suspecting something is amiss. It can't be Felipe; his Ford LTD Country Squire isn't parked in the driveway, so things are not looking good. Ricardo swallows hard, and Daniel warns him with a gesture of his head. "Let's call the cops, man," he whispers, but Ricardo is already out of the car and crossing the street, intent on going into the house.

They open the door slowly and close it without making a sound. They creep down the corridor, backs against the right hand wall, and see opposite them the father and son's bedrooms, empty and all messed up, like everything's been turned over in search of something valuable. Nothing strange here, though: the rooms are exactly as their owners had left them. They reach the dining room, which leads into the kitchen, which leads into the garage, and suddenly the noise they're hearing is totally familiar. Someone is playing the fucking drums!

Complex rhythms, graceful triplets . . . This thief clearly has hands that know what they're doing with a pair of drumsticks. Ricardo takes a big knife from the marble worktop and looks at his friend with a baffled expression on his face, as if to say, "I guess this is what we're supposed to do, right?" They walk around the washing machine, and they're standing right in front of the wooden door that will lead them straight to this jazz-junky criminal, a Ginger Baker-style burglar, whom they plan to scare the hell out of with a blunt carving knife and faces oozing anything but confidence. They speak under their breaths. "On the count of three, I'm gonna kick the door open and we scream like madmen, OK?" says Ricardo, "Three and you kick open the door, or you kick on three?" answers Daniel. "Three and kick." "Shit man, OK."

One . . . Two . . . And then the fucking door opens from the other side, scaring the hell out of the both of them as well as the hairy brute in the garage. Ricardo's knife hand trembles and he tells the monster of a man standing in front of him to get out. The huge intruder puts his hands to his chest, which is when they see a second thief by the amplifier with Ricardo's bass guitar in his hands. No one moves. Daniel is in shock, Ricardo waves the knife around, the hairy brute gets his breath back, pressing his hands together by way of an apology, and the guy by the amplifier is still holding on to the bass as if this whole thing has nothing to do with him.

"We just wanted to play a little, guys," says the hairy brute, pointing to the drums.

"Get outta here," replies Ricardo in a trembling voice.

"We're gonna call the fuckin' police!" shouts Daniel from the kitchen.

"There's no need, honestly, we're off. Put the guitar down, DD," the hairy brute addresses the other guy without taking his eyes of Ricardo and the knife.

The second thief, with his long mustache and gold-rimmed glasses, stands up unhurriedly, revealing his near two meters of height. He's wearing a cap that makes him look like a redneck, but he's wearing a Black Flag T-shirt, and there's no way Ricardo and Daniel would have missed that. The hairy brute has a goatee and black tortoiseshell glasses and is a little shorter than the other guy but much stockier and barefoot. He picks up a pair of low-top Converse and opens the door that connects the garage with the back of the house while apologizing one last time. The two-meter-tall mustachioed redneck leaves without saying a word. And that's it, they're safe. Nothing got out of hand.

✳

The pair are still standing in the garage without daring to play their instruments. Daniel frowns, staring at the bass drum. There are the sticks the other guy was using without his permission, and he feels intimidated, as much because someone else has sat down at his drums (and who knows how many times!) as because that imposter could play a hundred times better than him. Ricardo, with his hands on his hips, looks at the ceiling and suddenly shouts, "It's the fuck-ing cook from the Hamburger Hut! Goddamn! With his hair down I didn't recognize him at first! But it's him for sure!" He's excited, like he always is when he remembers something. He has a memory for faces and never forgets one. If Ricardo says that the intruder works in the Hamburger Hut, it's because he works in the Hamburger Hut.

"Danny, are you still up for moving to the bass?"

"What? Don't you want . . ."

"Are you still up for it or not?"

Daniel's frown deepens. He knows a drummer like that would really raise the level of the band, and he likes playing the bass.

The next day, when they leave the university, they head over to the Hamburger Hut and confirm that the hairy brute does indeed cook those double hamburgers with cheese they love devouring so much. The guy is wearing his hair up in a bun and doesn't have the black tortoiseshell glasses on. When he sees them come in through the door he snorts, curses under his breath, and puts the spatula down next to the grill. He asks someone to keep an eye on the meat. He won't be long. He signals them to come outside of the diner. He's tense but tries to stay calm.

Ricardo takes a step forward, he's nervous but smiling. He can't help himself. Daniel stays behind his friend. For the first time, Ricardo takes control and Daniel realizes that he's perhaps not ELPASO's natural leader.

"I told you that we only wanted to play. It won't happen again, honestly."

"We know, man . . ." says Ricardo.

"So what the hell are you doing here?" interrupts the thief/drummer/chef.

"Do you wanna join our band?"

"What?"

"I said, do you want to join our band?"

"You guys have a band?"

"Yeah, man, the other day you scared the hell out of us, but we were also blown away by what we heard!"

"I was just practicing . . . I had to sell my drum kit and, well . . . My brother and I were listening to you play once and we thought about breaking in to . . ."

"Awesome! Join the band. You can play every day. Come on, what do you say?"

"Fuck! OK! But on one condition . . ."

"What?" asks Ricardo, excited.

"My brother would have to play the bass. I only play with him."

"Cool!" shouts Ricardo.

"Cool?!" protests Daniel. "I'm supposed to be the bass player, not that redneck!"

"We'll both play guitar," Ricardo tells him. "You had to start with a new instrument anyway, so let's make it the guitar. What's your name?"

"I'm Will."

"Good to meet you, Will! I'm Ricardo, the singer and guitarist, and this is Daniel, the ex-drummer and future solo guitarist."

"What the fuck," Daniel holds his hand out to Will, "you can call me Danny."

"Shall we rehearse tomorrow?" asks Ricardo excitedly.

"I finish up here at five."

"We'll see you at my place at half past, then."

"Deal."

"Deal."

Second Movement
(1985–1988)

POCHO!

A SMALL CANVAS, MORE OR LESS the size of a magazine, flies across the stage without touching anything or anyone. It spins through the air like a ninja star. It passes first between Ricardo's face and his microphone and then between Will's hi-hats and left arm. The drummer looks at his brother, who's holding his note, the pick scratching sharply over the fourth string of his bass guitar, the faintest of smiles giving away his enjoyment of the scene. Will shakes his head and turns around to hit the tom, four bars and the song's over. Ricardo turns to the drums and looks at Will. Will looks back. Will looks at DD, Ricardo also looks at DD, and he begins to play the bass riff that starts the next song. DD couldn't give a shit about the battle that's erupted in the crowd. In fact, he's getting off on it. He enjoys watching people knock each other around and wants to carry on playing. Ricardo and Will join in, but, before the first verse, the guitar and the bass fall silent, the spotlights turn out, and the sound of shouting and fighting can be heard over the rhythm of the unamplified drums. The power's been cut, and one of the owners of the art gallery is trying to get the people out of the room while trying to save the few pieces of art that are still intact. "Get outta here, you fucking assholes!" he screams. Oscar, the guy who had programmed ELPASO's first performance in Juárez, asks the band to get their things together and leave ASAP. No one talks about money, both sides know that the little that has been made will go toward cleaning up and, maybe, repainting the walls.

No one in the band could have imagined that their first concert would be such a disaster. First, there was the problem of the lineup: Daniel had been "otherwise engaged" for a while and hadn't rehearsed the songs with two guitars like Ricardo had wanted. Will and DD had integrated into the band brilliantly, and the songs sounded much more robust and punchier with the new rhythm section. Ricardo had thought of arrangements that needed a second guitar, but it didn't look like Daniel was up for the challenge. "School's got me by the balls, man," he'd said, but everyone knew that if anything had him by the balls it was the blonde he'd been spending his evenings with for the last few weeks. "The dude's in love. It's normal." The other set-back was the language. Ricardo had doggedly translated all the lyrics of the songs (their own and the covers) but still hadn't learned them properly and often forgot parts. His pronunciation was OK, but not good enough for the Mexican audience awaiting them in the art gallery that had been temporarily converted into a concert hall. "*Pocho!*" they shouted at him.

Pocho is a derogatory term that Mexicans use to define a Mexican or Chicano who has problems talking in Spanish or does so with a pronounced American accent. For Ricardo, who was going through a period of total self-redefinition, the label hurt like hell. The grand-child and son of Mexicans he may have been, but that wasn't good enough. It was a familiar feeling. He was being made to suffer thanks to his origins, his social class, and his physical appearance. Mestizo, poor, fat, and now . . . *pocho*. The old Ricardo would have recoiled and hated everyone for this, but the new Ricardo had more of a fighting spirit and a clear aim in mind: to change the world through music, and he was going to do it caterwauling in Spanish. That's why he contacted María, a friend of Daniel's family, who gave Spanish classes at her home, where he went religiously once every week.

The fateful night in Juárez had a few more surprises in store for the band. Two crucial people for the group's future had been watching them play among the smashing, shouting, and general destruction. These two guys had picked up on the magic emanating from Ricardo's songs and thought it was a cool idea to sing in Spanish. One was Greg Adams, guitarist and founder of the Rhythm Pigs and one of Ricardo and Daniel's heroes. The other was Octavio Quintana, an unnerving and mysterious guy who offered to play lead guitar. "I think your songs would really benefit from a second guitar," he told Ricardo. "Yeah, me too. Why don't you come over to my place tomorrow and the four of us can rehearse a while?"

RHYTHM
PIGS

13 SONG LP OUT NOW ON
MORDAM RECORDS

**AVAILABLE FROM ALL FINE
STORES AND DISTRIBUTORS**

EVERYBODY LOVES THE RHYTHM PIGS

I WENT TO EL PASO FOR the first time in March 2015. We'd been driving for almost eight hours from Austin, each doing three-hour shifts at the wheel. Louis, Jordi, and me. On I-10, there's a point when the desert dissolves and warehouses start appearing, along with large parking lots with trucks for sale and the obligatory Hooters and Walmarts. I was lucky enough to see all this from the passenger seat with my nose pressed against the glass. On the television screen that my window had become I watched the lampposts zip by at a greater speed than the restaurants, which, in turn, whizzed by faster than the buildings and distant mountains, like a giant zoetrope.

Jordi slowed down and, outside a diner with a sign that read "*Chih'ua Tacos y Cortes*," we turned right. I saw the large parking lot of La Quinta Inn (one of the many motel chains we used) and just next to this an illuminated billboard with red letters inviting passersby to the Foxy Nude Show. We joked about having a drink in the strip joint, but never did. We took our room key, emptied the Ford Focus we'd rented in Dallas, and drew straws for the double bed that was just about big enough for one.

The next morning we had the classic, never-changing motel-chain breakfast: coffee, a Texas-shaped waffle, syrup, Cheerios, awful-tasting orange juice, and scrambled eggs with bacon. The telephone rings. Greg Adams tells us he's about to arrive at the motel parking lot. He says his car is big enough for all of us and we can leave the Ford there.

A dark red pickup pulls up outside reception, the driver's door opens and closes, and we see Greg silhouetted against the light. He's a tall, solid guy, around fifty years old, with a once-dark head of hair now revealing more gray hairs than brown. He's got blue eyes and is wearing a short-sleeved gray cotton T-shirt and jeans. He's wearing brown cowboy boots, which we hear clicking on the floor as he approaches. With a friendly look of measured enthusiasm, it's clear he's intrigued to find out about these three thirty-somethings born 5,700 miles from El Paso when he was already playing the circuit who now want to interview him. Greg is our first interview in El Paso and the third since we arrived in Texas. We follow the same routine that worked in the previous two: I introduce the three of us with my limited English, I tell him Lou is our official translator, and the conversation between the two of them begins to flow. Lou explains that we know Daniel Álvarez and that we would like to know a little more about ELPASO (the band) and El Paso (the scene). We tell him we know his band, the Rhythm Pigs, are well-known on the border and that it is an honor for us that he's agreed to meet. He smiles and invites us to get into his pickup, and we set off on an incredible tour, alternating between iconic places of the eighties punk scene and the obligatory sights of this Texan city. He takes us to the Koke House, Old Buffalo, and Club 101. He tells us that he was blown away by Teenage Popeye at a concert where he was working as the sound guy and that he decided then and there that he wanted a band too, just as had happened to Daniel and Ricardo. He's passionate about his music.

There was a magical moment when he took us to the Rathskeller, which was halfway through being torn down. That same day they were

94

going to demolish the entire block to build a CVS Pharmacy, and we were lucky enough to get a few pan shots while Greg explained how he'd begun there playing with his first band, Civilians In Action.

Rob Norred was one of Greg's best friends, and they both made the leap into punk at the same time. They often created fake flyers for nonexistent concerts and posted them up around the city, fantasizing that one day they would do the same with posters of real shows. They met Ed Ivey and set up C.I.A. (aka Civilians In Action), a raw, in-your-face punk band. Steve'O'Cide, one of the city's best-known graphic artists, drew the logo for the band and did some promotional flyers with a photo and their contact details. Daniel and Ricardo saw them for the first time in the Sancho Bros. Ballroom playing with the Victims (later One Second Zero) and Aftermath. Shortly afterward, Civilians split up. Robert Norred teamed up with John Williams and Mike Gray to form Red Zone, and Ed Ivey (bass), Greg (guitar), and Jay Smith (drums) started the Rhythm Pigs, the band that would put El Paso on the punk map of America.

In 1984 they record a first sensational EP titled *An American Activity,* and Jello Biafra himself places them at number one on his list in the magazine *Maximum Rock'n'Roll.* Mordam Records signs them, and they become the label's first big band, along with Faith No More (a band they would later become great friends with), and begin touring with them and other bands like Dead Kennedys or Short Dogs Grow. They play with the Melvins and Skin Yard, Black Flag, Jerry's Kidz, and most of the groups that fueled the fascinating underground scene in the US in the 1980s.

They release *Rhythm Pigs* and *Choke on This* and travel to Europe to play, increasing their legendary status in their hometown. In El Paso, everybody loves the Rhythm Pigs. Although they live in San Francisco, they've always considered themselves a group from El

Paso and come back to play whenever they can, making sure a local band opens for them.

On July 27, 1986, they are scheduled to travel through El Paso to play at Sound Seas, and Greg, who saw ELPASO in Juárez, proposes they open the show. Ricardo excitedly accepts. There are nine months to go, so he has time to work on his Spanish, polish the songs, and try Octavio out as the second guitar. "Did you really like us, Greg?" he asks for a third time. "Sure man! You're different, your songs are great, and you started a riot, what more could you ask for?" Shit, Greg, you're the man.

OCTAVIO

OCTAVIO WAS A GOOD-LOOKING GUY. He could have lost a few kilos, but he was strong and had an extraordinary magnetism. He wore a wool beanie that kept a tight hold on every one of his black curls. A long mustache underscored his nose, drawing attention to his meaty lower lip. His eyes were narrow but full of light, giving him an intense stare. He was always raising his eyebrows and laughing out of one side of his mouth. He couldn't speak English, but he understood it, and if he was ever with an American he made this clear: "*Te entiendo perfectamente, gringo cabrón.*"

He wore a Mexican *guayabera* with beige pockets and a T-shirt with the album cover of Kiss's *Rock and Roll Over* underneath. Below the waist he wore pleated brown trousers and white Nike Wimbledon Bruin sneakers with a blue Swoosh. He carried a black Gibson Les Paul in one hand and a six-pack in the other. He got the right man when he threw the six cans at Will (the ELPASO drummer was the band's main consumer of barley juice), they looked at each other knowingly, and Will returned one of the Budweisers, imitating a pitcher throwing a baseball.

Ricardo was bubbling with excitement and was dying to get down to rehearsing their songs with another guitar. The fact that the group was expanding from three members to four meant they were really in business now. Punk and hardcore and their philosophy of less is more was represented by three-member bands: Minutemen, Hüsker Dü, and the Rhythm Pigs were a few examples. Including a second guitar that could create complex arrangements or solos was considered a sacrilege in the first half of the eighties. That kind of stuff was for European bands, not for a group that wanted respect on the American underground scene.

Daniel was in the garage looking ruffled, as if he'd realized that Octavio might take his place as "the most important person in Ricardo's life." The last few weeks had been quite tense. Ricardo's uni-lateral acceptance of DD as ELPASO's bass player got to Daniel, even though that was clearly the condition for having Will as the drum-mer. And Ricardo felt somewhat let down by Daniel's total lack of commitment as guitarist, and they still hadn't talked about Octavio's possible inclusion in the band. Despite the tension, it was important for Ritchie that Daniel was there. His opinion about ELPASO's music was still a basic need for the project to keep moving forward.

The band chose "John Wayne Gacy" as the first song to rehearse. Octavio listened to the first verse and chorus, and when the song came back to the initial chord progression he was already into it, playing the riff as if he'd been doing it all his life. The song is a short one, no more than a minute and a half, but they extended the last part to enjoy Octavio's improvised rockabilly picking. That was when Daniel's body language turned from distrust to amazement, and when his friend Ricardo caught his eye all he could do was nod. They both knew it: this guy from Juárez was definitely in.

They tried out a few new songs that Ricardo had half finished, and the sound was awesome. They played for nearly four hours, going through the covers and the repertoire of their own songs. Octavio was an exceptional musician and sang well too, maybe bet-ter than Ricardo. He tried out a few harmonies and they all finished their first rehearsal together feeling more than satisfied. They left the house and headed for a local bar to sink a few beers. Daniel grabbed Ricardo's arm and looked him in the eye, "Man, today was fucking awesome . . . Do you want me to work on getting us a gig at Liberty Lunch in Austin?" Ricardo's affirmative response to Daniel's question led to the band's first tour. But, above all, it meant Daniel's definitive move into the official position of manager of ELPASO. He had designed the band logo and was now ready to design the group's rise to the Olympus of punk. It was just a question of time, and, as usual, Daniel had a plan.

GOOD VIBRATIONS

THE DIRECTORS JOE BERLINGER AND BRUCE Sinofsky
directed what I've always considered one of the best documentaries
in the history of rock 'n' roll. *Some Kind of Monster* describes the tur-
bulent times Metallica had to negotiate at the beginning of this cen-
tury, while they were recording what was to be their eighth studio
album. I've never formed part of a successful band, but I have been
a music-loving teenager who pored over encyclopedias and biographies to the point that I could memorize the names, surnames,
chronologies, and discographies of most groups and solo artists in the
world of rock 'n' roll and its offshoots. Thanks to that investment of
time (and money) I think I now have the legitimate authority to create my own theories and believe them to be well-founded. In general,
the stories that make up the biographies of successful bands are nothing like those of the groups I have played with. But, when you look
at the early days of one of these future supernovas, like U2, Nirvana,
or Metallica, you could imagine drawing parallels between their
early years and the band that you and your friends tried to get off the
ground. Nothing could be further from the truth. While these people, against the odds, have a gift for being in the right place at the right
time, the rest of us, by comparison, are blind to such opportunities.

What I believe makes Berlinger and Sinofsky's film so great is
that, at times, the most famous heavy metal band in history comes

across as a group of aspiring musicians in a stifling, stuffy rehearsal studio. There is a fantastic scene where Lars Ulrich shamelessly tries to wind up James Hetfield under the inoffensive gaze of Kirk Hammett and producer Bob Rock. James, the singer and guitarist, tries to contain his anger and tells the drummer that if he keeps going down that road, things are going to get messy. Kirk, the band's solo guitarist, mutters a few timid "Come on, guys," and "Let's not go there," which evaporate in the room's oppressive atmosphere. Just as the tension reaches its peak, Lars Ulrich maliciously sticks his finger in the wound, causing the definitive explosion of Hetfield, who then leaves the recording studio, slamming the door behind him. After this, the story comes back to their glamorous and successful adventures in rock, and the band gets back together, Hetfield returns, and they sign up a bass player for an insane amount of money.

My point is that for a few minutes and for the first time in my life I felt like I identified with a rock star. I could rewind that scene and change places with almost any of those guys. I've been the asshole poking at fellow band members. Of course I've been the target of some mean bastard in a band who has managed to drive me to the breaking point, but above all I've been poor Kirk Hammett, trying to mediate between two amateur musicians who, for some strange reason, want to humiliate each other in a cold, half-sound-proofed hovel on a weeknight. Because trying to ensure everyone gets on with one another in a crappy band is not easy. There are no royalties, no groupies, no sponsors, and no image licenses. The little money involved is always outgoing and is normally never seen again. The concerts are often poorly attended, and the studio recordings never sound as powerful as you'd like.

That is why the solid sound that ELPASO were able to achieve at the beginning of 1986 is so remarkable. Everyone in the band, it would seem, was in the right place at the right time. There were talent, personality, and good songs. Ricardo had secured his place as the unquestionable leader of the band, and everyone else was in agreement. Octavio connected with Ricardo's songwriting style and gained further favor with the ELPASO front man for being an out-and-out Mexican. Will and DD formed a thunderous and virtuoso rhythm section: the drummer spoke through his elbows, and the two-meter-tall bass player simply smiled and nodded. Black Sabbath was an influence for all of them, and they loved playing Tony Iommi's riffs. At the end of each rehearsal, Ricardo looked at Will, who would sing the chorus of "Good Vibrations" by the Beach Boys: "I'm pickin' up good vibrations / She's giving me excitations," and the others would rush in with the other layers of harmonies the song weaves in as it progresses: "Oom bop, bop, good vibrations." DD would go for the falsetto, and everyone soaked up that sense of brotherhood and good vibrations that could be felt bouncing around the the garage in El Segundo Barrio.

Daniel, for his part, was delighted to be in charge of managing the project. He had carte blanche, and the other guys trusted him completely. Will had given him a contact in Denison to include a concert there on ELPASO's first Texan tour. His to-do list went something like this:

TEXAS TOUR
- Talk with Joe about playing at Liberty Lunch in Austin
- Call Rob to play in Denison
- Get a sound guy
- Get an amp for Octavio
- Get a replacement guitar
- IMPORTANT!: Get a van

Ford Custom Van

FORD ECONOLINE

"THE FORD ECONOLINE, THEN? PERFECT!" These were the used car salesman's exact words before extending his hand and shaking Ricardo's vigorously, as if to stop him from backing out. "You won't regret this, kid!" he exclaimed. But it was too late. The kid was already regretting it. He'd saved like mad. Many months of penury and isolation. No treats. The efforts of years saving for a car he'd always wanted, a 1973 Chevrolet Caprice. The blue Chevy that would take him to the East Coast, New York maybe. Or Florida. Ricardo had always wanted to visit Boston; the city that had spawned Mission of Burma would have been a safe bet. The idea was to leave Texas behind. The destination was flexible, but it had to be a long way from El Paso and all the bullshit he'd put up with there. The band was going well now and Guadalupe, the photographer, had become the closest thing to a girlfriend he'd ever had. He fantasized about one day being able to take it all somewhere else, killing two birds with one stone: he could carry on with the project and finally leave the city he was born in.

Spending his life savings on his dream car would have been a bold statement, but Daniel had a knack for getting in the way of Ricardo's plans. He was able to deliver the perfect argument, obliterating his friend's protests like a gust of wind blowing down a house of cards. Or like the controlled demolition of a building. It's an amazing sight.

They place the packs of dynamite strategically all around the structure and detonate them one by one until the whole block seems to be guzzled up by the earth, tons of rubble and clouds of dust that might once have been—who knows?—a factory, a theater . . . A real, meaningful construction, reduced to NOTHING. And that's what Daniel did. He detonated Ricardo's arguments until they would finally collapse, turn to rubble. In this case, the 1986 tour was the dynamite that transformed his 1973 Chevrolet into ELPASO's Ford van.

"Think about it, Ritchie. How else are we going to transport Will's drum kit? Plus, with a big enough van we could sleep in it and save ourselves a night in a motel." Phrases like, "That's the rattletrap that'll get you out of Texas," were to eventually lead Ricardo to that overzealous handshake. "Let's go to my office and sign the papers. Then the Econoline'll be all yours, kid."

They left the parking lot and drove along Alameda Avenue with the setting sun staining the sky with orange streaks as it disappeared behind the Franklin Mountains. Daniel thumped the dashboard to the beat of R.E.M.'s "Harborcoat." The tape with the *Reckoning* of Michael Stipe's group had just christened the van's cassette player. Ricardo was driving, feeling pretty pissed. It annoyed him that Daniel had cajoled him yet again, but, at the same time, he couldn't hide the excitement he felt behind the wheel of the dark red van at the idea that it would take them on their Texas tour. Out of the corner of his eye he looked at Daniel, who began singing the song's chorus: "Please find my harborcoat . . . can't go outside without it." They both burst out laughing in unison and carried on singing as they joined the tide of cars heading downtown.

✳

First Denison, at Rob's place. Then on to Dallas and afterward to Austin. San Antonio and, maybe, Fort Worth. They could perhaps fit in the Railroad Blues in Alpine before closing in El Paso. Seven shows between February 8 and 22, 1986, which would include the possibility of opening for Scratch Acid and Killdozer in none other than Liberty Lunch in Austin. World domination has to begin someplace, and that place was Texas.

Many people moved to the West Coast. The Plugz and the Rhythm Pigs had chosen Los Angeles and San Francisco to settle in and worked hard to make a name for themselves in California. Daniel had a plan for rising to the top that included playing in every far-flung corner of the state, especially in small places like Alpine or Denison. He had the theory that if you became a hero in those places, the guys from the same Texan cities, when they headed off to the rest of the country to go to college, would do so with them in mind as their "favorite group." Daniel had thought it through as if he were planning the spread of an epidemic. A Texan kid infected with the ELPASO virus would go off to study in Portland, meet the folk there, and make friends with one of the university's radio DJs. "You never heard of ELPASO? They're awesome! They're from El Paso, Texas, and sing in Spanish. You should play them one day." The DJ puts the group on the radio and they become a small phenomenon. A Portland band hears them and decides to write to the group to invite them to play a show together. This pattern would be repeated throughout America, and ELPASO would slowly become a cult band that, sooner or later, a label like SST Records would sign and organize a tour for across the country. A second album, a European tour, and, who knows, maybe a third LP with a really big record label. But for the time being these were just castles in the sky, and they had to focus on rehearsals, preparing a good setlist for the tour, and closing the dates. Daniel had begun to illustrate some of the flyers promoting the concerts, and Ricardo had started his Spanish classes. They were ready to go down in history.

'86 TEXAS TOUR

IN MY FAMILY HOME, WE DIDN'T get a car until I turned nine, and, even once we had it, we never covered any great distances. I think the first vacation I ever went on was a few years later, in 1993, when we traveled more than 550 miles in the used Peugeot 205 that my father had bought from his boss. That was when I realized how important music can be for a long journey. That small car was missing rear seatbelts, air-conditioning, and democracy. There was only one musical authority: the driver's. "When you're old enough to drive and have your license, you can choose the music." My brother and I looked at each other, sighed, and set to quarreling over nothing.

In 1999 my father got rid of that Peugeot, and in 2001, just after turning nineteen and with my license slotted snuggly into my wallet, I bought it back from a local mechanic who had bought it from the person who'd bought it from my dad two years before. In Nameless I was the first member of the band with their own car, so I often did the rounds picking everyone up before rehearsals, and we loaded up the white, fifthhand Peugeot 205 with our humble instruments each time we had a concert. I tried to be faithful to the car's musically author- itarian origins, but my copilot would just stick on whatever he felt like. Sometimes the drummer would bring his own cassettes, com- pletely overlooking my magnificent collection, meticulously labeled and organized in plastic briefcases.

With my two teenage bands (Nameless and Claim) we never played outside Barcelona. The closest I ever came to a first tour was a few consecutive concerts in Madrid and Zaragoza with my last project. After a few years without much musical activity, I decided to be true to my childhood dream and record an album. But properly. With long days in the recording studio, problems with the mixing, and arguments over song orders. To do this, I put down my bass, the instrument I had carried with me my whole life, and became inseparable from my old acoustic guitar and the pink Moleskine notebook in which I scribbled my first lyrics. I made a few demos at the home of one of the members of Claim and, thanks to the internet, the pseudo-folk numbers I'd just written began to take shape. Some specialized broadcasters played my music, and I managed to bring together the three friends who would accompany me in my last band, Anicet— named after the African-Spanish basketball player—which would give me my most glorious moments in a fairly unimpressive musical career.

After a few months playing and polishing the set that would become our first album, we got into the studio. We recorded what was undoubtedly the finest album we could have produced at that time. Its impact nationally was acceptable, and we accepted the inevitability that our first small tour to present our debut album would not be a great success. We managed to schedule three dates in just six days, which had us driving almost eight hundred miles for the first two performances. Some twelve hours on the road.

We loaded the van the night before and headed off at sunrise in the direction of Madrid. It was February 2013, and the soundtrack for the journey came from a few CDs and the extended playlists each of us had on our phones, thereby further complicating the choice of what music we would listen to throughout the trip. Cassettes had their drawbacks, sure, but no one ever changed the music mid-song. And if the cassette was an entire album, you would listen to it from start to finish. The new musical era is killing albums, with everything revolving around immediacy, playlists, and recommendations. None of that does anything for peace and harmony among the members of an amateur band with disparate music tastes. Those eight hundred miles were a nonstop to-and-fro between songs, insults, and rebukes. It was a beautiful experience. We did two good concerts and came home hoping to one day return to the two cities with a new album.

February 10, 1986. Denison (TX)

The final showdown pits Beat Happening's self-titled album against *Tim* by the Replacements. Great bands like Black Flag, Sonic Youth, and The Judy's went out in the qualifiers. Now there are only two tapes left and one cassette player. Ricardo is defending the yellow album, complete with a rocket-riding cat, while Daniel, the driver, is gunning for the first material the Replacements have released on an international label. The Davis brothers are also in disagreement over the music that should be played in the van and, faced with the two-all draw, all Octavio can do is, literally, sweat. "Explain your arguments again," he says while he gets comfortable in the back and opens a paperback edition of *Little Boy Blue* by Edward Bunker. "What an asshole . . . didn't you say you couldn't speak English?" Will shouts at him. "*Pero lo entiendo perfectamente, gringo cabrón,*" he replies as the others burst into thunderous laughter.

Ricardo is backing the authentic sound of Beat Happening and claims "Foggy Eyes" as one of the most punk songs he's ever heard, despite not following the standard arrangements of the style's most emblematic bands. He also cites the fact that the album was

115

released by a small record label, K Records. "For me, right now, Beat Happening are like Minor Threat and K Records like Dischord." DD applauds, Daniel and Will boo, and Octavio carries on with his book.

"It's my turn," says the driver. "We can all agree on that bullshit about parallels between one band's self-released album and another. I like them too, but, fuck, Ritchie, we've got more than ten hours to reach Denison and we need a little movement... We don't want to be reduced to tears by Calvin Johnson's sorrowful wailing!" Will begins to hit the windows while at the same time shouting out Daniel's name as if he were part of a crowd wildly cheering on a political speaker.

"Replacements," says Octavio under his breath.

"What?" shouts Ricardo, clasping his head in his hands. "You motherfucker!"

"Come on! Danny, put the tape on!" exclaims Will, handing him the cassette.

"I'm sorry, Ricardo, but I really wanna hear 'Bastards of Young.' I love that song."

"You're the boss, Octavio, put on side B, Ritchie."

They stop for the night in Lubbock and the next morning drive on to Denison. Their idea is to arrive for lunch and leave everything set up a few hours before the start of the concert. It's Monday and, according to Rob, the owner of the place they'll be playing in, people will go and get drunk as long as they can get back to their homes at a decent time. Rob is an old high school friend of Will's and also used to be a musician. He now offers the barn adjoining his house for alternative shows in Denison. It's a strategic venue for groups from Oklahoma who decide to come down to play in Dallas and want to do a second concert to raise a bit more money to pay for gas on the return journey.

With everything set up they drive into downtown Denison, and

Will tells them stories about his childhood there. DD just smiles and nods each time his brother asks him for confirmation. He doesn't look very comfortable and rests his head on the window watching the buildings pass by.

※

Ten punks line the front row watching the members of ELPASO as they pick up their instruments and turn on the amps. The rest of the audience is spread randomly about the barn. There are a few rednecks around a table with drinks strewn across it, knocking back the *ponche* and staring malevolently at the musicians. For the concert flyer, Daniel had drawn a caricature of President Reagan with a Hitler mustache and Nazi jacket raising his left hand in the classic Vulcan greeting. It was highly likely that those guys wearing cowboy boots had voted for him two years before and weren't at all amused by the leaflet mocking their beloved Republican president. Aside from the punks and rednecks are the most numerous group in the audience: college students who, mostly, had been DD and Will's friends from class and who are blown away when ELPASO deliver their first song of the night. Ricardo screams into the microphone and strums the guitar while the rest of the band follow him flawlessly. They are a tight and captivating wall of sound that fills Rob's barn, bringing smiles to faces and provoking gestures of approval among the crowd, including the Reagan voters.

The band fires songs into the music-thirsty crowd like punk-seeking missiles and heads start to shake and the front row launches into a small but intense pogo, which pleases Ricardo and Octavio no end. As there's no stage, from time to time the smallest punks are fired toward the musicians, who happily return the pogoing public

117

with a shove. Everyone recognizes the opening riff to "Corona" (the Minutemen song the band covers in Spanish), and they all shout and start dancing to Will's drumrolls. Daniel watches in excitement from the corner how the magnetism and talent of ELPASO radiate through Rob's barn and imagines the small, thirty-odd-strong group thrashing about in the room, recommending their friends see this cool band from El Paso who do "Chicano punk" in Spanish.

February 12, 1986. Fort Worth (TX)

Jumpers are a strange group; the bastard children of the Butthole Surfers, they move between punk and performance. The five members are naked from the waist upward (guys and girls) and completely painted in black. They shout, bark, and pound their instruments as if they were in the middle of an unnerving primitive and freaky mating ritual. The crowd loves them, dancing and shouting along. They're totally into the dynamics of the Jumpers' show: if they're supposed to raise their hands, they raise their hands. If their supposed to bang their chests like gorillas, they bang their chests. You want us to spit at the ceiling? We spit at the ceiling. Ricardo is in a state of shock and can't fully understand what is happening.

"Hey Danny, what the fuck is that guy doing?"

"I don't know, but I'm flipping out!" replies Daniel while slurping on his can of Dr Pepper.

The lineup is completed with ELPASO and Dislexyc Jow Blobs, an indie-rock group from Dallas who have just released their first EP and are musically reminiscent of R.E.M. at the time of *Fables of the Reconstruction*, only with psychedelic lyrics that verge on the absurd. Texas had these things. Young people were screwed in Texas, immediately treated like weird creatures. Maybe that's what pushed them to want to be even more extravagant. If there was anything that typi-fied groups from Texas, it was their facility for being odd.

The night was nothing short of spectacular, and the three per-formances were all met with a wildly enthusiastic crowd. ELPASO's set steadily picked up as they played, reaching its crescendo with an electric version of "Guyana Punch" by The Judy's. It was the only song they hadn't translated into Spanish, and it was sung surprisingly well by none other than DD. He grabbed hold of his bass and leaned over the mic from his colossal height, wearing his black tortoiseshell glasses and the cap he never took off, even in bed. He sang with a soft voice at the same time as he picked the notes on his bass in the first part of the verse; Octavio came in with an arpeggio and the high harmonies, which were the cue for the drums to start up. The song strolls along inoffensively and steadily until "Freshen up" is repeated and grows into a marvelous and accelerated punk chorus, electrify-ing the crowd and forcing them to dance to the screams of "Guyana punch, uh-oh, uh-oh-oh". The concerts all finish like that, on a high, with the crowd dancing to the rhythm of the song that The Judy's released in the early eighties and which ELPASO have turned into one of their favorite covers.

The guys loved watching Dislexyc Jow Blobs and ended up drinking the night away with them in the neighborhood's crappiest bars. They had breakfast together and Ricardo proposed they play again at the Circle Ranch the next day. Daniel had closed the show in Dallas without any other group on the bill, and these guys were locals. They could call up some of their friends to fill out the room a little, and they'd divide up the money from the ticket sales. Dislexyc Jow Blobs accept the offer, and the two vans leave Fort Worth and head for Circle Ranch. It's Thursday, the tour is a minor success, and that night there is no concert, a sure bet for a party.

February 14, 1986. Dallas (TX).

"Hello?"

"Lupe?"

"Ricardo! How're you doing?"

"Good, we're about to start a concert."

"Oh, yeah? How was the sound test?"

"Good, good. Dislexyc played first, it's looking good. We're gonna fill the Circle Ranch."

"That's awesome, Ritchie!"

"Yeah . . . it's fantastic. Lupe, listen . . . Remember what I told you the other day?"

"What do you mean?"

"All that bullshit about friendship and sex and my inability to commit."

"Yeah, sure . . ."

"Yeah well, that's just bullshit. I love you and I want to be with you, I mean I want us to be together. I know we're always together but I mean, I don't know, I want to be, like, your boyfriend, I guess . . ."

"You guess?"

"No, shit, I want us to be boyfriend and girlfriend, Lupe. Last night we saw a couple arguing, they were shouting at each other because he'd hooked up with one of her best friends, or at least that's what we understood, and she, well, she was going off, screaming like a banshee, and, I don't know . . . For a second I thought about our non-relationship . . . You know, you could . . . you know?"

"Well, to be honest, Ritchie, I don't know. Can you be a little clearer??""

"Look, since we've started seeing each other more often I haven't been with anyone else, and I don't feel like it either. Sometimes

I have to make the effort not to call you and behave like a nonboy-friend is supposed to behave, or whatever the fuck it is I am. I want a stable and monogamous relationship with you Lupe, that's what I want."

"Wow . . . I don't think anyone's ever asked me like that before, but, well, I want a stable and monogamous relationship with you, too, Ricardo."

"Yeah? Great! Listen . . . I gotta go, Daniel's at the door of the concert room waving his hands around like an asshole, and I think it means I'm supposed to be going in. Happy Valentine's Day, Lupe. I can't wait to see you."

(Laughing) "Happy Valentine's Day, Ricardo. Break a leg!"

February 15, 1986. Austin (TX)

This might be one of Daniel's greatest achievements as manager of ELPASO. Getting the band onstage as openers for Killdozer and Scratch Acid at Liberty Lunch in Austin was a strategically brilliant move. These were two of the star bands of the independent label Touch and Go Records, and Liberty was perhaps the most awesome music venue in all of Texas. When he and Ricardo began rehearsing and writing songs, they looked through their notebooks from the time Daniel was at the University of Texas at Austin and created a small directory of contacts they thought might be useful for future music- and management-related needs. Martin, Daniel's best friend from his time in the Texan capital, helped book shows there and promised to get a good date for ELPASO.

When the time came, he proposed a show with another group on a Thursday, which was often a good day for little-known bands. They could play for around an hour and record the whole concert, so that they'd have their first demo tape: *ELPASO Live in Austin*. But Daniel was sure it would be better for ELPASO to support two strong bands and wanted a little under half an hour onstage. He was convinced that if faced with a demanding public, the band would rise to the occasion and was in no doubt at all that twenty minutes was enough for them to show what they were capable of. And that's what happened.

They played six songs and left everyone wanting more. With the three previous concerts they had learned to measure the audience, and they mercilessly unleashed one song after the other, making everyone at Liberty Lunch jump and shout and leaving a lasting impression on the crowd, the organizers, and the members of the other bands. In fact, David Yow (the singer from Scratch Acid) said something along the lines of, "Your show blew me away, man. You have definitely got what it takes to go a long way." Goddamn! David fucking Yow!

February 16, 1986. San Antonio (TX)

It was when they arrived in San Antonio that they realized something was up with DD. We're talking about an almost entirely expressionless and extremely quiet guy. Daniel would have sworn he hadn't heard him utter more than two consecutive sentences in the two years they had spent together as a band in El Paso. The first day in Denison brought back some pretty unpleasant memories from his childhood, and in Austin this feeling was a hundred times more intense. Over coffee at a gas station between the capital and San Antonio, Will told the others about the tumultuous life he and DD had led in those cities as kids. They were sitting at a table right next to a window overlooking the road, with plastic cups filled with disgusting coffee that was hot as hell. Surrounded by shelves of crucifixes, cowboy hats, and

Texas flags, they listened to Will give them the full version and, in a way, justify DD's attitude during the tour.

Octavio nodded, as if Will was telling them something that resonated with him, too. Ricardo, for his part, had also lived with an inexperienced and unprepared father who was abandoned by his partner, and he also felt a sense of rejection toward El Paso, similar to what DD had felt in Denison. Music had brought them together, but the weight of the past had made them brothers. Everyone except Daniel. At that table, lost between Kyle and San Marcos, Daniel Álvarez knew that something was beginning to grow among the members of ELPASO, and he wasn't going to be a part of it.

That night at Taco Land they played better than ever. San Antonio was perhaps the best concert of their career. Their conversation in the gas station was still alive in their heads, and the rage they all felt came through the speakers like a stampede of runaway buffalo.

February 17, 1986. Alpine (TX)

The owner of the Railroad Blues let the band leave all their material in the room and pick it up the next morning, Tuesday. Tim wore a red flowery T-shirt and a pair of yellow-lensed Ray-Ban Shooters. He was bald but had left the little hair he had to grow long. Not many people came to the concert, "It often happens on Monday night, boys," said Tim, "here's your cash." One of the good things about the Railroad Blues was that Tim always paid the bands a fixed amount, even if the concert was a complete disaster. He had a decent sound system and Daniel, who was the band's soundman, recorded their first live demo. There wasn't much to do on a Monday night in Alpine, so they headed for the Motel Bien Venido on Holland Avenue, where they had booked rooms for the night.

When they arrived, Mr. Patel asked for Ricardo Salazar. "There's a call for you guys." Ricardo recognized his home phone number and ran off to call his dad. Felipe asked him how the concert had gone and about what time he was expecting to arrive in El Paso and told him that something had happened to Debbie. For Daniel and Ricardo, Debbie was one of the most important figures in ELPASO's short history. She worked at Jalisco Café with Felipe, and the band's first chords came from her guitar. When she lent them the instrument, she made them promise that when they were a successful band, they would sign that white Fender Stratocaster so she could sell it and buy a new car. But that wasn't going to happen now.

That afternoon, Debbie had taken her 1967 Coupe Torino with the intention of driving to Canutillo to visit a friend but had the misfortune of crashing into a couple of nutjobs who'd run the light at the intersection of Talbot Avenue and Burns. They smashed into the driver's door, and Debbie was killed instantly.

Ricardo burst into tears, hung up, and looked at Daniel: "Danny, man, Debbie's dead."

FUCK ME, ALIEN

MY FIRST REAL ENCOUNTER WITH DEATH was when I'd just turned eight years old. I heard the key turn in the lock and ran out to welcome my dad. It was what he always did: he'd hug me and, if I was lucky, pull out a comic from his wad of newspapers. Something like the *X-Men* or the latest *Iron Man*. But that day, he slammed the door shut and strode right past me, without even turning his head. He went into his bedroom, and my mom, with a scared look on her face, asked him what had happened. My father said simply, "Gabriel has died." And he began to weep uncontrollably. He sobbed and shouted, his hands covering his face. My mother and I looked at him, terrified, from the bedroom door. There in the dim light of the room, that invincible giant whom I admired so much was falling apart at the seams in a crying fit that seemed liked it would never end. Seeing someone cry for the first time is not an experience I would recommend, especially if their tears have been caused by some kind of tragedy. Gabriel had had an accident and left a young wife and two kids, aged four and two, without a husband or a father. My father was weeping for them. And, of course, for his friend. But the idea that those three people would have to deal with this drama caused him an immense sadness, which is what made him cry in front of me for the first time in our lives.

Something similar happened to Ricardo. He was crying for

Debbie, of course, but, above all, he was crying for his father. Felipe had found a lot of support in his friend from work. She was like a little sister to him and a kind of auntie to Ricardo. Taking the tape of the Alpine concert to Debbie's place would have been at the top of Ricardo's list of priorities on getting back home, after the high of finishing his first tour as leader of ELPASO. "Do you remember all those afternoons when we called you up and came by your place to pick up your guitar? Yeah? Well, this is why. Thanks Debbie." That's what Ricardo could have said to her. But it wasn't to be.

They bought a case of beer and sat together in one of the motel rooms to drink. They got drunk and tried to celebrate the small success of their tour of Texas. They sang "Good Vibrations" by the Beach Boys, dedicating it to Debbie, and one by one feel asleep. All except one. Ricardo, drunk, got into the van and drove a few miles to Marfa. He parked the car in the middle of the desert and got onto the roof of the Ford to look at the stars. The tears were flowing slowly from his eyes and trickling down his cheeks when he caught sight of some strange lights whirling around the sky above him. Yellow, white, orange. He'd heard of the Marfa Lights but had never seen them. UFO nuts were sure they were alien lights, but for Ricardo it was a spiritual experience. For a moment he thought that one of those lights might be Debbie and figured that to go to heaven from El Paso you had to cross the Marfa desert. Maybe all the souls of the dead in Texas have to travel to Marfa before ascending to Eden. Maybe Marfa is where the "Stairway to Heaven" begins.

Lying on the roof of the Econoline he began to hum the Led Zeppelin classic and fell asleep. He dreamed he'd been abducted by aliens, right there in the desert. The martians were humanoids and looked a bit like Jeff Bridges in *Starman*, wearing flannel shirts with black and red checks and talking just like Daniel. They jabbered on at him about the infiniteness of the universe, finally convincing him to go with them to their spaceship and let them stick all kinds of martian instruments up his ass. He woke up. It was still night. He put the key in the ignition, started up the van, and went back to the motel.

They slept little and badly and the next morning picked up the instruments from the Railroad Blues with the intention of getting back to El Paso before lunch. Daniel was driving and Ricardo watched him. He saw his profile framed in the van window. Behind them the desert dropped away at full speed. He remembered Jeff Bridges violating him with those strange alien instruments and thought how, with his gift of verbosity, Daniel was capable of persuading him to stick something up his ass. He took out a notebook and pen from the glovebox and started writing:

In the middle of the night, I'm driving along the highway, and I think I can see you coming toward me. I know you love me, I know what you want. I know you're looking for me, so you can abduct me. You fly over me, I'm paralyzed by the light, it engulfs me to the point I don't know where I am. In the desert, perhaps in the universe, maybe in my head, but I see you. Now my mind is blank, my brain has stopped working, it doesn't want to live. It was that night, on the highway, you were looking for me to abduct me. Fuck me, alien. Fuck me, alien, baby. Take me with you, alien, to nowhere.

It was midday when they reached Ricardo's house. Felipe was waiting for them at the door and helped them unload their stuff from the van. They put it all in the garage, called Pizza Hut, and ordered several family-size pizzas. They ate while Felipe told them about what had happened to Debbie. The funeral was being held that same afternoon at the Canutillo cemetery and they were all invited. In the end only Felipe, Ricardo, and Daniel went. They made a cassette recording of the concert at Alpine and bought a pretty bunch of pink roses. They parked the Econoline on the corner of Fifth Street and Vinton Avenue and went into the cemetery. Felipe gave Debbie's mom a big hug and kissed her little sister. The friend Debbie was on her way to meet when she had the accident was crying, sitting on a chair next to the coffin. Ricardo put his right arm around his father's neck and pressed his head against Felipe's. Daniel stood unmoving and awkward next to his friend. He'd never been to a funeral, and it seemed sad and shabby. Daniel thought Debbie deserved a grand burial, with people celebrating her life and with the Ramones blasting at full volume. But it wasn't like that. It was a gray day and the wind came and went, lifting up the dust and sand in the cemetery. One of the gusts swept up so much sand that it created a brown cloud so thick you could hardly see a few meters in front of you. Daniel thought he saw a silhouette through the dust of someone leaning on the other side of the fence that surrounded the cemetery. As the cloud dispersed he saw the person more clearly. It was a man dressed in a brown suit. He looked homeless and had long, greasy, graying hair and a bushy white beard. Beneath the suit he was wearing what looked like a once-white sleeveless shirt. He was barefoot and stared unblinkingly at Daniel with an unnerving intensity. He nudged Ricardo with his elbow. The guy grabbed hold of the fence and started shaking it slowly while muttering something inaudible. Daniel looked around him, but everyone had their heads bowed. Nobody seemed to be paying any attention to the homeless guy. The priest was reciting some psalms when Daniel looked back at the fence. There was no one there. He looked all along the fence but could see no trace of the man in the dirty suit. He'd vanished into thin air.

"Ritchie, did you see that weirdo over by the fence?" Daniel asked Ricardo as they left the cemetery. "I didn't see anyone," he replied. "Shit, man, he was staring at me . . . He totally freaked me out."

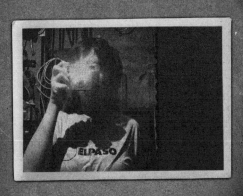

LUPE

IT'S AMAZING HOW A DROP OF rain is able to trickle *up* a car's windshield. The wind and aerodynamics help it to travel up the glass in search of the other drops that have accumulated outside the dry area created with each swipe of the wipers. The black arm holding the brush sweeps across the windshield, dries it, and then that poor raindrop has just enough time to start moving up the glass before the hand strikes again and pulverizes it. Ricardo is fantasizing about spermatozoids and salmon. The water drop pirouettes like a spermatozoid and heads back up the windshield like a salmon swimming against the river current. Then he looks at Lupe, who is driving, and thinks they could have salmon for dinner. He loves Lupe's profile. A mane of long, straight, jet-black hair reaches down to her shoulders. She has large, dark eyes crowned by stunning black eyebrows. Her nose is wide and pretty. Ricardo lets his gaze slide down her pronounced cheekbones before reaching Lupe's mouth . . . And what a mouth! Her lips are full, especially the lower one, and often trace a faint smile, even when she's serious. He remembers the first time he kissed them. It was in that same car, the Plymouth Valiant that she'd inherited from her grandmother. They also had sex, but for him it was impossible to forget the electricity he'd felt as their mouths came together. "I think I could come just from one of your kisses," he tells her. "What?!" she exclaims, her eyes widening without taking them off the road. "I love your mouth and when you kiss me. It turns me on so much." They both laugh, and she shakes her head in denial.

On the cassette player, "Kiss Off" by Violent Femmes is playing, one of the girl's favorite groups and one of the many bands she's introduced him to. It's raining lightly but the pavement is still wet from the previous day's storm. For a while they drive behind a truck driving to the left of them whose wheels are throwing water from the road up into the right-hand lane. It's impossible to overtake. The Plymouth leaves the highway close to Sheffield and stops behind the long grass growing on either side of the road. They turn off the engine, lock the doors, and begin to kiss. He bites her top lip and Lupe grips hold of the hair at the back of his neck. They slide across to the back seat and she straddles him, as she did the first time they fucked. The difference is that now they're making love. A year and a half has gone by, and their relationship is getting closer and closer. They've had plenty of sex, but they've also talked. They've seen a heap of films together and jumped together in countless concerts. They've argued, but always make up afterward, their relationship getting stronger with every row. She's taken photos of him, and he's written songs for her. A few weeks ago they made their relationship official and now, on their way to the Caverns of Sonora, they're fucking in the middle of the interstate while the rain pitter-patters on the roof of the Plymouth Valiant.

CAVERNS OF SONORA

"IT'S GETTING LATE,"LUPE TELLS RICARDO. He looks at her and kisses her on the tip of the nose. "Come on, then, I'll drive for a while." They get dressed and roll down the windows a little, now all steamed up with the rising temperature inside the car. They've got a little more than an hour before they arrive at the Caverns of Sonora. They've driven the three hundred miles to Sheffield, and it's almost twelve o'clock midday. It looks like their improvised love-making has livened up the sky, which is now clearing, rays of sunlight beaming through the clouds, forcing them to feel around in the glovebox for their sunglasses. The dry, barren landscape turns greener as they approach Sonora. They leave the interstate at exit 392 and take the road that leads to the caverns. Two large masts rise in the distance. At the top of them the American and Texan flags fly. They park next to a sign that reads: "Welcome to the Caverns of Sonora. Welcome to the Underground Experience." Ricardo laughs at this. He's also going through his own underground experience with the band. Lupe reaches for her camera and the leather backpack she keeps the film in. She's been into nature photography for some time now and these caves are something else. Bill Stephenson, who founded America's National Speleological Society, said that the beauty of the Caverns of Sonora is so stunning that not even a Texan could exaggerate it.

As it's a weekday, there aren't many people. Just a few school kids, giggling and ignoring their teacher as she tries to give them the lowdown on stalactites, and certain groups of future speleologists, talking with a zeal that Ricardo finds unnerving. "What a bunch of nerds," he says. Lupe takes photographs nonstop, loving every moment. Ricardo watches her, mesmerized by her beauty, lit up by the spotlights and with millions of rocky spikes hanging overhead. He thinks about how the rocks look like tears and wonders if the earth cries. "Does the underground cry?" he considers. "Maybe it did the day that Hüsker Dü signed their contract with Warner Bros. to release *Candy Apple Grey*," he replies to himself. He likes the album, it has some good songs, but he can't forgive the fact that a group that flies the flag of "do-it-yourself" music and punk ethics has succumbed to the siren calls of the big record labels. Ricardo is all for breaking the artistic and musical norms of hardcore and punk, but turning your back on the small labels and the people who have helped to get the scene off the ground is a lack of respect. Not like that. Not for money.

Lupe is still discreetly snapping away, and the group of school kids begins singing the typical songs kids always sing on school trips. Ricardo is fascinated by the acoustics of the place. "It would be incredible to record an album in here," he says to Lupe. "That's the kind of thing those famous bands you hate do," she snaps back. He eyes her suspiciously and sinks back into his thoughts. They would never let him set up everything to record an album in there, but they could manage the vocals and harmonies of a song. He could write a song about the underground and title it "Caverns of Sonora." Ricardo was on a creative streak and almost everything that happened around him was susceptible to being turned into a song. The films he watched, the bar conversations he overheard . . . Everything could be reflected in a well-written, heartfelt lyric. Ricardo had somehow become a songwriter. At first, music was more aesthetic, a way of making a statement. He played to set himself apart from the rest and, at the same time, make a name for himself. But after a couple of years he had also found in songwriting a way of giving his version of things. Suddenly, what sparked a new song wasn't a riff or a chord roll, but an idea. The need to give his opinion on the state of the American underground had led him to see a song in those caves and tears in the rocks. He ran over to tell Lupe, like someone who's just had a revelation. This was to happen on many occasions, and Lupe would almost always react in the same way: "Sounds like an awesome idea, Ritchie. Do it!"

Unable to contain his smile, he looked around him. Lupe accepted that, as far as her boyfriend was concerned, the outing had finished. He would be champing at the bit to get out of there in search of a notebook into which he could vomit the verses hammering on his brain. Ricardo was standing on one of the walkways that marked the route through the caves, lost in his thoughts and staring into space. The girl smiled and brought her Pentax MG to her right eye. She focused manually on Ricardo's face through the lens and took a photo of him. She pressed down on the trigger that stops the film advancing and shot a second photo of the rocks on the ceiling of the cave. That double exposure would turn out to be an intriguing photograph, the figure of Ricardo blending with the rocks and varied textures. It was used for the cover for ELPASO's first demo.

✳

There had already been moments of tension. Daniel couldn't take criticism or not being in control. The fact that the cover for the group's first demo was a photo he hadn't taken bothered him. And what was more, Ricardo wasn't convinced by the obvious title that Daniel had suggested for the tape: "Live in Alpine." It's true that it was the live recording of some of the songs they had played at Railroad Blues in Alpine three months earlier, but it is also true that it was a hackneyed, somewhat unoriginal name for their first recorded material. Ricardo proposed "Mountain" and pushed for Lupe's photograph on the front cover. He was being honest when he said it had nothing to do with the fact that he was in it. He simply thought it was more aesthetic and simple, and his criteria ended up winning over Daniel's. And once again it all happened very quickly. Danny didn't deal with it well. He was happy to play the role of ELPASO's manager, his musical opinion was still critical for the band, but he had the feeling his relationship with Ricardo was shrinking at the same time that Octavio and, especially, Lupe became increasingly strong influences over his old friend and sharer of dreams. Furthermore, Daniel often displayed an extraordinary stubbornness, which is why he turned up at Ricardo's house one day with an example of a design for the cassette of *Mountain*.

He'd chosen collage. He positioned a mountain on a gray-blue sky. Over the top of this he'd stuck the group's logo, separating the "EL" and the "PASO" and positioning a small cutout beneath on which he had typed the word *Mountain*. Lastly, over the letters and the mountain he positioned a cutout of a Greek statue, on which he had stuck the head of a bull. He outlined the whole thing with black pen to make it more uniform and put it into a cassette case. When Ricardo saw it he couldn't help but smile. "You never give up, eh?" Danny said nothing, staring at his friend and waiting for a reaction. "I don't know . . . I think I prefer Lupe's." "OK," replied Daniel, snatching the tape from Ricardo's hands and jumping up from the couch in the dining room. "I'll see you tomorrow," he said as he closed the door.

The next day they'd arranged to meet at the Hamburger Hut where Will worked, and Daniel brought a mockup of the tape with Lupe's photo. The cassette cover looked excellent, and Daniel had decided not to put anything on it—undoubtedly the right thing *not* to do. He did, however, give the photo a black frame that blended with the spine of the cassette, displaying the band's name and title of the demo. On the back part was the typed-out track list, cut out into small white rectangles stuck on the same black of the frame and spine. They all agreed it was very cool. Now Daniel's anger had died down, he was happy with the final result. He held the cassette up over the bar to show Will, who nodded his head from the kitchen. He was wearing his hair up in a bun and a hairnet over his head. He was sweating, and his eyes were streaming tears from the onion he was chopping. He couldn't stop blinking, and it took him three attempts to focus and see the cover properly. He looked at Daniel and shot him a "It's fucking sick, man." Daniel turned to look for Ricardo, who was sitting at one of the tables by the window that overlooked Broaddus Avenue. Ricardo answered the look with a drumroll using a couple of spoons and the glass of Coca-Cola with vanilla they'd served him, along with a coyote howl. It was something they'd done since they'd met at Ysleta High School, and it meant that everything was dandy. They opened the notebook Daniel often used for band business and began a list with all the magazines, radio stations, fanzines, and influential people they would have to send the demo to. There was little over two months before the concert on July 27 with the Rhythm Pigs at Sound Seas, and the idea was for the demo to be circulated enough to bring more people to the show.

Send *Mountain* to:
- Mordam Records
- SST Records

- Dischord Records
- New Alliance Records
- Homestead Records
- K Records
- Matako Mazuri Records

- Maximum Rocknroll
- Flipside
- Urban Decay
- Boston Rock
- Alternative Press
- The Rocket (Bruce Pavitt)
- We Got Power!
- Forced Exposure
- The Big Takeover
- Mucky Pup EP

- Tesco Vee
- Greg Adams/Ed Ivey
- Jello Biafra

MEAT PUPPETS

THE STREETS OF EL PASO HAD been filled with black-and-white copies of Steve'O'cide's illustrated poster for the Meat Puppets concert at Sound Seas. On Wednesday, May 14, the group from Phoenix came to the city to present *Up on the Sun*, the album that SST Records (one of California's most influential record labels, which, interestingly, would end up moving to Texas in the future) had released a year before.

Steve'O'cide drew a caricature of Curt Kirkwood, the Meat Puppets' singer and guitarist, on a circle filled with stripes and with the details of the show around it. Beneath the band's name were the names of the other groups: Hernia Briefs, Moral Crips, and Mike Jennings's band, Abandon Ship. Mike managed Sound Seas, was one of the biggest names on the local scene, and also led this magnificent band, which flirted with ska, reggae, and dub with superb musical prowess.

At the concert were all the members of ELPASO, Daniel, and Lupe with two friends. The room was full to bursting, and the local bands played their sets in a friendly atmosphere and to a crowd in the mood to party. When Shandon Sahm, the drummer of the Puppets, sat at his kit, the crowd began screaming like madmen. Then Cris Kirkwood came onstage, picked up the bass, and began a few improvised lines in which Sahm joined with a syncopated bass drum and snare rhythm. Curt Kirkwood hung his Gibson Les Paul Honeyburst around his neck and picked over the base rhythm that floated around the room. The bodies moved like waves, and the melodies coming from Curt's guitar plowed through them, wrapping around the heads of the crowd and shaking them in time to the bass drum. Then, the leader of the group from Arizona held a note, tensing the fifth string and stretching it outward as if he wanted to tear it from the Gibson's neck. Sahm pounded one of his drums four times and, knowing intuitively to come in on the fifth beat, the trio from Phoenix dived into the first verse of "Lake of Fire," the tenth song from *II*, one of the band's best and most mythical albums. From the extensive and virtuoso repertoire of that concert, two other songs from the same album stood out: "Plateau" and "Oh Me." These three songs would end up forming part of another album, one of the biggest in rock history, when the Meat Puppets were the only group that Kurt Cobain invited to the *Unplugged* album he recorded for MTV in New York on November 18, 1993.

I'll take this opportunity to come back to the sixty-minute TDK tape on which I recorded that album at the end of the summer of 1995. My cousin wanted to give his sister some music as a present, and there we both were in the only shop in the neighborhood that sold cassettes, with *Ten* by Pearl Jam in one hand and Nirvana's acoustic album in the other. I think she would have preferred Pearl Jam, but for some strange reason we asked them to gift wrap Nirvana.

We got back to my uncle and aunt's home, went into my cousin's bedroom (who at that time had a black mini hi-fi system with a dual cassette deck all to himself), and took off the paper and the plastic wrapping from *Unplugged in New York*. We took out the tape, pressed play, and heard that opening ovation, a great applause surging from the dark speakers, bringing a smile to our faces. It lasted around

146

fifteen seconds. A voice said something in English that I didn't understand, we heard the first chords of "About a Girl," and when Kurt Cobain sang, "I need an easy friend," my heart stopped and the hair on my arms stood on end, as if pulled by the music. I wanted to cry, laugh, and jump all at once, but I just sat there on the floor, unmoving, my legs crossed and hands on my thighs. In my thirteen years of life I'd never felt anything like it. Never had a song moved me so much and so quickly. The song finished with a rapturous applause, and the classic riff that introduces "Come as You Are" fired from the stereo, pounding into my hippocampus, along with the other tunes that were to take residence in my brain forever. After four or five songs I told my cousin that I couldn't go home without that album. I ejected the cassette that was in my Sony Walkman WM-FX103 and asked if they had any sticky tape in the house. The cassette was a TDK D60 and contained a pastiche of soulless summer hits. Back then, to stop us accidentally erasing whatever we'd already recorded, we would often break the tabs on the top part of the cassette. But to record a new album it was enough to tape over the tabs. And that's just what I did. We rewound the two cassettes and chose the machine's silent, double-speed recording mode. In less than half an hour I had my pirate copy of *Unplugged in New York*.

I remember every detail of those dialogues, the guitar melodies, the cries from the crowd . . . Anything that can be heard on that album has been etched onto my mind. Even now, I cough along with Kurt when I listen to *Unplugged*. At the time, I liked the whole album, but there were three songs that particularly grabbed my attention. A couple of long-haired metalheads were invited to play with them, whom Kurt introduced as the "Meat Puppet" brothers, and they stood out above the others. Then I found out they were a group and that the three songs were theirs and not Nirvana's.

Kurt Cobain always said he'd gotten into punk rock when he saw Black Flag playing at the Mountaineers Club in Seattle in 1984. When I looked into that tour, I found out that that concert took place on Friday, April 27, and that the Meat Puppets were one of the opening bands. Who could have told the Kirkwood brothers that night that one of the kids in the crowd would change the direction of rock history seven years later and that, thanks to him, three of their songs would become the favorites of a thirteen-year-old boy brought up in the suburbs of a city like Barcelona.

My love affair with the Meat Puppets would come full circle in December 2012, when I was lucky enough to seem them live, at a small acoustic show they did at the store owned by the BCore record label in Barcelona's Gràcia district. There were no more than thirty of us there, brimming with emotion when they played "Lake of Fire," a feeling that I shared with Daniel Álvarez when he spoke to me about the Meat Puppets show in El Paso. It was the only time that, while talking with him, I could say: "I saw them live too and they were awesome."

✳

Daniel and Ricardo come out of Sound Seas before the others. They sit outside on Laurel Street just in front of the train tracks. "That was sick, Ritchie. There were loads of people watching Abandon Ship. If we can get the same numbers on the day of the gig with the Rhythm Pigs, it'll be awesome, man." Ricardo looks at his friend sideways and smiles. "I really liked the Meat Puppets. Greg Adams told me once they were one of the bands that most impressed him live, and fuck if he wasn't right," says Ricardo while trying to peel a sticker off the wall next to his right ear.

At that same moment, Daniel jumps to his feet and shouts "Did you see him, man!?" "Who?" answers Ricardo, confused. "That weirdo from Debbie's funeral! . . . There, in the dirt alley behind Sound Seas!" Ricardo cranes his neck but sees nothing in the alley, which is dark and silent. "Holy fuck, Ritchie, I swear to you, he was staring at me again," exclaims Daniel feverishly as he crosses the tracks and approaches the punk leaning up against the lamppost. "Excuse me, man, did you see that scruffy guy with the big beard who was over there just now?" "I didn't see anything, man," answers the punk. Daniel and the punk dissolve into the darkness and you can just about see their faces, half lit up intermittently by the flickering yellow light of the old lamppost. They talk. The punk just rolls a cigarette while nodding to everything that Daniel, who is waving his hands around like a man possessed, says. They're both drunk, the punk a fair bit more than Daniel, and end up sharing the cigarette and laughing about God knows what.

Ricardo doesn't smoke. He never has. He used to drink beer and had gotten drunk pretty often at college, but now drunkards and their antics made him feel uncomfortable, and although anyone who's ever seen him under the influence says he's a happy drunk, he's decided to give alcohol a rest. It's been a year and a half since he last took any drugs. He often says he's not against other people taking them, but he judges those who do. He's had pointless arguments with Lupe and Will, and Daniel no longer talks to him about whether or not he's taken anything. Despite all this, he is often seen as someone who looks likely to be a drinker and a drug-taker. Everyone looks surprised when he tells them he doesn't touch either, and no one believes him when he claims never to have smoked. "Maybe it's my appearance," he wonders on such occasions. He normally has a grade-one buzz cut and has a mustache and goatee you'd expect to find on the classic Chicano gangster. He wears checked lumberjack shirts over white cotton T-shirts and jeans. On his feet are always a pair of blue Adidas Campus, like the ones made popular by the Beastie Boys.

That same night, while Daniel philosophizes with the punk, a pale-faced kid not much more than fourteen years old who can't pronounce his "r"s, approaches him for a cigarette. "I don't smoke." The kid doesn't seem to like the answer, and without another word he lays a right hook on Ricardo's chin. The punch hurts Ricardo, taken completely off guard, and he pushes the kid. "What the fuck are you doing, you little brat!" he shouts. "Have you got a problem, you half-caste asshole?" someone shouts at him from a short distance away at the intersection of Laurel and Mills Avenue. "Shit . . ." he thinks. He's been lured into a trap by some skinheads. They sent the kid brother in the hope their target (Ricardo in this case) would react in a way that would justify giving him a beating. The shove is good enough for them, and the four guys run toward Ricardo. The people coming out of the Meat Puppets concert make a space forming a ring around the ELPASO singer to watch the action. Trying his best to look unfazed, Ricardo turns to the side to avoid being kicked between the legs and holds his house keys in his fist so his punches don't break his fingers. These are the only two things his father told him about fighting. That and to try to take out the biggest first, although in this case there were four equally big oafs hurtling toward him, so his only aim was to survive.

The first blow falls, and to the surprise of the onlookers it doesn't come from any of the five contenders. Will Davis, who has just come out of Sound Seas, has knocked down two skinheads with a single slug, Octavio lets fly with a left-handed uppercut that splits the third nazi's nose, and DD already has the fourth one in a perfectly executed wrestler-style headlock. The attack is all one way: from the fists of the ELPASO members directly to the faces and stomachs of the four fascists. DD shows his dance partner no mercy, while Octavio and

Will take care of the other three. Like in a Bud Spencer and Terence Hill movie, the long-haired drummer and Mexican guitarist are perfectly coordinated, as if every movement has been choreographed and rehearsed. Ricardo is in a state of shock, and Daniel has pushed his way through the gathering crowd and is inside the circle of people, next to his friend. The pair can only watch as their fellow band members give the thugs a thorough pasting. They've never been in a fight like this before. They wouldn't know where to start. Lupe, for her part, has taken it on herself to dress down the mini skinhead who started all this by punching Ricardo for not having tobacco.

Slowly, and with every crushing blow, the four loudmouths back down and instead of the aggressive taunting they began with are now raising their hands in submission, begging to be allowed to slink away. Will threatens them all with a kick up the ass if they ever come back, while Octavio and DD dust off their clothes. The crowd, mostly punks and indie fans, applaud the show and hurl insults at the skinheads. Daniel pushes Ricardo toward the rest of the band, and Will intercepts him with a bear hug. Will is famous for his squeezes, and it fills Ricardo with a sense of warmth, triggering memories of being a lonely kid with no friends. Submerged in the drummer's body mass, he imagines a make-believe scene: today's Ricardo (leader of ELPASO, Lupe's boyfriend, with friends ready to defend him at the drop of a hat) stands in front of a young, beardless, fifteen-year-old Ricardo and hugs him with all his strength while telling him not to worry, that all that anxiety, hatred, and bullshit he has inside will one day change. He'll meet Daniel, they'll set up a band, and the ball will start rolling. Today's Ricardo then invites the young Ricardo to sit down and wait for a third, future Ricardo. "He'll be here soon," he tells him, "And I'll bet he has some big news for us."

ED IVEY

THE TIME BETWEEN THE FIGHT AND the Rhythm Pigs flew
by. They were three months of long rehearsals, during which their
first demo, *Mountain*, began to appear among the recommendations
and articles of some of the Texan fanzines. They got back into their
rehearsal schedule from before the Texas tour. After Debbie's death
and with the release of the demo they'd had some downtime, and it
had been a while since they'd played together.

During the weeks leading up to July 27, 1986, they realized the
leap in quality that Octavio was giving the band. For one thing, thanks
to his left-handed uppercut, he'd won Will's unconditional respect.
At first, the drummer was distrustful of Octavio and the mysterious
aura that surrounded him. They had no idea where his money came
from. They all guessed he spoke English better than he let on, and
they still didn't know whether he preferred women or men. He was
all enigma. Tensions were high between the ELPASO drummer and
guitarist. Both competed absurdly for the prize of the band's "hard
man," which led to some uncomfortably tense moments in the van.
But the fact that neither blinked an eye before pouncing on the skinheads brought the two together. They admired each other as musicians and now as people, too. With DD everything was simpler: if you
won my big brother over, you've got me too.

Ricardo was fascinated by Octavio. And during those rehearsals a creative energy bubbled and sparked between the two. Ricardo had brought a couple new songs to the garage: "Abducción en Marfa" and "Caverns of Sonora," which talked of his paranormal experience with the desert lights and gave rise to the doubts he had about the alternative scene and its relationship with the dangerous American music industry. To help the song develop, Ricardo told Octavio about *Kidd Video,* an NBC animated series in which the titular band gets trapped in the Flipside, a parallel dimension dominated by a contemptuous, ruthless, and fat music executive called Master Blaster. In each episode, the band tries to escape from that universe to get back to the real world. The animation perfectly illustrated what Ricardo wanted to say with "Caverns of Sonora." Kidd Video was the American indie scene being swallowed up by a predatory music industry, embodied by the villain, Master Blaster. Octavio quickly understood Ricardo's abstract ideas and masterfully translated them into melodic riffs and complex arrangements. These two songs catapulted the group to a new musical level.

For Daniel, the concert at Sound Seas was also a chance to reclaim his artistic ability with the design of the show's flyer. At that time in the city, as well as the omnipresent Steve'O'cide, there was the extremely talented BillBo. They had both worked on two of the Rhythm Pigs' classic works: BillBo was the man behind the artwork of *An American Activity EP* (1984), and Steve'O'cide had come up with the cover of *Rhythm Pigs* (1986), the El Paso band's first album with Mordam Records.

For the poster, Daniel continued with the idea that he'd started on with the blue leaflets from the Texas tour: Mexican iconography and punk aesthetics. For the concert on July 27, he drew a portrait of Frida Kahlo in black marker. From the artist's face, positioned right in the center of the paper, surged a mass of black ink, which covered a third of the design and which then became her hair. The groups' logos fitted neatly into this black space, at the bottom the Pigs', which was bigger, and above that ELPASO's, accompanied by the concept: "Chicano punk!" All the text was written in white ink on the black background. Between the logos the poster read "13-song LP out now on Mordam Records." Frida's bust was formed by a black dress decorated in white patterns. In the spaces of paper on either side of Kahlo's face was information on the show: place, date, time, price, and the classic "all ages!" Lastly, at the bottom of the poster, concert-goers were informed that the consumption and sale of alcohol was prohibited, which was positioned together with the Sound Seas management team.

※

During the Texas tour they developed a habit that passed into a pre-show bylaw. The band formed a group hug, like American football players when they want to give one another instructions or encouragement. Will gave the note, and they all harmonized the chorus of "Good Vibrations" by the Beach Boys. What had previously finished off their rehearsals, they were now using to start their concerts. They spurred one another on until the energy of the four of them joined together, drawing them together into one. A four-headed hydra capable of setting any stage alight. Then Will would go onstage to sit at the drums and begin playing, shaking his blond hair around like a man possessed and pounding his drumsticks like a caveman. His brother, DD, stood in front of the bass amp wearing his thick-rimmed glasses and bicolor cap. He hung his Fender Precision around his neck and joined the composition with a looping bass line that moved in perfect synchronization with the rhythm resounding from the drums.

Octavio very slowly turned up the volume on the Gibson. He had the guitar close to the amp, which the Les Paul fed back into with increasing stridence and strength, getting the public increasingly worked up. Ricardo stuck his mustache to the microphone to announce that they were ELPASO, a Chicano punk band from El Paso, Texas. He placed his Stratocaster's strap around his head and turned to look at Will, who was waiting for the signal. He pounded the snare with both drumsticks, while DD and Octavio silenced both the bass and the feedback. For a few seconds Sound Seas was in silence, which was broken by Ricardo's "one-two-three-four," the cue for the opening blast of "John Wayne Gacy," their most orthodoxly punk number.

ELPASO's repertoire flowed. They were playing at home. This was better than Juárez, better than Dallas, and better than Fort Worth and Denison. This was even better than the powerful concerts they'd played in San Antonio and Austin. El Paso understood them, and their bicultural musical concept went down well on the border. What was more, it was an enthusiastic, lively crowd. They jumped and shouted. They pushed one another and gave back the energy that Ricardo and his band fired at them through their songs in Spanish.

They closed with their version of "Corona" by Minutemen, and the crowd rewarded them with a huge ovation. They swapped places onstage with the members of the Rhythm Pigs. A few years before they had looked on in admiration from in front of the stage, and now they were on it with them, exchanging remarks about the amps, cymbals, and cables they shared for the show. Jay and Will talked excitedly about Will's drum kit and how good Jay's bass drum sounded. Octavio offered one of his guitar jacks to Greg, who thanked him with a hug. Ed Ivey, the Pigs' bass player and singer, came up to Ricardo to tell him how impressed he was with the band's performance. He was really pleased that Greg had invited them to open the concert and said they'd exceeded all expectations. Ricardo wanted to cry. He just looked at him in amazement, like he was floating in a cloud. Ed's words were sincere, and he could hardly get out a "Thanks, Ed," taking him back to that shy and retiring teenage Ricardo who found it hard to show his affection. They looked at each other in silence when the Rhythm Pigs' singer finished talking. Ricardo went red and stuttered a question about whether he'd mind him writing to him from time to time. "Sure, man! It'd be awesome to hear what you guys are doing!" he replied excitedly. "After the gig, I'll give you my address . . . Oh, and . . . congratulations! You guys played a sick show!"

A sick show. Fantastic. Awesome. Madness. Magnificent. Different words, different mouths, but the same intention. It was perfectly clear that with their performance that night at Sound Seas, ELPASO had slammed their fist down on the table and become one of the city's interesting bands. History was repeating itself. Daniel reminded Ricardo what they had felt when they saw Teenage Popeye playing with the Ramones or the Rhythm Pigs opening for Black Flag. In those two shows, the local bands had impressed them more than the headliners. Ed Ivey, Greg Adams, and Jay Smith's band presented their first album with Mordam Records and showed why they were one of the most respected and sought-after groups of the American underground. They jumped up onto the stage after ELPASO and scorched the crowd with frenetic rhythms and trance-inducing riffs. The lyrics were chanted back at them like hymns, and the pride of being from El Paso flooded the hearts of everyone in the room. They recharged their batteries in their hometown and got back on the road to add more cities to their "visited" list. They didn't disappoint, but then neither did they surprise. The Rhythm Pigs had taken it on themselves to prove they were every bit as good as everyone thought. Like the Ramones in '79 and Black Flag in '84. "We surprised them,

Ritchie. They shit their pants. Nobody was expecting to see such a good band, man!" Daniel said excitedly, "This is starting to get interesting!"

As darkness descended, covering Texas Avenue, the crowd began to filter out of the club. Ricardo was kissing Lupe by the stage when Ed Ivey approached with one of the Frida Kahlo flyers that Daniel had illustrated. "Excuse me, guys, here's my address." On the back of the poster was his address scribbled in red permanent marker, which could be seen inverted from the printed side of the leaflet: "Write whenever you want, Ricardo. I'll do what I can to help." They'd heard what a great guy Ed was and about his commitment to emerging bands, and here was the proof.

❃

In my case, it was Manuel Calderón who talked to me about Ed Ivey for the first time, in March 2015. I was looking for contacts in El Paso online. There were just a few days to go before my trip to the border, and I only had four interviews organized. On Facebook I came across Manuel, who was working for Sonic Ranch (one of the best recording studios in the south of the US), and he agreed to a morning interview in one of the studios before beginning a session with an indie-folk band from Idaho. He wrote in perfect Spanish and just when I was about to sign off, Manny typed in Ed's name. He referred to him as "The Godfather" of punk in El Paso, and he encouraged me to write to him. They had met once at Sonic Ranch on a project that had brought the Rhythm Pigs' vocalist back to El Paso. He had been living in San Francisco for years, but whenever possible he came back to his home city. Jordi, Lou, and I agreed to send Ed a Facebook friend request and also wrote him a private message outlining our intentions and needs. We flew from Barcelona to Miami and from there took a plane that left us at the Dallas-Fort Worth International Airport at around midnight on March 7, 2015. We slept in one of the airport hotels, and the next morning we rented the Ford Focus that would help us get around Texas for the next two weeks.

Austin was the second stop on our journey, and we arrived on a Sunday night, March 8, after driving the almost three hundred miles from Denison and with the jet lag from our flight hammering at our temples. It was raining. Lucky for us, the apartment we rented in the state capital was spacious and surprisingly upscale. We went inside and opened our bags, our belongings slowly spreading across the living room floor. T-shirts, notebooks, cameras and video cameras, trousers, and sneakers were all over the floor, draped across armchairs and stools, and littering a large part of the marble kitchen island. We decided on burgers for dinner, which we bought at Wendy's, whose giant illuminated sign shone in through the window from the other side of the street. Jordi got the laptop ready to download the audio and video files from the interview we'd done in Denison that morning. His Dave's Double with cheese was going cold when he showed us one of the notifications that Facebook had sent him: "Ed Ivey has accepted your friend request." We celebrated, raising our cardboard cups filled with mountains of ice and the remains of our Coca-Cola. We also saw that he'd replied to the message we'd sent telling him we wanted to talk with anyone who'd participated in the punk scene in the city between 1979 and 1990. He forwarded our message to all his contacts, and more than fifteen people had already written back to us. Thanks to Ed Ivey we were able to interview the members of Red Zone and Kathy Smith and Clutch Cardon from One Second Zero. We were invited to the home of Mike Nosenzo from Teenage Popeye and were treated to a day in El Paso with Greg Adams, Ed's fellow

band member from the Rhythm Pigs. Most of the people we interviewed lived in El Paso, Austin, or Dallas, so it was relatively straightforward to fit around everyone's schedules. The only person who
lived outside Texas was Ed Ivey himself, who was in San Francisco,
and it was looking like an interview with him was unlikely to happen. Then, he mentioned he would be coming to Austin to work on
South by Southwest (one of the world's biggest music events) a day
before our flight home, so we reorganized our route and came back
to Austin from El Paso before returning to Dallas to take the plane
back to Europe. The detour meant a lot more driving hours, stretched
nerves, and extra expenses. It was a nightmare trying to find a hotel
for those dates because of the massive influx of festivalgoers, and it
was pouring down rain when Ed Ivey opened the door of the house
where we were going to conduct the interview.

He welcomed us heartily and in pretty decent Spanish, too. He
was able to speak and understand it, and even described to us some
of the Spanish punk bands he'd been happily surprised to hear during
their tours around Spain. He was a small guy and wore jeans and a
shirt with brown sleeves. His eyebrows arched, forming a crease in
his forehead, which, in turn, seemed to be pushing back his hairline,
from which an endearing fringe fell in the center of his head. His
white temples stood out against the rest of his hair, which, despite
the gray, was still dark. Small eyes hid behind fine-rimmed, metal
glasses that were settled on a small, squat nose. He was cleanshaven,
but from the tip of his chin hung an all-white goatee more than four
fingers long that bobbed up and down when he spoke. He was both
charismatic and to the point. He talked to us about the letters he'd
exchanged with Ricardo and how much he'd liked ELPASO's music.
He asked us about all the people we'd interviewed before him and
was glad to hear what we had to say. He was genuinely pleased to have

been able to help us and wished us luck with our endeavor. As we were leaving, he grabbed me by the arm to get a closer look at my digital Casio wristwatch. His father had had one just like it and, for an instant, the memory caused a flash of emotion. I smiled at him, we hugged, and I thanked him for the umpteenth time for the help he'd given us. "Take care," he said and closed the door. I stood outside the house, blinded by the sun. I looked up into the sky, shielding my eyes from the brightness. The gray clouds had all burned away during my conversation with Ed, and for the first time since we'd arrived, I saw blue taking charge of the skies over Austin.

SAN FRANCISCO

IN SEPTEMBER OF THAT YEAR, RITCHIE decided not to enroll at university and take a year's sabbatical. He still lived with his dad and started to look for a full-time job. Lupe spent most of the time with him. For the Salazars, she was another member of the family.

For a while now DD had been working at the Hamburger Hut with Will, and Octavio had moved into the apartment they were renting in the center of the city. Daniel, for his part, started a second degree at UTEP and shared a room with two guys who would eventually submerse him in the border's art circles. One was Argentinian-born Roger Colom and the other was Rubén Verdú, a Spaniard who had left Barcelona to travel to Odessa and ended up studying art at the University of Texas at El Paso.

The band had already scheduled a number of shows for the following year, and after their first demo was well-received they were working on the songs that would become their first studio EP. They also decided to move their headquarters to Octavio's mother's house in Juárez.

In one of the letters that Ed Ivey and Ricardo Salazar exchanged between July and December 1986, the former invited the latter to spend a few days in San Francisco and while he was there take the chance to see Bad Brains. The bill for the show included D.R.I. and the Rhythm Pigs, and it took place on Friday, November 28, at The Farm, one of San Francisco's temples of punk. This was a good opportunity to extend their list of contacts, venues, and cities where they could play, as well as enjoy a first-class show.

Bad Brains were one of the most pioneering bands of all the American hardcore and punk scene. Originally from Washington, DC, its four members embraced Rastafarian culture and began playing concerts they organized themselves in the basement of the house they shared in the late seventies. In the mid-eighties their albums were taking the scene by storm, and the band was on everyone's must-watch list. In 1984 they split up, only to get back together to release *I Against I* with SST Records a couple years later, and their gig in San Francisco was a unique opportunity to feel the buzz of a live performance. Furthermore, for Ricardo, Bad Brains had the added racial bonus: a group of Black guys playing punk and flirting with reggae on a scene essentially composed of white guys. Cool.

That, without a doubt, was the kind of trip that Ricardo and Daniel should have made together, and it would have been up there with all the other legendary concerts that populated the two friends' collective memories. But Danny wasn't going and, stranger still, Ricardo thought this was fine. The van was his, and he had every right to use it without the band's permission. Lupe really wanted to go to California and so, against the odds, the two friends were not going to be headbanging together in front of the stage at The Farm in Frisco.

✳

The tide of fans pushes forward and starts shouting when the lights dim, and the colored spotlights fire shafts of blue, orange, and red light. Darryl Jenifer holds his bass while Dr. Know slams down on his guitar, apparently measuring the volume of his amps. Both have incredibly long dreadlocks and look at each other knowingly. Earl Hudson, from behind his drums, marks the rhythm for what's coming next by endlessly striking the hi-hat in perfect time. The guitar joins in and the band explodes into "Coptic Times," with H.R. screaming down the mic for the first verses of the song that opens their 1983 album, *Rock for Light*. The crowd start pushing one another, and the first silhouettes can be seen flying over people's heads. Fists raised in the air and frenzied cries hopelessly aspiring to harmonize with the voice of Bad Brains' lead vocalist, the rage-filled caterwauling serving only to raise the temperature of the cramped space. The musician's dreadlocks whip through the air, and H.R. thrashes about the microphone. It's like an accelerated, violent version of Bob Marley when he launches into "Attitude." The song lasts little over a minute and sends the crowd into a frenzy, the bravest getting up onstage before falling into the sea of shaved heads, mohawks, and baseball caps like ungainly trampolinists.

Lupe stoically withstands the mayhem exuding from the very walls of The Farm. Three years ago, in the same city, she saw Violent Femmes at a concert she thought at the time was pretty far out. But Bad Brains create a level of insanity in this live performance that leaves Lupe fearing for her life. There are times when she feels she has no control over where her body is moving, and she is terrified of falling and being trampled by the mass of punks. The opening notes sound for a reggae cover of the Beatles' "Day Tripper," and the atmosphere calms for a moment, a trancelike sensation streaming through the space. Ricardo crouches down to let Lupe get on his shoulders. She resists for an instant but as she rises above the crowd she realizes the oxygen is much more breathable from up there, looking across the tops of the heads moving to the rhythm

BENJAMIN VILLEGAS

of Darryl's bass. The repertoire progresses with "Secret 77," "I and I Survive," and all the band's other earth-shattering songs. The voice of Paul "H.R." Hudson rises up above the bawling crowd in the band's last song, "Banned in D.C." Naked, sweaty torsos emerge from the front rows, twisting with the screeching of the frenetic, yet precise, picking of Dr. Know. The song finishes and H.R. slams the mic stand into the floor, a deafening ovation rising up from in front of the stage. Lupe is still on Ricardo's shoulders, and she smiles and shrieks in delight. He's also roaring at the stage as he staggers, trying to keep his balance. "What did you think of fucking Bad Brains?" Ricardo asks. "Wow! They were unbelievable," she replies. "Total fucking madness!" they both shout in unison. They look at each other and laugh, sinking into a passionate kiss infused with sweat, punk, and adrenaline. Around them everything seems to be moving in slow motion and fading into darkness. If this were a rom-com, a spotlight would shine on them as they kiss, The Farm would be the school gym, and "She's an Angel" by They Might Be Giants would be playing as the final credits scroll slowly down the screen.

✳

The Bible. That was the name often give to the notebook containing all the names and phone numbers of the people who managed the venues and booked the underground shows throughout North America. Ed Ivey lent his "Bible" to Ricardo so he could note down the contacts he thought would be most interesting. The Rhythm Pigs were a respected group and sought after throughout the country as well as on the Canadian punk scene. To have their backing would be a massive boost. To be able to call up all those people and start a conversation with "Hi, we're ELPASO, Ed Ivey from the

166

Rhythm Pigs gave us your contact info . . ." meant starting on the right foot.

Ricardo was fascinated to find the numbers of legendary groups from the Texan punk scene like Cringe and Mulletto from Dallas, The Hugh Beaumont Experience and Skuds from Fort Worth, Rejects from San Antonio, Huns from Austin, Really Red from Houston, Uncalled 4 from Waco, or Vomit Pigs from Daingerfield.

The list went on with bands (some of which no longer existed) from all over the country:

- Angle from Salt Lake City (Utah)
- Antler Joe & The Accidents from Fort Myers (Florida)
- Black Flag from LA (California)
- Bad Brains from Washington, DC
- Critical Mass from Miami (Florida)
- Descendents from LA (California)
- Fingers from Pittsburgh (Pennsylvania)
- Jerry's Kidz from Albuquerque (New Mexico)
- Minutemen from San Pedro (California)
- Melvins from Seattle (Washington)
- Peer Pressure from Greenwich (Connecticut)
- Queers from Portsmouth (New Hampshire)
- Short Dogs Grow from San Francisco (California)
- Tapeworm from Stamford (Connecticut)
- Unnatural Axe from Boston (Massachusetts)
- Village Pistols from Greensboro (North Carolina)
- Weirdos from LA (California)
- (…)

Lupe and Ricardo spent a week in San Francisco enjoying their first vacation together before driving to Los Angeles. On Saturday, December 5, they had tickets to a show at Scream to see one of the city's most promising bands: Jane's Addiction.

At the end of 1986 the alternative scene underwent a period of transition. Faith No More had taken a different path with *We Care a Lot*, their debut album with Mordam Records, which represented a new way of understanding the use of guitars. In LA, the Red Hot Chili Peppers had already released a couple of albums with EMI, and everyone was talking about Jane's Addiction before they'd even released an album. The show at Scream was greatly perplexing for Ricardo. The guitarist, a guy called Dave Navarro, performed and played as if he were an aging rock star. His Gibson Les Paul had a whole range of effects with countless distortion and delay pedals, and he really milked the solos, which was unforgivable according to the rules of hardcore. And as for Perry Farrell, the band's front man... The guy, around thirty years old, was bare-chested and sang in a voice that was unusual for punk bands, using falsetto and shrieking, his voice breaking up as he sang. It was a combination of faltering rhythms and never-ending instrumentals. Ricardo thought his head was going to explode. Lupe, however, loved them, and after the gig this dichotomy was the subject of a heated conversation between them in the van as they left Los Angeles on Interstate 10.

Getting into an argument when you've got eight hundred miles of driving ahead of you is not advisable. Hours and hours of road time were filled with differences of opinion regarding the group they'd seen the night before. Jane's Addiction represented everything that threatened to destroy Ricardo's musical universe. Lupe lived and consumed music outside of the unwritten rules that her boyfriend lived by. Perry Farrell's band had seduced her because she had no prejudices regarding the way people in bands she liked sang or played the guitar. She just allowed herself to be guided by the charm, class, charisma, or choruses of whoever was invading her ears. She was free. Ricardo, on the other hand, was shackled to his rules. He was trapped under a mountain of absurd ideas that were increasingly less connected with music. He was uncompromising, and it took him forever to acknowledge when someone else had a point.

Lupe loved him, which was why she tried to get him to be more flexible. "You can't put limits on talent," she would say. She also valued ethics and songs that said something, but she didn't see the problem with ELPASO having a guitar solo in it. She thought that, in a way, they were wasting Octavio's talent and was sure it was all down to fear. Fear of rejection, of looking the fool. Fear of not fitting into a scene that looked like it was starting to collapse anyway. "Fuck them, Ritchie. Do the music that comes to you, and that's it."

✳

"OK, you're right," said Ricardo, while an enormous truck roared passed them. "What?" shouted Lupe. "You've got a fucking point, I said! I'm scared shitless of not fitting in, and I think I've let myself be influenced by the fucking 'unwritten law of hardcore' and by Daniel . . . And, I admit, Jane's fucking Addiction were awesome. So there you have it." Lupe's face lit up as she tried to avoid an enormous smile spreading beneath her nose. Both were standing by the roadside, waiting for a guy called Luke from Silverback to come and fill the tank with a few gallons of gas. Carried away with their argument, they failed to see the fuel indicator had fallen to empty, and their concentration lapse left them on the side of the interstate a little over an hour and a half from El Paso. Luckily, an old guy in a green Dodge truck had stopped and promised them he would send them Luke, a mechanic from Akela (New Mexico) who often helped drivers forced to stop on the side of the highway.

And that's just what he did. Almost without a word, Luke pulled up behind the van in his black pickup and got out with the motor still running. He lowered his more than one hundred kilos onto the shoulder and got out a couple of red containers that looked tiny in his enormous hands. His blackened fingers opened the Ford's fuel tank, and he poured in the gasoline without saying a word. On the back of his shirt was a dreadful logo comprising the word *Silverback* and an awful illustration of a gorilla repairing a car with the hood open. Once the containers were emptied, he took the money from Lupe and turned away. He threw the gasoline can into the back of the pickup, sat in the driver's seat, and waved goodbye with his enormous black hand while accelerating away and vanishing down I-10.

*

The sun is setting, they start up the van and drive to the nearest gas station. They fill the tank and put on the original cassette of *Freaky Styley* by the Red Hot Chili Peppers that Lupe bought in Tower Records on Sunset Strip. "Jungle Man," the album's first song, makes the Ford Econoline's sound system vibrate. It's funky, but it has something. Hillel Slovak's guitar is incredible, and it shimmies around Flea's sexy bass line. Lupe moves her head to the beat of the song and looks at Ricardo, who's thumping the steering wheel as he drives. He's playing the bass drum and snare with his fingers and nodding his head. "Holy shit, it's good!" he says. "Of course it's good, Ritchie!" Lupe replies, "the world is full of amazing music, darlin'. Open your mind!" He laughs and starts singing: "I am a jungle man. I am a jungle man. I am a jungle man. I get all the bush I can."

Ricardo and Daniel had always felt they were part of the more open punk factions. They understood and respected the musical experiments that bands like Black Flag or Minutemen had undertaken throughout their careers. But it was hard for them to accept that the alternative scene was changing and that a lot of what they had believed to be infinite had disappeared or was on the verge of doing so. Ricardo began to understand this thanks to Lupe and was ready to make changes to ELPASO for the better, but first they were going to pay homage to the scene that had seen them grow as musicians. Driving through New Mexico with the Red Hot Chili Peppers blasting from the stereo had enlightened him, and he had decided to record a demo with Spanish covers of his favorite songs. They would title it *Gimme These Songs!* And it would comprise:

- "Don't Want to Know If You Are Lonely" by Hüsker Dü
- "Corona" by Minutemen
- "Guyana Punch" by The Judy's
- "That's When I Reach for My Revolver" by Mission of Burma

That was how Ricardo operated. It could take an age for him to acknowledge something, but, when he finally did, his mind gradually opened and the light would flood into all corners of his hyperactive brain. The group needed a new demo and to bring this stage to a close. *Gimme These Songs!* would kill both of these birds with one stone. They were just a few weeks before the end of the year and he already had his resolution for 1987.

1987

SATURDAY. JANUARY 3. TWO WOMEN IN their fifties. The one on the left has glassy green eyes; her features are multiplied in small wrinkles, turning her face into a topographical map of her life. Each line tells a different story. On either side of her aquiline nose are cheekbones that preserve the beauty they conveyed thirty years before. Her yellowing teeth can be seen every time she opens her thin, almost imperceptible lips. Her hair emerges from white roots that blend into an auburn color that does little for her. Fuck fifty! She's over sixty and talks in a distracted and monotone voice. The woman on the right is in her fifties. She could be the daughter the other woman had during a wild and most probably difficult adolescence. Who knows. The words of the younger woman clash with those of her friend and hang in the air between them. There is no communication, but there is friendship and affection. The fifty-something-year-old has prominent breasts that Will finds particularly arousing. Beneath the green veins that run across her hands are the remnants of an attractive girl who was undoubtedly popular and successful in high school. She has unruly, somewhat thinning, blond hair, through which a pair of pretty little ears can be seen. Her mouth is wide, and the corners fall almost down to her perfect chin, which, for the time being, has escaped the ravages of time. Her blue eyes are half shut inside her almond-shaped eyelids, ending in crows' feet that

173

have clearly been flourishing for some time. The whole composition is dominated by a pair of fine eyebrows that form symmetrical arches, tracing two beautiful curves over a somewhat bewildered gaze.

She reminds Will of his mother, making him feel uncomfortable with the early signs of an erection in his trousers. She's been smiling at him for some time now, ignoring her friend, who is stirring her coffee back and forth with a metal spoon, striking the cup and marking a perfect 6/4 time. Will feels the woman's turquoise eyes burning through his shoulders, his arms, and his lips. They make him tremble in a way he hasn't trembled for a long time, and his well-versed pickle-slicing technique is affected by Oedipus, whispering in his ear to fuck her. Fuck her, Will. He shakes his head in an attempt to rid himself of this invasion of pseudo-incestuous ravings. He puts the knife down on the marble and stares at her. With her body facing her friend, she stares back at him and smiles cheekily. She makes a subtle gesture with her head, indicating the restroom door. He shakes his head but can't suppress a smile, his lips thinning to show his teeth. The blonde says something to her friend and gets up from her seat. She walks toward the restroom and winks at Will. "Fuck," he says under his breath. "I'm just going to the restroom, Armando." Without knowing how, he follows her to the Hamburger Hut bathroom, opens the door, and sees her eyes looking back at him in the mirror of the women's room. She's putting on red Maybelline lipstick, like in an ad with Lynda Carter, while she holds his gaze. He's aroused but rooted to the ground. This is too much for him. She takes off the blue turtleneck sweater she's wearing, revealing an incredible pair of enormous breasts bursting from the black bra that Will is desperate to tear off her. And that's just what he does, surrendering himself to this amazing woman who reminds him so much of Maureen Davis, his mother. She lets him dominate her, as he grips her firmly by the hips but kisses her nipples with gentle tenderness. He looks at her when he realizes he's about to explode, used to taking it out before reaching the end, but she smiles and asks him to do it inside her and Will comes, gasping, and she grips his blond hair tightly, presses her forehead against his, and also reaches an orgasm. They are both shaken by the electricity of the moment and are left trembling as if struck by lightning in the middle of a violent storm. The spasms dissipate, and they kiss and embrace one another. Will is still inside her, with no trace of what was the most powerful erection of his life. They feel no need to speak.

She gets up and cleans herself with a piece of toilet paper. He pulls up his jeans and goes through to the dining room of the Hamburger Hut, where everyone seems to be scrutinizing him. It looks like they weren't as discreet as he'd thought and a memory from his childhood in Brenham comes flooding back to him: shut up in a wardrobe with Marsha at a birthday party and emerging to cries of "William's got a girlfriend! William's got a girlfriend!"

THE BORDER

THEY HAD REHEARSED IN JUÁREZ, IN a back room of
Octavio's mother's home. Will didn't sit at his drums that day. For
several weeks he'd been absorbed by the quality sex he was getting
from Ruth, the woman he met in the bathroom of the hamburger
joint. It seemed to annoy DD that his brother was going around like
a fifteen-year-old who'd just lost his virginity, and their new roommate, Octavio, said you could feel the tension in the air when the pair
would shut themselves away in the bedroom at all hours of the day.

Everyone in the band thought it was a good idea to launch a
demo with the Spanish covers that Ricardo had suggested. Octavio
was especially keen. He'd never been into a recording studio and was
dying to have his guitar-playing recorded onto an album. That evening, like every rehearsal evening, they walked to the border to cross
back into the US and get a few beers downtown. From Octavio's
home in Juárez to the apartment he shared with Will and DD in El
Paso you had to walk a little over fifteen minutes, if there were no
unusual holdups at the border. They knew most of the police who
worked there, and they'd never had any problems.

Leaning with his back against the wall, one of the customs offi-
cers chewed intensely on a tuna and mayo sandwich. His lower jaw
rhythmically grinding every bite that he tore from the sandwich he'd
made himself that morning. He was holding on to his snack with both

hands, staring into space as he always did when he was at his post. His glasses enlarged his eyes to the point that they filled the prescription lenses. Those immense eyes fell on Octavio. In his forties, the officer still had strong, hairy forearms that could always be seen protruding from the short-sleeved shirts he wore both in winter and in summer. He had to tighten his belt to keep his trousers, which were far too big for him, above his waist, and he wore sneakers to be comfortable while he worked. Years of wearing his police cap had worn away at his hairline, which was now sparse and feeble. "Excuse me, sir, could you come with me, please?" the officer said to him as he used his ring finger to wipe the remains of the mayonnaise from the corners of his mouth. "Shit . . ." replied Octavio. "I'll just be a minute, wait for me."

Ricardo and DD (who were already on American soil when their friend walked off behind the officer) waited for over half an hour and didn't leave until another officer told them their friend wouldn't be going with them. They left, oblivious to how serious the situation could be. A new intriguing element was going to be added to the list of unknowns that came with the guitarist and his increasingly murky aura of mystery. If Octavio didn't turn up in the next couple of days, they'd have to record the demo without him.

✳

We decided to cross the border on our second visit to El Paso, in May 2016. Joel Quintana (one of Octavio's cousins we'd met the year before) invited us to set foot on Mexican pavement, knock back a couple of cocktails, and, while we were there, put an end to many of our preconceived ideas of the bridge that divides the United States and Mexico.

To start with, we always had the feeling that crossing the border was just an administrative procedure. Like at an airport. It might be the viewpoint of a tourist, which is what we were, but it never seemed that complicated. I guess that watching movies had led me to fantasize about a much more dangerous and unpredictable border, with cars filled with drugs or dead bodies trying to cross from one side to the other. It couldn't have been more different. What you see most are people crossing the border to work or shop, and young Mexicans who come in and out of their country every day to study in America. The two cities are, in fact, one, El Paso Street turning into Avenida Juárez once you pass the dividing line. A single coin was enough to tread on Mexican soil, and a few blocks down the road we were in the Kentucky club ready to wet our whistles with a few margaritas, which were every bit as good as the posters outside had promised. The place is considered one of the city's cult venues because of its more than one hundred years of history and its reputation as the bar that invented this world-famous cocktail of tequila, triple sec, and lime.

We talked about the escalation of violence that the city had suffered in recent years, and Joel told us with a heavy heart about how his family in Juárez had encouraged him not to cross back and to stay in the US forever. A great many people in El Paso have family on the other side of the border, and many of them have lost family members in the drug war that was unleashed in the city in 2008. It was plain to see that the people desperately wanted to show that the violence had calmed down. The fact that young people were once again returning to the bars at night and new businesses were slowly beginning to open were two clear signs of the new sense of security the people from Juárez were now feeling. Most would agree with the headline in The New York Times in 2013: "Ciudad Juárez Gets Back to Living."

GIMME THESE SONGS!

ON JANUARY 22, THE GROUP SHUTS themselves inside the studio with the intention of recording the four songs that will make up the *Gimme These Songs!* EP in a single day. Daniel is armed with a video camera, and two days have gone by since Octavio was stopped at the border. They are still none the wiser.

At the same time, in Harrisburg, Pennsylvania, the Republican Budd Dwyer (accused of bribery) takes out a pistol in the middle of a televised press conference and commits suicide. Before midday, Ricardo, DD, and Will have recorded definitive takes of three songs. They go out to a nearby burger joint to find all the restaurant's customers in silence, moved and watching the old television that is fixed to one of the walls. The news of Dwyer's suicide shocks them too, and they begin to speculate about the Republican's possible innocence. "If that asshole shot himself claiming his innocence, maybe he was right," says Will. Several of the customers agree with him, while others turn the argument around and think that his suicide was irrefutable proof of his guilt: "You've gotta be pretty sure they're gonna put you away to stick a Magnum in your mouth and blow your brains out."

The atmosphere is eerie, and the absence of any news about Octavio makes the already unnerving lunch even weirder. Ricardo doesn't even want to finish his double hamburger with cheese. He's gone from feeling pissed at Octavio for not telling them anything to seriously worried about what could have happened to his friend. Will and DD say they have no idea where he got the money to pay the rent. They just know that he pays every time without fail and always in cash. Daniel (who still doesn't get along that well with Octavio) puts on the table what no one else has ever dared to ask the guitarist: "Maybe he's gotten himself into some kind of trouble with drugs. That would explain the problem on the border and the wads of cash that fill his pockets without him ever lifting a finger." Although Will and DD love Octavio, they've always suspected what Daniel has just voiced and so say nothing to counter his accusation. And everyone knows that silence gives consent. Ricardo, however, explodes, accusing his friend of being grossly unfair to a member of ELPASO. He takes it as a betrayal and tells Daniel that his only motivation for saying such a thing is because he's jealous he's not in the band. "Where the fuck do you get that bull-shit from, Ritchie?" replies Daniel in disbelief, "Just 'cause he's a good guitarist doesn't make him a fucking saint, does it? I've been working on the design for the EP for days, and I've left Rubén and Roger pre-paring one of our performances by themselves to come here and give you assholes a hand. I don't need to play an instrument to feel like one of the group, OK?" Ricardo's unblinking eyes are fixed firmly on Daniel as he smashes his right fist into the table, the cutlery flying into the air, and through gritted teeth tells his friend, "Well, you can fuck off with your fucking artist friends. We don't need you here at all." Daniel's ears go red, he frowns, and with blood-filled eyes he gets up, throws a twen-ty-dollar bill onto the table, and leaves the restaurant, slamming the door behind him. Ricardo is still muttering insults when he looks up and sees that all the diner's customers have stopped looking at the latest news on the suicide and instead have turned to watch the fight between him and his old friend. "Fucking stuck-up asshole . . ." he whispers. Will and DD remind him they have to get back to the studio to finish off the songs. They pay and get to-go coffee, their favorite drink for dealing with the work they have ahead of them.

※

They have pizzas for dinner and drink beer on the red leather sofa that Joseph has right in front of the mixing desk. "Don't stain the uphol-stery with pepperoni, you assholes!" All that's left to do are Octavio's vocals and guitar solos, everything else is ready in powerful live takes that ELPASO, as a trio, blasted through in little over five hours. They sound awesome.

Ricardo, in the recording booth and with a neat 1980 AKG C-414 mic stuck to his lips, guesses that someone is ringing the door-bell because of the red light above the door. Joseph, on the other side of the glass, makes hand signals that he interprets as a: "Wait a second. I don't know who the fuck that could be at this time, but I should go and open the door." The Davis brothers seem to be shout-ing at each other, but he doesn't hear them, all the mics are muted. All except his. In fact, all that he can hear is his amplified breathing.

The ELPASO singer looks at the clock hung above the sofa. It's nine in the evening. The door to the room opens and Joseph stumbles in, pushed by whoever is behind him. The guy's silhouette is lit up as he crosses the threshold into the room, and Octavio's unmistakable mustache, curly hair, and the Mexican guitarist's contagious smile come into view. "Did you miss me, motherfuckers?" he exclaims as he hugs the Davis brothers. Ricardo is still in the booth and can't hear anything, but he's relieved. His friend is OK and has arrived just in time to record his parts on the guitar.

※

Recording. At minute 2:06 of the cover of "That's When I Reach for My Revolver" by Mission of Burma, Octavio drags his pick along the neck of the distorted Gibson Les Paul for four seconds. It's like a distant rumble of the thunder that's on its way. He holds a few notes before launching into a melody that progresses as his fingers fly across the strings. Ricardo has his eyes shut. Will and DD look at each other while they nod and smile and Joseph is pressing buttons to give the guitar solo that Octavio is in the middle of improvising more volume.

After half a minute of picking, the guitar comes to an abrupt end with an inharmonious chord. Octavio frowns and looks up to see the others; he doesn't look satisfied. Ricardo, by contrast, is beside himself and pleads with his hands for the guitarist to keep playing, to kill the guitar slowly before the next chorus. And that's what he does. Joseph stops recording and turns around to see the satisfied looks on the other band members and says, "Guys, that is a sick first take. I think that's a wrap. We've got ourselves a great album!" And he's not wrong. The EP is powerful and direct. It is brilliantly performed, and the band manages to make the songs of others their own.

"They just blow you away!" cries Will after hearing them all for the first time. "Someone tell that to Dwyer!" replies Joseph ironically. Everyone is smiling except Ricardo. The joke is macabre and he likes that, but the image of Dwyer killing himself takes him back to his argument with Daniel in the burger joint. He regrets putting his friend down like that. He accepts that something is happening. There's too much tension. "I'll call him tomorrow," he thinks. And that's what he does. They talk, sort it out, and Daniel designs a nice collage for the cassette of *Gimme These Songs!* but their relationship is never the same again. Something short-circuited between them the day Budd Dwyer shot himself in the head in front of America.

STRANGE SENSATIONS

IT'S HARD TO IMAGINE GROUPS LIKE the Foo Fighters or Green Day feeling nervous months before a show. They're bands who spend their lives doing back-to-back tours with barely a few days between concerts. Filling up major venues all over the world, three or four times a week throughout the year must help to normalize the lead-up to a performance. For small, unknown groups who struggle to fill up a concert hall, it's not quite the same.

I clearly remember when we organized our first major performance with Nameless. We were seventeen years old and had just recorded our first three-song demo. It was 1999, and we were playing a mix of alternative rock, punk, and Metallica covers. We'd played a couple of times at school, and a local radio presenter suggested we open for a major national progressive rock band. His program was coming up on its fifteen-year anniversary, and he was hoping to celebrate it by holding this concert. We agreed on the performance five months before the date of the gig and waited for the big day with an intense mix of excitement, nervousness, and anxiety. We decided on a strict rehearsal schedule that led us to faultlessly performing the setlist we'd prepared. We had little over thirty minutes to show our strength, speed, and musical talent. We came up with a cover of "Seek & Destroy" by Metallica that included the entire song "No Remorse" in the middle. It was more than ten minutes of heavy metal orgy that we knew would delight the crowd we'd be playing to. During those months I managed to get my index and middle fingers to strike the bass strings at the same speed as Cliff Burton when he recorded *Kill 'Em All*.

On the day of the concert, a drunk guy got up on the stage and started howling the chorus of "Seek & Destroy" in between a pathetic series of "yeaaahs" meant as a dreadful attempt at imitating James Hetfield. It was something that might seem funny now, but at the time it made me feel frustrated and uncomfortable. After so many months fantasizing about the performance, I felt profoundly put out by this fat ape ruining our cover, preventing the rest of the crowd from fully enjoying our music. To make matters worse, I made mistakes in a few songs, and Jonathan went crazy on the drums and sped up too much on a song that was meant to sound much slower and weightier. Though the crowd left on a high and we received what seemed like genuine praise from the show's organizer and the big bands, we felt somewhat disappointed. Just a couple days before, we had performed a faultlessly sublime repertoire in the rehearsal studio. "If all these people had heard us on Thursday, they would have been even more blown away," I thought. Five months of working and waiting went up in smoke in thirty minutes of performance. There were no record labels calling us up. There were no talent scouts or managers waving contracts all ready to be signed. There was nothing. We were rehearsing again in less than a week despite not having any shows lined up. A month later we organized a gig in a cycle of emerging groups. This time we "only" had three months to prepare for the performance, so we decided to add a day each week to our rehearsal schedule.

✷

During the first months of 1987, ELPASO were in a similar situation: at the end of May they were going to open for both Suicidal Tendencies and Descendents within a space of fewer than seven days.

They had four months to prepare the two shows. As well as the rehearsals, they had set up a couple of gigs with local bands, and in February they were to play with Uglor and Abandon Ship in El Paso and in April with Red Zone in Albuquerque, New Mexico. The few copies of *Gimme These Songs!* they'd sent to magazines, fanzines, and record labels had yet to bear any fruit. Ricardo had used his time to start setting up a national tour, calling the contacts that Ed Ivey had given him in San Francisco.

Daniel was not wild about the tour idea. His plan had always been for the group to grow first in Texas and gain popularity in Austin, Dallas, and Houston, and then move farther afield and conquer the rest of the country. But now Daniel's guidance and plans had lost their influence, and, after his trip to California, Ricardo was sure that it was time for him to get behind the wheel of the ship. "Leaving Texas will be great for us, Danny. California is amazing, and we've got a heap of contacts thanks to the Rhythm Pigs. And things are really interesting in Washington and Oregon. There are loads of cool bands in Seattle we could set up concerts with. I have a feeling that amazing things are going to happen to us on the West Coast."

February 23, 1987. El Paso (TX)
Uglor + ELPASO + Abandon Ship

The Canon NP-1215 photocopier in the university's art department spat out the yellow paper that Daniel had loaded. Inside the machine, the black toner was impregnating the paper, reproducing single-color versions of the collage that was being scanned on the glass. Each swipe of light that half escaped from the side of the lid announced a new copy. The monotonous sound of the photocopier made Danny's head spin as he pressed the green button that set the mechanism in motion each time a new flyer came sliding into the out tray. He did this around fifty times, grabbed the pile of flyers, and felt the warmth that the recently copied paper gave off. He put the original on top of the copies and left the department, greeting all the people he knew as he sped through the university corridors, showing the copies to one of the guys he bumped into. "It's cool," he said. Daniel thanked him for the comment and feigned a smile in an effort to hide his displeasure at his design for the ELPASO show with Uglor. For a while now he'd been on autopilot whenever Ricardo asked him to do something. In the beginning, he was totally inspired to come up with graphic material for the band, but that excitement had turned to apathy. He was incapable of saying no to his friend, and so he responded to his requests with work that wasn't about to grab anyone's attention. Evidently, from their performance on the night of the concert, Daniel wasn't the only one in ELPASO lacking in enthusiasm.

From the end of the seventies, the biggest musicians and bands from the border had started swelling the list of names in El Paso's punk diaspora. Tito Larriva and Charlie Quintana from The Plugz (icons and pioneers of Latin punk) left Texas to set up in Los Angeles. Teenage Popeye reached high levels of popularity in the city but, in their efforts to expand, left for Austin and toured Europe. Something similar happened to One Second Zero and Red Zone. The Rhythm Pigs of Ed Ivey, Greg Adams, and Jay Smith chose San Francisco as the springboard into their whirlwind career in the American underground, relentlessly releasing albums and touring the US. Everyone helped to create the breeding ground needed for the scene to grow in these cities. Hence, the importance of the night of February 23.

Playing at Sound Seas were three of the bands hailed as the heirs to the city's first punk generation. Uglor, Abandon Ship, and ELPASO were seen as promising local bands, and a concert with all three of them on the bill was the perfect opportunity to gauge the local scene in 1987.

It's worth pointing out here that the significance I'm attaching to this show stems from a global vision I've developed as I've delved further into El Paso's underground history. At the same time, the local bands that would form the scene of the early nineties were coming together. Kids who were getting their first instruments and flirting with a few chords and the primitive rhythms of whichever prepubescent was starting out on drums. Most of these guys had never seen Teenage Popeye and admired the Rhythm Pigs because of what they had become, but had never set foot in the Rathskeller. They'd only ever seen the façade of the Koke House. They just about managed to set up a few concerts at school and in the backyards of their parents' homes. They dreamed of getting onto the stage at Sound Seas and, perhaps, opening for one of the major bands that might be playing there. They were to be the city's third punk generation, but it was yet to be decided who would lead the second. That was why the show with Ricardo's group, Uglor, and Abandon Ship was so important. That also explains the repercussions of having delivered such an awful concert that night.

From Uglor's double-bass drum kit came the devilish rhythms that defined the music of Grant Dorian's band. Grant had played with Daniel and Ricardo and had been a potential ELPASO drummer before the Davis brothers turned up in 1984. Sander Starr was bawling into the main mic, and the long hair and sleeveless T-shirts from the Misfits mixed with the darkness of the songs. If this had been a battle of the bands, Uglor would have run away with first prize. They were powerful, proficient musicians and charismatic. They intimidated the crowd, like a wild and dangerous animal you can't help but approach.

Abandon Ship, once more, displayed their solid relationship with psychedelic ska/reggae. Mike Jennings, Pat Tucker, and Gene O'Reilly flowed in syncopated time, generating a unique atmosphere. ELPASO's songs, however, sounded dull and weak. Octavio, as always, tried to save the performance with his rock star lashes and virtuoso guitar-playing, but it was impossible. They all agreed that the concert had been a bad one. The worst. They'd put everything into the shows that were coming up after, which they somehow believed were of primary importance. Until then they had approached every gig as if it were the biggest of their career. Their underestimation of that performance could be seen in Daniel's flyer and their performance onstage. Their mistake lay in their belief that it was far more important to open for Descendents than to share the stage with two relatively unknown local bands, like them. Underrating them meant underrating themselves.

<h2 style="text-align:center">April 18, 1987. Albuquerque (NM)
Red Zone + ELPASO</h2>

It was Saturday morning. Dawn was breaking in El Paso and the morning light bounced off the bodywork of one of the cars parked in the middle of the road, in front of the apartments where Will, DD, and Octavio lived. Ricardo had double-parked the Ford Econoline and was feeling around in the glovebox looking for the sunglasses that would protect his eyes from the blinding glare of the sunlight. On the brown leather of the passenger seat, five coffees steamed and trembled with the vibrations of the engine. Through the speakers boomed the heavy chords of the song "Heater Moves and Eyes" by the Melvins. Lupe had subscribed to a fanzine from the Northwest, and they had sent her a cassette of *Gluey Porch Treatments*, the debut album of the band from Seattle. The tape had been in the cassette player for weeks, and the members of ELPASO were hooked. As Ricardo slammed the van door shut, it was like the music had been plunged into deep water, but the dense low notes of Buzz Osborne's band managed to slip out and creep along the orange-colored streets of the city.

Ricardo followed the invisible trace of the Melvins' chords along the pavement, and a long shadow cut across his thoughts. Immediately a second black silhouette joined the first, and he saw that both were cast onto the road from the sneakers of DD and Octavio. Ricardo took off his sunglasses and greeted them with a nod of his head, laughing. They'd brought with them five more coffees.

"I bought coffees too, you assholes!" exclaimed Ricardo.

"Yeaaaaahh!" sang Octavio at the same time as he pretended to play the Melvins' chords.

"What about Will? We're pretty tight for time."

"We don't know anything about him. He didn't sleep at home last night."

DD frowned and knocked back the espresso in his right hand. His eyes watered and his cheeks reddened both from feeling pissed and from the temperature of the coffee.

"Motherfucker!"

"We think he's with Ruth. For days they've been at each other's throats, shouting and threatening each other at all hours. I hope he remembers the gig. He's out of it at the moment."

"Goddammit . . . DD, does Will have a car to get to Albuquerque if we leave now?"

DD shook his head while he put the other coffees in the van. The Melvins flew out from inside the Ford as soon as the door opened, along with an intense aroma of coffee, which made Octavio close his eyes in anticipated pleasure of his favorite beverage. Apparently, the Davis brothers' Lincoln Continental sedan had been in need of repairs for some time now.

"Maybe Lupe could lend him her Plymouth?" asked Octavio.

Ricardo hesitated for a moment and then cursed under his breath, shaking his head. "She can't, she's got plans with a friend in Horizon City. Fuck! What the hell are we gonna do? We have to leave now, or we'll never get there on time . . ."

Playing in New Mexico had a lot going for it. One thing was that you could leave the city on the same day as the show. They had a journey of about five hours ahead of them and had arranged with Mike Gray to meet at the door of the venue after lunch. They would unload all the equipment and set up. They could start with the sound checks before six, and the performance would end around ten. If they cleared up everything quickly enough, they could load up the van by eleven and be home by three. Saving themselves the expense of staying overnight in Albuquerque was, undoubtedly, another big advantage. Now it all depended on Will. If he turned up on time, everything would go ahead as planned.

They waited in silence. Leaning up against the side of the Ford, they stared at the floor, pondering over what to do. Will was always punctual and was often unforgiving when the others weren't. Just two days before the show with Red Zone, he predicted that Albuquerque would be a big gig for ELPASO. They were taking his full drum kit. As an opening act it was quite normal to come up against a band, promoter, or venue manager who would only let you set up one drum kit onstage, in which case the headliners would always use theirs. If that was the case, you had to dismantle your kit and take the snare, the stool, and the cymbals separately.

Will Davis was a powerful drummer. He was skillful and elegant but would hit the drums with great force. He put holes in drumskins, split cymbals, and regularly splintered sticks. They'd had major run-ins with drummers from other bands who complained at how hard Will would strike the bass drum. "Crybabies," he'd think. He got caught up in endless battles with the owners of the different drum kits he played, although he usually gave up and ended up taking the sting out of the squabble through his playing. These situations really got on his nerves, and he made a promise to himself never to play on another drummer's kit again. "I play with my own fucking cymbals, or I don't play." But none of that was going to happen in Albuquerque. His leaving them in the shit like this without so much as an explanation created a strange atmosphere among the band.

Ricardo looked at Octavio and thought about his arrest on the border and about how he somehow miraculously managed to get to the studio at the last minute. He thought about Jerry West's shot at the beginning of the seventies against the New York Knicks. A stroke of genius. The Lakers player brought the game to a draw at the last moment with a half-court buzzer-beater, although his team would then lose in overtime. Maybe if they went, Will would turn up out of the blue a minute before they had to start. He would sit down at his kit and, without further ado, give the performance of his career. For Ricardo, this was an absurd idea. He preferred the idea of reaching the end of the game with enough of an advantage not to have to rely on a winning shot. Basically, because those shots don't always go in.

"Guys!" They all turn around. The voice is coming from the other side of the van. "I'm sorry! I overslept and had to stop for gas! I thought you'd go without me!" The three expectant faces drop, changing from hope and excitement to resignation as they realize that the voice is Daniel's and not Will's.

"So you're not thrilled to see me, you assholes . . . At least I brought coffee!" he says holding up a blue thermos in his left hand.

"Very original, Danny! You can leave it on the passenger seat with the other hundred gallons of caffeine." Still breathing fast, Daniel hugs DD and Ricardo and greets Octavio with his usual indifference.

"Where's Will?"

"That's the million-dollar question! And the answer is: we've got no fucking idea."

Daniel turns toward DD, who looks away like a child ashamed of something his friend's done. The situation is tense. With people slowly beginning to emerge onto the streets around them, Ricardo suddenly slams his hand down on the van's bodywork and jumps in front of Daniel.

"Why don't you play the drums today?"

"What?"

"You know the old setlist back to front . . ."

"Don't fuck with me, Ritchie, I haven't played for years."

"So what?"

"What, what, what?" interjects Octavio.

"We can fiddle with the setlist a little and make the concert a bit shorter."

"I don't know . . ." whispers Daniel, his hands squeezing his cheeks together. "I'm not sure about this at all, man!"

"Can you think of anything better?" Ricardo's tone hardens. "There's no way I'm standing these guys up. Not them. No fucking way."

On saying this, Ricardo realizes he's giving up on putting on a good show. He's just thinking about avoiding Mike Gray and the other guys from Red Zone seeing them like a bunch of assholes. He doesn't want to let down Ed Ivey, who suggested them as the opening band. The others look on in silence, their lead singer glaring inquisitively at his friend. Octavio and Daniel agree with resignation. There's no other option. Everyone's eyes fall on DD. He's never played without his brother, and if the bass player bails out, then the show's over.

The two minutes it takes for the younger Davis to answer seem like an eternity for Ricardo. Everything in the street stops. The footsteps of the passersby sound like explosions reverberating around a cavern, and Ricardo feels his eyes blink in slow motion. Even the wings of passing birds seem to slow down as the seconds seem more like hours, days, weeks. Ricardo feels as if he's the only one who can actually move at normal speed in this bizarre time dimension. His stomach contracts, and his legs tremble. If he could go back to being the shy child he used to be, he would run over to the other corner of the room at school where no one could see him and cry with rage. His tears would flow down his reddened cheeks while his friends chanted taunts at him. He would try to get his breath back amid the sobbing and would dry his eyes with his sleeve, waiting for it all to be over. Waiting for the response. The response from the mother who abandoned him. The response from the teacher who humiliated him for being overly sensitive. The response from a world that seems to want to make everything more complicated for him. DD's response.

That's why he wants to throw up when the bass player nods his head. The tension suddenly dissipates, and his stomach returns to its normal size. The people, birds, and eyelids move at the speed they're supposed to, and Ricardo, who would happily pass out, grits his teeth and gives the van a kick. The Melvins stopped playing a while ago.

He opens the back door and signals for everyone to get in. He invites Daniel to sit in the front. "That's the drummer's seat," he says, giving his friend a wink. The inside of the Econoline smells like coffee. Ricardo starts the engine and turns the cassette of the Melvins over. He puts his foot down on the accelerator, and the dense and dark chords of Buzz Osborne's band leave an invisible jet stream along the trail that leads them to Albuquerque, New Mexico.

They drive along Overland Avenue to El Paso Street. Ricardo turns the steering wheel abruptly to the left without slowing down. Everyone suddenly slides to the left inside the van, and the instruments hit the inside of the bodywork. Daniel grabs the handrail above the window with both hands, and the cups on his lap spill onto his pants. The coffee doesn't burn him, but it leaves a brown stain on his jeans. Ricardo takes his eyes off the road to see what has happened next to him. From the back of the van all that can be heard are the sounds of clanging metal and Octavio's curses in Spanish. The sound of a horn brings him back to his driving, and he's forced to jerk the wheel over again to avoid hitting the car, whose driver is angrily sounding his horn at him for drifting into his lane. Ricardo manages to bring the Ford back in line and apologizes to the others. He stretches his back until it cracks. He slides his backside forward, his body falling over the steering wheel. He squints his eyes, trying to make out what's happening at the end of the street, next to the Plaza Theatre. "What the fuck is going on there?" he asks. Daniel, who is trying to dry his pants with the paper towels that came with the coffee, raises his head and looks at what appears to be a body slumped at the doors to the theater. They slow down and travel a couple hundred feet at a little over five miles an hour. There's no doubt about it. When they get to the intersection of Sheldon and Mills Avenue, they can clearly see Will's body lying unmoving on the ground. His back is leaning against the wall, his legs stretched out on the sidewalk, and his head has dropped onto his left shoulder. Ricardo, his hands trembling, pulls up the hand brake and kills the engine. He opens the door and gets out. There are a few people standing around the drummer's body. Octavio and Daniel also get out but stay quietly by the van looking pale. DD pushes them out of the way and runs to his brother. Ricardo is asking what's happened, and the two guys next to Will don't know what to say. "He was here when we got here," says one of them. Ricardo puts his right hand to Will's neck to feel for signs of life, and as soon as he touches the flesh beneath the left-hand side of his jaw, the ELPASO drummer raises his head, his eyes rolling in their sockets, and gives Ricardo a slap.

"Don't touch me you son of a bitch," he mumbles. He can hardly open his mouth. His breath, which stinks of alcohol, impregnates the space around his body and hits his friend and brother full in the face.

"He's wasted!" exclaims Ricardo, laughing nervously. "The motherfucker is totally wasted." DD takes a deep breath, gets up, and gives his brother a vicious kick in the thigh. Daniel runs over and grabs him before he unleashes a second blow. Ricardo does too. They manage to get him away and calm him down. "Chill out, DD. He just needs to take a cold shower and sleep it off." The younger Davis pushes his friends off him and runs over to the van. Daniel gets his breath back and follows him with his eyes. His hands are on his hips, and his chest is pumping with adrenaline. At the same instant that he sees DD get into the vehicle, he recognizes a silhouette behind the Ford. An old man with greasy, graying hair and an unruly white beard, wearing a white undershirt beneath a brown suit. The phantasmagorical figure whose fleeting appearances had terrified him years before was back and just a few yards away from him, stony-faced and staring right at Daniel. "Give me a hand here, Daniel. We gotta get him home." Daniel agrees without taking his eyes off the tramp, but as soon as he crouches down to get Will's left arm over his shoulders, the guy behind the van vanishes.

They manage to drag Will to the Ford and get him inside. DD, pained and pissed, doesn't even get out of his seat. Ricardo sees what's happening as a sign. He swallows his pride and realizes that without Will there's no way they can give a decent show. Suddenly, the idea of going to Albuquerque and letting someone else take control of the drums seems totally absurd. Daniel sees the doubt in his friend's eyes and asks, "What are we gonna do about the gig, Ritchie?"

"I'm gonna call Mike now and cancel. Let's get this asshole into bed."

May 23, 1987. El Paso (TX)
Suicidal Tendencies + Short Dogs Grow + ELPASO

The depression that Will sank into after his breakup with Ruth marked the two weeks between the canceled concert with Red Zone and the short performance they'd committed to playing before the sets of Short Dogs Grow and Suicidal Tendencies. The ELPASO drummer wandered around the Hamburger Hut like a lost soul. His boss gave him a few days off, which he spent sprawled out on the sofa among cans of beer and pizza boxes. He kept the blinds down in an effort to make it feel like it was permanently nighttime. All he wanted to do was sleep. The bluish light from the television flickered across his face as he stared back at it blankly. His eyes seemed to be looking right through it. In fact, they seemed to be looking right through the walls and the building, his gaze lost in the desert and drowning in the Pacific. He didn't sit at the drums once. The group ruled out performing on May 23. Ricardo spoke with Mike Jennings to tell him that, in the end, they wouldn't be playing. Mike told him it didn't matter and encouraged Ricardo to come along and watch Suicidal Tendencies play. He did. And he loved them. He also enjoyed watching Short Dogs Grow; they were an impressive band. Ricardo felt a wave of frustration wash over him as he watched the bands from the crowd and wished he could have been onstage. Having to cancel a second concert was a real hammer to the head for him. He had to do something. They couldn't miss their chance to play with Descendents as well.

He left the concert and went straight over to see Will. Octavio opened the door, and Ricardo walked straight past him before he could finish saying hello. He stood in front of the mass of facial hair, grease, and tomato stains that was decomposing on the sofa. DD came out of his room to hear Ricardo throwing the empty cans from the coffee table so that he could sit down in front of his brother.

"What the fuck do you think you're doing, Will?"

"Leave me alone, man. You're blocking the TV."

"There's no way I'm leaving until you tell me what the fuck you're gonna do."

"I don't wanna do anything, Ricardo. I'm tired. Just let me live in peace, man."

"Live? You wanna live? It looks to me like you want to die like a dumbass motherfucker. You spend all day trying to sleep. The house is all blacked out so you can get your eyes closed by seven. Everything you're doing is the exact opposite of living, so don't tell me to let you live in peace, you asshole."

Ricardo's words seemed to spark the faintest flicker of light in Will's eyes. He looked Ricardo in the eye and sat up on the sofa for the first time in days.

"Fuck, man, I don't want to die."

"Well, then get yourself out of this shit, Will."

"I can't, Ritchie, I'm all screwed up. I don't know how."

"You told me once that playing the drums saved your life."

"Yeah, it did . . ."

"Well, play the fucking drums, then, Will. In eight days we've got a golden opportunity opening for Descendents. Let's blow their minds."

"But I'm useless . . . I can't even lift up a slice of pizza. How do you expect me to wield a drumstick?"

"Let's go to Juárez to rehearse tomorrow. Can we?" said Ricardo as he turned to Octavio.

"Sure, no problem," he answered.

"Get yourself in the show and think about what I told you. I'll see you tomorrow. You, too. Get some rest." Ricardo stood up and grabbed one of the half-empty bags on the floor by the sofa. He filled it with cans and folded up the cardboard boxes to put them in, too. "I'll throw this shit out," he said as he left the apartment.

The door slammed shut, making Will jump. He'd been drowning in his own misery for days now, but at no point had he thought of all that as suicide. He'd never wanted to shoot himself in the head over a girl. Ricardo's words stirred something up in him. His obsession with sleeping to avoid feeling the anxiety in his stomach was undoubtedly a sign that he didn't want to live. The idea that he'd been dead for the past two weeks made him retch. He ran to the bathroom and vomited. He threw up a repulsive mix of pepperoni, beer, and bile. He also vomited some of his anxiety. Not all of it, but enough to let him pick up his drumsticks the next day.

May 31, 1987. El Paso (TX)
Descendents + ELPASO

Milo Aukerman comes out onstage at Sound Seas and positions himself between Stephen Egerton and Karl Álvarez. He's wearing a yellow Bad Brains T-shirt and beige, pleated pants. He pushes his black tortoiseshell glasses onto his nose and grabs the microphone with both hands. "Thou shalt not commit laundry," he says. They kick off with "All-O-Gistics." "Thou shalt covet thy neighbor's food. Thou shalt not create ties with the scathed. Thou shalt always go for greatness. Thou shalt not commit adulthood. Thou shalt not partake of decaf. Thou shalt not suppress flatulence," the band come into the song one after the other. "Thou shalt not commit hygiene. Thou shalt not have no idea. Thou shalt commit thyself to an institution. Thou shalt not take the van's name in vain." And when Milo howls, "Thou shalt not allow anything to deter you in your quest for all," the fuse is lit and the song explodes.

Ricardo watches the Californian band from the side of the stage. He's happy. Guitar in hand still. The ELPASO show was almost perfect. They managed to get their act together, and the weirdness of the three previous concerts went up in smoke with a reenergized performance and slick guitar-playing. The crowd jumped, shouted, and sweat. Will played better than ever. This was exorcism for him, and he threw up the last of his anxiety pounding the drums like a madman. His strength impressed everyone, including Bill Stevenson himself. The sweat flew from this arms and forehead, while his long blond hair whipped through the air. With every bang of his head, the ELPASO drummer brought rhythm to the song, the strands of hair that escaped from under his hat shook in the air, releasing showers of sweat that disintegrated from his drumskins. He was agile and unstoppable, even playing through the breaks between songs.

DD, infected by his big brother's renewed energy, played and sang with precision, elegance, and intensity. The notes from his bass fired like torpedoes into the eagerly awaiting crowd. Octavio once again proved his prodigious talent as a guitarist. He did everything he was meant to—and did it to perfection. He ended the night surfing the crowd after pouncing bare-chested from the stage, his classic Gibson Les Paul leaned up against the amp feeding back and producing noises that further excited the audience. This was a punk orgy led by a solid and mature master of ceremonies that was forged into what would become a unique night of music. For Ricardo, impressing Descendents and giving everyone in the crowd a legendary performance that was etched onto their retinas and would live on in their memories meant everything. He announced each of their songs with the title, saying nothing more. "John Wayne Gacy." Will marked the entry with the hi-hat, and the group exploded into one of punk's most primitive and authentic tunes. Ricardo was in full control of his voice now, his vocal cords no longer contracting with the fear of getting it wrong, like they did in the group's first performances. He sang. And really well. He defended his compositions and his discourse with a deep voice and almost perfect Spanish. He finished the gig with a succinct "Thanks," which could hardly be heard among the ovation that Sound Seas gave the four members of ELPASO.

When he unplugs his *Fender Stratocaster* to get down from the stage, he bumps into Milo. "How did it sound?" he asks. "Sick, man!" replies Descendents' vocalist. Karl Álvarez congratulates him and the drummer, Bill Stevenson, asks him to wait after the concert. "I wanna talk to you about something," he says winking knowingly at Ricardo, who, in turn, nods without saying a word. He just stands there watching one of his favorite bands getting ready to start playing. A drop of sweat trickles down his forehead, flowing to the end of his nose, where it hangs. He can feel it suspended there, enjoying the slight tickle it gives him in its struggle not to plummet to the floor. He doesn't blink. All he can think about is the day he got soaked by the sweat of Henry Rollins while watching Black Flag. Of the high from the acid. That night he saw Bill Stevenson for the first time. In 1984, the drummer of Descendents used the time his band stopped playing to join Black Flag and took charge of the drumsticks during the performance of Henry Rollins and Greg Ginn's band in El Paso. Tonight, that unreachable figure talked to him directly. One musician to another. He knew who he was and invited him to talk privately after the show. "If only Lupe had come," he thinks to himself. Both she and Daniel couldn't come at the last minute. There was no one to document their best show. Not even a photo. The memory of that day would be marked only by Daniel's landscape flyer, on which Ricardo had scribbled the setlist. A repertoire they could perform on the American tour he was just putting the finishing touches on.

He comes back to himself when the drop of sweat releases from the tip of his nose. He's lost all notion of time. He must have been standing there for a while. Guitar in one hand, setlist in the other. From his privileged position he enjoys the panoramic view of the venue. In a single glance he takes in the crowd and Descendents performing "All-O-Gistics." Together. It's the perfect image. He contemplates it, and an enormous smile spreads across his face. He decides it's time to put away the damn guitar.

✳

Ricardo and the others help clean up after the concert. In the atmosphere of an empty Sound Seas, you can still feel the vibrations from the electric performances of ELPASO and Descendents. Bill Stevenson, bare-chested and with a white towel slung over his shoulder, approaches Ricardo and helps him lift one of the guitar amps.

"Have you recorded anything?"

"Yeah, an EP with our Spanish covers and an old demo with some live songs we recorded last year."

"You should send a demo with new material to Greg from SST."

"Greg Ginn?"

"Sure man. Greg Ginn. He's putting together a new label right now called Cruz Records, for more alternative stuff. I think he'd be really into what you guys do."

"Fuck, that would be incredible. We're big fans of all the bands on his label. We saw you and Greg play when you came through with Black Flag in '84. It was amazing."

(laughing) "Thanks! That was a crazy tour. I don't remember much about that time."

"Me and my friend Daniel were blown away. In fact, that concert was basically our inspiration to start the band."

"Is Daniel the guitarist? He's really good, man."

"No . . . That's Octavio. Daniel is our designer. He's in charge of the artistic side of the band. He started playing the drums before Will arrived. He's a big fan of yours. It's a real shame he couldn't come tonight."

"Yeah, it is. Hey, we gotta go. We're off to Florida tomorrow and we need to rest. Write to Greg Ginn and send him whatever you have. I'm sure what you guys can offer would have a place in the Cruz Records catalog. I'll try to talk to him, maybe we could get you guys to open for us on tour with our new band. We're releasing an album at the beginning of next year."

"Fuck, Bill! That would be amazing . . ."

"It'd be my pleasure, Ricardo. Let's see what we can do."

"Thanks, man. Enjoy Florida."

✳

Night falls on the city, and the lights from downtown El Paso illuminate the way back. Ricardo drives the band's van. Empty. He's left the others at their place and is on his way home. He's feeling relaxed. There's no music this time. He's desperate to tell Lupe about his conversation with Bill Stevenson. He's excited but serene, too. His father is almost definitely going to be asleep, so he'll have to wait till morning to tell him. He has the strange feeling that the stars seem to have aligned for him. Maybe what has taken such a long time to happen is finally on track. If you stumble, then you have to get up and walk more steadily. That's what happened to him. He tripped up, but he's back on his feet and is striding forward toward his goals and ambitions: to record and release an album with Cruz Records, go on tour with the new project of the members of Descendents, and to give the North American underground scene a kick in the ass. Make a name for himself. Maybe even fulfill his old dream of leaving El Paso. Perhaps he could follow in the footsteps of his local idols and move to California. Ed Ivey said great things about the Melvins and Skin Yard and his experience of playing in Seattle. It'd be awesome to play there. The traffic lights light up his face. From red to green. With his right hand on the steering wheel he lets his left hand move with the wind as he drives unhurriedly homeward. He tries to grab hold of the air. He always liked doing that. As a kid in the car with his dad, he would often hang his arm out the window and try to snatch at the air that was pushing his hand back.

He parks outside his front door. There's a light on inside. Lupe must be awake. He gets out of the van and closes the door gently, the sound causing a rat to race across the road. He smiles and hears the door to the house open. He turns to see Lupe's silhouette against the light. He walks toward her and as he gets closer sees that she's sobbing and breathing sharply. It's the kind of breathing of someone who's been crying intensely. Ricardo picks up his pace, his stomach contracting. He thinks about the feeling of grabbing for the air. There's something about it that's enjoyable, but it's frustrating. The speed of the air makes you think you might be able to catch it, but when you close your hand it's always empty. There's nothing in it.

He reaches the front door. Lupe can't look him in the eyes. Her nose is red, and there's a wadded up tissue in her right hand.

"What's going on, honey?"

"Ricardo . . ."

"What's wrong?!"

"Ricardo, my darlin' . . . I'm pregnant."

Third Movement
(1988–1990)

1988: THE YEAR PUNK BROKE

OF ALL THE MUSIC DOCUMENTARY DIRECTORS, Dave Markey is perhaps the closest to the underground movement of the eighties and early nineties. He is known for having integrated the do-it-yourself ideology into his audiovisual work. Writer, producer, editor, and director for most of his projects, he leapt into the limelight of independent music with his film, *1991: The Year Punk Broke*. This film revolved around the tour that took New York-based Sonic Youth around Europe in the summer of 1991, sharing the bill with groups like Nirvana and Dinosaur Jr. As the film progresses, this lineup of future stars of American indie is completed with cameos from Mudhoney, Courtney Love, Babes in the Toyland, and the other New Yorkers, Gumball. Punk veterans like Bob Mould (Hüsker Dü/Sugar) and Ramones also have their slot in the story. Markey alternates between raw live performances by these bands and interviews and comments from many of their members. In more than one of these is the idea that 1991 was the year in which punk broke, a recurring concept that would eventually provide the name for the documentary.

Kim Gordon asserts as much from the stage in one of the shows and Thurston Moore proves it twice by way of an interesting example: according to him, Mötley Crüe were traveling from stage to stage around the world playing a woeful cover of "Anarchy in the U.K." by the Sex Pistols in front of crowds numbering in excess of fifty thousand. For Moore, things take a turn for the worse when, asked about this, John Lydon's (the singer of the Sex Pistols) reaction is simply to laugh. These affirmations are something of a premonition given they were made months before Nirvana's unpredictable bombshell. The film was released in 1992, in the middle of the grunge whirlwind, and automatically became one you simply had to see. Geffen Records uses some of the scenes shot by Markey in the music video for "Lithium," the third single on *Nevermind*. The image of Kurt Cobain leaping into Dave Grohl's drumkit left an impression and excited millions of teenagers, including yours truly.

Ricardo and Daniel went through the punk breakup that Kim and Thurston are talking about, only at a slightly different time. For these two friends, everything they believe in, and that was predicted by Sonic Youth, is shattered in 1988, the year in which their reality starts to fall apart.

During those twelve months, three of the most important albums of the future of independent music are released. Dinosaur Jr. release *Bug* and the Pixies *Surfer Rosa*. Both are well-received in the US and the UK, expertly bringing together pop melodies and raucous guitar-playing. They are at once beautiful and intense and offer two youth anthems in "Freak Scene" and "Where Is My Mind?" To these two masterpieces should be added the acclaimed *Daydream Nation*, the last album on an independent record label for the omnipresent Sonic Youth. The album is at the top of the year's best album lists and contains "Teen Age Riot," one of the best-known songs on the track list. The group from New York is now one of the nexuses between the old and new schools, the latter formed by revolutionary bands that are emerging from the American underground. They are close to the effervescent Seattle scene and strike up a friendship with one of the labels that changes how music is produced independently:

Sub Pop Records. *Daydream Nation* also produces the tour that indie music demanded, and the work turns Sonic Youth into role models for a new generation of musicians and artists that would subvert the punk movement. Together with Dinosaur Jr. and the Pixies they create a new trend and set the path to follow. A path that would see alternative music reach its peak just a few years later.

In 1988, the definitive breakups of Hüsker Dü and the Rhythm Pigs, two of Ricardo and Daniel's main influences, are announced. Ed, Jay, and Greg's band, the boys' idols and neighbors, return to the United States after one of their European tours and decide to put an end to an adventure that was already five years in the making. Nineteen eighty-eight is also the year that sees the beginning of the Rollins Band and Fugazi, the new projects of Henry Rollins and Ian MacKaye after Black Flag and Minor Threat, respectively. Many of Ricardo and Daniel's favorite bands have disappeared from the scene: Big Boys give way to Poison 13, and David Yow starts the Jesus Lizard after the breakup of Scratch Acid.

Industry and money settle into a community that had previously done everything by itself. Away from the business world. A clear example is R.E.M., who sign a ten-million-dollar contract with Warner Bros. and release *Green*, the album that includes their first two number ones, with the songs "Stand" and "Orange Crush." Everything starts getting professional. The founders of Sub Pop show a talent for marketing and business that is unprecedented in the underground. One of their most successful initiatives is the creation of the Sub Pop Singles Club, a paid monthly service in which club members are mailed singles from the label's bands. In 1988, for example, two singles are released that would eventually become collectors' items: "Love Buzz/Big Cheese" by Nirvana and "Touch Me I'm Sick" by Mudhoney.

My **TOP FIVE** favorite albums released in 1988:
1. *Bug* by DINOSAUR JR. (SST Records)
2. *Ultramega OK* by SOUNDGARDEN (SST Records)
3. *Green* by R.E.M. (Warner Bros.)
4. *Sub Pop 200* by VARIOUS ARTISTS (Sub Pop Records)
5. *Daydream Nation* by SONIC YOUTH (Enigma Records)

❉

In El Paso, a new generation of bands starts to grow, playing in high school gyms and people's backyards. A promising example is Phantasmagoria. May 17, 1988. Mesa Inn. The young band, led by guitarist Tony Alarcón, show their talent at a concert headlined by veteran group MDC and in which Ulgor also play. That night, the members of Phantasmagoria take the stage, together with an entire generation. They're here for good.

The city sees new spaces opening up and clubs that offer live music and help develop this new wave of musicians and alternative concertgoers. From amid this burgeoning scene emerges the figure of Joe Dorgan, one of the main architects of the underground's professionalization at the border. He begins to hire bands and organize gigs in The Lost Iguana, and a year later, in December 1989, he opens the city's ultimate club: Club 101. This venue would host the likes of White Zombie, Nine Inch Nails, and Die Warzau. Most of the kids from this new generation would start off among the usual crowd at Club 101 and later end up performing onstage there.

For ELPASO, 1988 was a fateful year. Their trajectory came to a complete standstill, and each member experienced those twelve months in a different way.

Ricardo Salazar

First, they're a little late. Then come some light periods that turn out to be bleeding and not menstruation. Tiredness. Nausea even. It took Lupe weeks before she suspected that those were the signs of a possible pregnancy. The pregnancy. A person was gestating inside her. A baby, fruit of the mix of her cells and those of Ricardo. When the test confirmed her suspicions, she broke down in tears. Her man was giving everything he had onstage at Sound Seas while she was stifling her sobs with a towel over her face. Sitting on the bathroom floor. She tried to contain her crying so that Felipe, the future grandfather, wouldn't hear her and come to the door to ask if she was alright. She didn't have dinner with him and instead just lay in bed staring out the window. It was in the early hours of the morning when she finally saw the Ford Econoline pull up outside the house. She crept silently downstairs, opened the door, and waited for Ricardo, her breathing still accelerated and her nose and eyes red from crying.

He didn't react. He fell into a mini trance that gradually turned to a mix of fear, worry, and sadness. They went up to his room without turning on the lights. The early morning light timidly lit the inside of the house through the windows. His legs were faltering, and he was incapable of holding Lupe's hand. He wanted to. But he couldn't. They sat on the edge of the bed. They were apart by barely a few inches, but for the first time in their relationship there seemed to be a great distance between them. Not a word had been spoken, but they both knew what was going to happen. They knew they'd have this baby. They knew that Lupe was going to have to drop her photography studies and that ELPASO's tour was going to have to wait. The Spanish classes. The rehearsals. The whole project would have to be put on hold.

Before his eyes, Ricardo saw that part of the film that shows what could have been but wasn't: the tour with ALL (the group that emerged from the dissolution of Descendents), signing with Cruz Records, and finally releasing the band's first album. Growing, producing more albums, and, at last, leaving Texas. All of that was washed away by the tears that slowly began to blur his vision.

They cried with relief. They laughed, terrified about what was to come. Abortion was never an option. For Ricardo, what his mother had done to him when he was so young still weighed heavily on his shoulders. He'd always wanted to leave all that behind by forming his own stable family. One in which the kid wouldn't suffer because of the parents. These thoughts had multiplied as his relationship with Lupe grew. She was perfect. He knew it would happen, but he'd wanted to wait, of course. Once she had become a highly sought-after visual artist and he a renowned musician, everything would have been easier. If that tiny thing floating in Lupe's insides had been born in California, and under the circumstances that he had dreamed about, it would have been perfect. But no. That tiny thing floating in Lupe's insides was going to be born in El Paso, Texas, on January 22, 1988. They named her Teresa, and she was a big baby with a lung capacity that took everyone by surprise the first time she wailed. "She's going to be a singer like her father," said Lupe. The mother looked amazing. As good as or better, even, than during the pregnancy, when already her natural beauty had multiplied a thousandfold. Ricardo looked at them, and when one of the nurses went to pick up Teresa to clean, weigh, and measure her, he gave her a sonorous slap on the arm. "Leave the child with her mother, they're just getting to know each other. Don't even think about touching her." He'd been away from the band, his notebooks, and his guitar for nearly half a year. He was working full-time at the Jalisco Café with his father. The grandfather, when he heard the news, couldn't help a smile escaping across his face. Felipe had always supported his son in everything. He would have understood if they'd decided to have an abortion. But the thought of having a granddaughter ... Nothing could have made him happier. And there he was sitting nervously in the hospital corridor. Waiting to see her face for the first time.

When Ricardo came out with Teresa in his arms, Felipe jumped to his feet and approached his son. He looked at the little girl and began to cry. "Not bad, eh?" the boy asked him. The grandfather's mouth was trembling, and he found it hard to get the words out, "Undoubtedly your finest creation yet, Son," he whispered. "Can I hold her?" Ricardo gently placed his daughter in the arms of his father. He was overwhelmed. For the first time, he was another link in the chain and not the last one. She was the most amazing thing he'd ever laid eyes on, and he made a promise, there and then, never to turn his back on this beautiful creature.

Daniel Álvarez

Daniel experiences the impasse at a distance. The birth of Teresa is too much for him, and he reacts to it in a strangely cold manner. He visits the baby at the hospital with the other members of ELPASO but feels awkward at the sight of his best friend in the role of father. Somehow, all that allows him to free himself of the burden that the group and his friendship with Ricardo were starting to become for him. If they don't play, there's no band. If there's no band, he can focus on school and the development of his own career as a performer with Rubén and Roger. And he does so without having to deal with his friend. No need for justifications. No consequences.

He has made a leap as a collage artist, and his most recent pieces are colorful compositions made from cutouts from illustrated books from the late seventies. Volumes on geology, biology, or history, which give his work an aesthetic homogeneity and the concept a kind of surrealism. He often works in large formats. Until now his designs have always been within the confines of 8 ½ by 11 inches.

He is especially fond of two of his recent creations: *American Kid Collage* and *American Border*. The first one revolves around a boy with a pistol, and the second is a representation of the north-south fusion found at the border.

He works so much at home that he's been studying for a while now at the UTEP library. The relaxed atmosphere there helps him to disconnect, and he can make good use of his time. He realizes there are some spaces that are better than others for creation and study. Sometimes he'll scan the faces sitting around the library tables and sketch them at full speed in the last pages of his notebooks, following their features, gestures, and faces with his eyes. Going over cheekbones, noses, and ears. Scribbling wide, slim, and square faces. Some quite attractive, others downright ugly. He likes the ugly ones most. He loves ugly couples. Ugly couples who fall in love and grope each other in dark corners of the library. His search for faces and their reproduction often serves to fill in the time between homework tasks. It's an exercise he learned in drawing class and nothing more. But one day, the game is taken to a new level. There's a face that he cannot draw. She hardly even blinks, and the blue ink pen he's sketching with slips between his fingers as a result of the difficulties this face is causing him. She's curvaceous. Tall. She has legs that go on forever, over which are some tight-fitting, faded jeans with holes in the knees. She's wearing dirty white Nike sneakers, and the bottom of her pants reveals a pair of beautiful ankles. Daniel likes them. Her knitted white pullover is wide and not very long. The sleeves hang down, but the cuffs fit snugly around the girl's wrists. White wrists, like her face. Like all her skin. Her straight, red hair falls across her shoulders and blends with the straps of her orange-tinged leather backpack, stuffed with textbooks. "What course could they be from?" he wonders. She has a smattering of freckles across her cheeks, which contrast with her wide turquoise-blue eyes that stare into the distance and that Daniel would dearly like to dive into and drown. She's wearing glasses with fine, gold rims that look amazing on her. They give her a look that is both intellectual and sexy. Her lips are sharp. The thicker upper one protrudes a little more than the lower. Daniel finds them completely irresistible and would jump at the chance to kiss them. She wraps a lock of her hair around the index finger of her left hand while she sits waiting for the librarian. "Annette Leduc?" he hears. The redhead stands up, further showing off her spectacular figure. She seems to have a friendly manner and talks with a French accent that Daniel finds all the more alluring. Before she leaves, the girl turns and her eyes meet Danny's. He takes a second to react and turns away abruptly in a failed attempt to pretend he wasn't staring. He throws down the notebook and pen and she, before going, sends him a friendly smile that lights up the building, the city, the whole world. He smiles like an idiot and nods his head at her. It's the first time he's seen her at the university and hopes with all his heart to see those turquoise eyes again someday.

DD, Will, and Octavio

For the other members of ELPASO, 1988 is as frustrating musically as the second half of 1987. The Davis brothers are into the idea of touring the States. Octavio is not so excited. The idea of leaving Texas seems to overwhelm him, which is why the birth of Teresa and the fact that all tour plans are put on an immediate standby seem to calm his nerves. What does bother him is not being able to work on the band's album. After his almost token participation in the demo *Gimme These Songs!* he is impatient to experience recording a full studio album.

Will gets over his split with Ruth, and he and his brother start working double shifts at the Hamburger Hut. The idea of leaving El Paso and starting from scratch in Houston or in another city is becoming increasingly tempting. As they're still living with Octavio in the shared apartment downtown, they need to generate more income to repair their car and save enough to get to East Texas and rent a house there. The brothers are still rehearsing with Octavio at his mom's house. Ricardo stopped rehearsals in December 1987, when he focused on the pregnancy and the preparations for Teresa's birth. The twelve months between the show with Descendents and the summer of 1988 fly past. A whole year in which the pages seem to literally fly off the calendar. In June, Will decides to call up Kevin, a good friend from Houston, to ask him about bands there that might need a bass player and drummer.

The brothers also toy with the idea of starting a group from scratch. Will and DD have their own material and work from dusk to dawn to avoid having to sell their instruments like when they left LA. Getting themselves a guitarist and starting their own band is not a bad option. Kevin puts them in contact with J.R., the owner of the Axiom, the city's biggest alternative club. He's the man with most contacts for the scene in Houston.

The hand of fate touches them on a Friday evening at the Hamburger Hut. Will calls J.R. from the diner, on his break between shifts. Before scribbling down the phone number on a piece of paper, he turns toward the door and hears it opening. His eyes pop out

220

EL PASO: A PUNK STORY

of their sockets when he sees Ricardo. He's with Lupe and Teresa. They haven't seen each other for months, and Will is surprised by his friend's dyed blond hair. "What the hell have you done to yourself?" he shouts across the diner. Ricardo and Lupe laugh and hug DD, who has come out to greet them. Will makes a gesture by way of an explanation that the call is an important one.

On the other end of the line J.R. tries to sum up the music situation in Houston for Will and the possibilities they have if they decide to move there. He's a smooth talker who gets easily excited, and he promises to introduce them to the right people and even offers them the chance to play at the Axiom.

"Don't sweat it, man. Let us get there first and set up the band!" replies the drummer. Will's face reveals his disbelief when, after he mentions ELPASO, J.R. gets all excited and starts shouting into the phone.

"I know you guys, man! I was given your demo of Spanish punk covers!"

"Seriously? You gotta be kidding me, J.R.!"

"Sure! I've been thinking of setting up a show at the Axiom with you guys for months!"

The ELPASO drummer can't believe his ears. His eyes are fixed on Ricardo, who has no idea what's going on with his friend. They smile. J.R.'s verbal tommy gun is still firing down the line. But Will is no longer listening. This could be the last chance to bring the band back to life.

THE AXIOM

THE TWO FIRST REHEARSALS LACKED FLUIDITY. All stops and starts for checking notes and chords. They had to begin some songs up to three times just to get the right speed for each. It was clear how much affection they had for their own music. A lot. They avoided describing this as a reunion, to avoid seeing what had happened months before as a split. They wanted to believe that the band had simply been cryopreserved for a year and a half. An impasse, maybe, but never a separation. "ELPASO has never ceased to exist," Ricardo would say to himself.

However, the Davis brothers were about to leave El Paso, and Daniel had done absolutely nothing related to the band for months. Even Ricardo himself, albeit unconsciously, used the word *revival* to refer to what they were going to do at the Axiom: he'd asked Daniel, "We're doing a revival of the band in Houston. Can you take care of the flyer?" The fact is, in order for something to be revived, it has to be dead first. ELPASO had died, and now they were trying to bring it back to life.

Daniel, who never really believed such a miracle was possible, accepted the job. He got down to work and even proposed taking the first promotional photos of the band. He took their pictures in front of two iconic murals in the city. He took the only two snapshots that show all four ELPASO members together. One in front of the mural in Segundo Barrio (painted by Los Muralistas del Barrio in the seventies) and the other in front of the mural on the 800 block of Sixth Avenue. The second is especially natural. It's a nice photograph that catches the four members off guard. Will is resting his head on Ricardo's right shoulder, and Ricardo, like DD, is smiling at something Octavio is saying. In the background you can see part of *AIDS*, the art piece that Carlos Callejo painted there a year before. Besides the photos, Daniel designed a great collage with the show information that he decided to photocopy onto red paper. Ricardo sent a parcel of fifty flyers to Houston, for J.R.

Musically speaking, everything started coming together again after the third day of rehearsals. As if the rust was being cleaned from the music they were playing with every strum of a guitar. Like getting back on a bike. Like good sex with an old partner. They also readopted their roles. Octavio and Will started insulting each other again as an absurd reaction to the affection and musical attraction they felt for each other. The four sang, for the first time in ages, the Beach Boys' "Good Vibrations." The song that served as an emotional thermometer. It was looking good. "Maybe Houston will work." "Perhaps we'll get a second chance."

J.R. had proposed they perform on a Friday. February 20, 1989, to be precise. They had tried to get a gig in Austin before or after that date, but it was impossible. Most of the contacts they used to set up the Texas tour in 1986 were no longer on the scene. The guy who got them the show with Killdozer and Scratch Acid at Liberty Lunch was now a door-to-door insurance salesman to, among other things, feed his gluttonous twins. There had obviously been a change of guard on the scene. It all helped to confirm their theory that punk had broken in 1988. They felt that everything was conspiring to remind them that the trail they had blazed until now may not have been of much use.

Their plan was to get the crowd interested again. If J.R. had been fascinated by their music, why wouldn't they conquer the crowd at the Axiom?

They organized a weekly rehearsal. Monday evenings. With eight weeks to go before the concert, they decided to set up a gig with Phantasmagoria in the auditorium of Coronado High School and try out with a younger audience. It was a weird performance. The teenagers who had gathered in front of the stage had no idea who they were. They knew nothing about the less glamorous part of the scene in the city. They idolized the Rhythm Pigs (as Ricardo and Daniel had done years before) and were now dedicated to supporting their contemporaries. Most of the fifteen-year-olds who saw the show enjoyed ELPASO's performance. The band sounded powerful and tight. Ricardo and Octavio decided to go onstage in semi-drag and gave it their all, with no delicacies, save for the sequins and tutu. They got a few laughs, but their listeners remained largely subdued. For Phantasmagoria, however, the kids were unleashed. They got up onto the stage and jumped into the crowd. They pushed each other and screamed out the choruses, giving wild ovations at the end of each song. The members of Phantasmagoria were not much older than their audience, but seeing them live you'd think they were veterans. They had confidence and knew how to play with the feedback.

The best news of the evening for Ricardo and his band was when, after the concert, a kid came up to them to tell them how much he'd enjoyed their music. "Hi, my name's Arlo. I loved your show! Do you have any T-shirts?" Ricardo was sorry he didn't have any, but did give him one of the few cassettes they still had of *Gimme These Songs!*. Arlo walked away looking very happy with his tape. The next day he took a white T-shirt out of his wardrobe and, with a black marker, drew the ELPASO logo right in the middle of it. He then walked around the city wearing his newly designed T-shirt. He stayed in contact with Ricardo, who gave him a copy of the live demo they recorded in '86. A few years later, Arlo went on to set up several different cult bands. He sang in Stinging Fish, played the guitar in Foss, the group he shared with Beto O'Rourke (future Texan congressman) and Cedric Bixler-Zavala (leader of At the Drive-In and the Mars Volta), and set up a Big Black-style duo with another renowned El Paso musician, Jim Ward.

Arlo welcomed us into his home in Los Angeles in May 2016. He opened the doors of his attractive apartment, which he shared with Aisling Cormack, his partner and fellow band member in the lo-fi pop group Fragile Gang. He gave us a fantastic interview in which he told us how exciting the early nineties were in El Paso. He showed a near-religious respect for anything to do with Ed Ivey and the Rhythm Pigs. All of his generation did. He excitedly remembered how his friend from At the Drive-In reached the top, making sense of two decades of working in the city's underground. He told us with a smile on his face how impressed he'd been with the members of ELPASO, dressed in women's clothing at that high school concert. He also let us take photographs of a bunch of flyers and cuttings from that time, when he was a musical activist on the border. As the sun set and the green palm trees slowly became black silhouettes against the orange evening sky, the couple suggested we go for dinner together at a vegan pizzeria in Silver Lake. It was close to Sunset Boulevard and, as they said, "we could talk some more." Listening to him talk was an absolute pleasure. We didn't doubt what he had to say for a second.

Arlo has a deliberate and relaxed aura that instantly draws you to him. He's hugely charismatic and listens to you with an overwhelmingly comforting enthusiasm and interest. As we said goodbye at the door to the restaurant, he invited us to go to Skylight Books, the bookstore where he works. We accepted and the next morning we were standing in Los Feliz, at the intersection of Russell and Vermont Avenues, with the idea of having some breakfast before going to the store. We gorged ourselves on pancakes with maple syrup at a nearby diner and, with full stomachs, decided to cross the threshold of Skylight. That, without a doubt, was the perfect job for a guy like Arlo. The shelves were arranged around an impressive tree standing right in the middle of the store. In his office, surrounded by boxes and books, he put on a few of his latest songs with Fragile Gang and gave me a copy of the seven-inch he released with Foss in 1994, *The El Paso Pussycats*. He promised to speak with Jim Ward so we could interview him during our next stay in El Paso, Texas. I proposed we try doing some music together sometime. "We could send each other tracks on the internet," I told him.

All these words could have been blown into nothing with one of the gusts of wind with which the Pacific refreshes the coast of Los Angeles. Once we'd gotten back in the car and had lost ourselves in the streets of Los Feliz, there was nothing to make Arlo keep his promise. Nothing at all. Just three days later we got an email from Jim Ward confirming the interview we'd been trying to set up for months. A year later, in May 2017, I opened my email to download the vocal tracks that Arlo had sent me and that would form part of our first musical collaboration. Musical and transoceanic. Our voices matched perfectly, and the final song turned out great. I wrote back to him and proposed we produce an EP together and, true to his never-ending enthusiasm, he replied, "Sure! That'd be fun!"

✳

They'd all managed to get a few days off to be able to get to Houston the night before the gig. Except Octavio, of course, who continued to support himself without a job that anyone knew of. For him it was never a problem to leave a day earlier. Ricardo, however, was leaving Teresa for the first time, which generated a small but intense internal conflict. Daniel and Annette, his French girlfriend, also formed part of the delegate that would cross Texas, taking ELPASO back to its natural habitat, the stage. With the Ford Econoline loaded to bursting with material and people, they crossed the US's second-largest state to the sound of *Ultramega OK* by Soundgarden and the self-titled Fugazi EP. Twelve hours crossing the South with powerful riffs thundering out from groups from up north. Octavio, DD, and Will preferred Chris Cornell's band, while Daniel and Ricardo were more into Ian MacKaye's new project.

During one of their pit stops to refuel and eat something, Ricardo called Lupe to see how she and the little lady were doing. She didn't pick up the phone. He forced himself not to worry, despite how strange it seemed that no one had answered. He tried again, unsuccessfully, and on the third attempt, just as he was starting to go out of his mind, Lupe answered and told Ricardo that little Teresa had gotten sick and they'd had to go to the hospital. She tried not to scare the new father, using a calm voice and recounting events as if they weren't that serious. It was a hypoglycemic attack. A harmless drop in blood sugar that had made the girl faint. They had to be alert in case it happened again during the next forty-eight hours and carry something sugary with them that would get her back on track if there was another drop. Ricardo thanked the heavens that Teresa was OK, but cursed the universe for not being able to be with her at home. The end of the journey was agonizing for ELPASO's leader singer. He wished with all his heart that this would be worth it.

They got to the motel at around eight in the evening. They divided up the three double bedrooms they'd booked and ordered some takeout. Ricardo spoke with Lupe before going to bed and as soon as he was up. He slept like shit. Exhausted from the long journey, he couldn't handle the strain on his nerves caused by his daughter's health and Octavio's stratospheric snoring. They ate the free breakfast that came with the rooms and went over to the Axiom to leave their material, so they wouldn't have to drive it around in the van all day.

J.R. turned up an hour late. He got out of the car clucking and gesticulating. His conversation stopped every few seconds. His comments were delivered like whiplashes and with each came rhetorical questions that made it even more difficult to follow him. He talked about cocaine, about his grandmother, about losing money on the last three shows he'd booked and the son of a bitch who was the sound guy. "He's fucking good at his job, but he's a bloodsucker. I asked him to give me some time to pay him for the last three gigs, and do you know what he did? Sucked my fucking blood! That's what he did. The asshole threatened not to come to set up the next concert if I didn't pay him first . . ." The guy had been a roadie in the seventies and he knew what these guys were like. He'd seen right through J.R. and all the world's club owners. "Either you pay me, or I don't come." Good philosophy. Will wanted to meet the sound guy because he'd played the Chinese lute for the Red Krayola, a psychedelic rock group from Houston that the elder Davis brother was a big fan of. He wanted to ask him about his experience with the band and about Frederick Barthelme, the band's drummer and author of *War and War*, one of his favorite novels.

Daniel and Annette wandered around the streets of Houston until the time of the concert. They'd spent the whole journey all over each other, and everyone thought it was a good idea that they disappear from sight for a while. The band had something to eat downtown and turned up at the venue at the time they'd arranged to set up and do the sound check. When they entered, they saw the sound guy surrounded by darkness. He was lit up by a couple of blue spotlights. He walked with a stoop, and the chain that hung from the back pocket of his dark Levi's clinked as it knocked repeatedly against his bony backside. It created a melody that harmonized with the sound of his bracelets and the metal earrings that studded his left ear. A sorry-looking ponytail tied up with a black rubber band tumbled down across the list of dates printed on a T-shirt from Led Zeppelin's last tour. He hid his receding hairline with an orange bandana that wrapped around his skull and joined up with short, thick eyebrows that fell across his heavily wrinkled and almost imperceptible eyes. The blue from his eyes fought against the red from his weary-looking eyeballs, presumably the result of excessive marijuana consumption. From his aquiline nose fell a perfect horseshoe-shaped mustache, the same brown as his hair, that hid his thin, dry lips, between which danced a small joint that had been stuck there for God knows how long. When he called them over, you could see the few teeth he had left were yellowing, the huge gaps between them a sign that sooner or later they'd all fall out, laying bare his horribly battered gums. The sound check was a barrage of insults and obscene language. Keith, as he was called, seemingly despised music and musicians. He was sickened by the guitar effects pedals. He insulted Octavio, suggesting he learn to play the "fucking guitar one day." Will was lapping up the scene from behind his drums. When they were done, he and Keith smoked a giant spliff in the alley behind the Axiom and talked about how cool Houston was in the seventies. The others shut themselves in the gloomy room that served as a dressing room and set to reading the names of all the bands that had played there before them. DD got hold of a black marker and scribbled the ELPASO logo. When he'd finished, Ricardo hurriedly wrote "Chicano Punk!" under the name of the group. DD and Octavio smiled and opened a couple of Budweisers that they found lying around. They were nervous about the concert and hardly said a word. Shortly, Will arrived and livened them all up with his awful redneck jokes. After what felt like an age, the door opened slightly and Keith's head pushed through, borrowing from Jack Nicholson in *The Shining*. "Little pigs, little pigs, let me in . . . Here's Johnny!" he said as he cackled with laughter. It was time to go onstage.

※

The last chord of the final song from the setlist blasted out from the speakers and vanished into the desolate concert hall of the Axiom. The polite claps of the only two people who had actually bought a ticket echoed around the room. It was pathetic. One of them was Ronnie Barnett, the future bass player of the Muffs and one of the most prosperous musicians to come out of the Houston underground scene. Ronnie and his friend felt a mix of sensations. On the one hand they'd enjoyed ELPASO's music, and they thought the band were onto something interesting. Their songs and performance were clear evidence of great talent. But they couldn't connect with the band. Seeing them play in an empty room turned the live ritual into something absurd. They even felt uncomfortable in their empathy for the four guys up there performing in front of an empty room. Their miserable ovation reverberated in the immense space. In the void. Ricardo still had his nose stuck to the microphone, sweating and panting after a grueling performance. The others put their instruments down, their heads bowed, and hurriedly headed for the dressing room for more beer. They needed alcohol to get through this disaster. When ELPASO's lead singer got his breath back and opened his eyes, the nothingness was still there. He had tried to ignore it throughout the show. He'd looked at the floor, at the other band members, or at the neck of his Stratocaster. Out of the corner of his eye he had seen Danny taking a few photos. His friend could get as close to the stage as he wanted. With half a roll of black-and-white film free he focused and, with the flash on, took a couple of shots. No more than ten. He got one of Octavio wearing a black beanie down to his eyebrows and his beige *guayabera,* holding on to his Gibson Les Paul. Of all the photos he took that night, the most significant was of Ricardo, in which the singer can be seen with his dyed blond hair against the backdrop of the legendary stage curtains of the Axiom. He's wearing a horrible short-sleeved patterned shirt over another, white shirt with long sleeves. He's screaming into the microphone, but his eyes are closed, and his face is leaning toward one side. As if he's trying not to look in front of him. As if he's desperately trying to ignore the emptiness that flooded over him when the show had finished. An emptiness that seemed to leap from the room straight into his chest. An emptiness that first left him feeling shaken, and then saddened. An emptiness that hit him like a ton of bricks when he thought of Lupe and Teresa alone at home. When he realized he'd not been there for his daughter's first serious medical scare. And all for nothing. That was the moment he started to fall apart, as he looked around him, unable to recognize anything or anyone. His brown eyes fell on Daniel and Annette, who looked like complete strangers. His chest began to expand and contract. Keith moved him out the way to unplug the microphone and asked if he was OK, but Ricardo was unable to process the words that were spat from Keith's disgusting mouth. The sense of anguish, which had been looming over his head like an enormous, hairy mammoth foot, smashed him to pieces. He hyperventilated, his legs gave way, and he collapsed. He was blinded by one of the spotlights and thought he was dying. Not a single image of the band flashed before his eyes. No sign of Teresa or Lupe. His first panic attack in a long time brought back the image of his mother, vanishing into the distance. Disappearing in the white light that dilated his pupils to way beyond their normal size. Darkness flooded his eyes, and the sparkle was snatched from them forever. On that night, thanks to that flop of such epic proportions, the generator that so often lit up Ricardo's gaze burned itself out.

It's humiliating having to beg to all and sundry for your show to have an audience. Everyone knows about the sickening symptoms of stage fright. People who freeze, vomit, or piss themselves when they have to stand in front of an audience. It's fucked up, there's no doubt about it. But at least you have a fucking audience to scare you. Going out onstage, with everything that implies, and seeing that not a single person in the world has decided that your music is worth coming for is monstrously humiliating. I remember a good number of concerts with a poor turnout. I remember performing, more than once, to a crowd of no more than a dozen people. But I'll never forget the day I played to a deserted concert hall. I can't think of a more punishing blow than that to the hopes of an aspiring musician. That was the detonator that set off a slow and apparently innocuous process of dissolution. It wasn't openly dramatic, but it plunged me into misery. It was with my second band, Claim, the project that came after Nameless. It was a band with which we'd achieved an extraordinary level of creativity. We got together in 2001, and a demo and ten concerts later, in June 2003, the group came to an end. Officially, because the two guitarists had to focus on their studies. Nobody dared to suggest the real motive.

Jonathan and I, drummer and bass player, respectively, stood in the middle of our rehearsal studio looking at each other like a pair of idiots. We didn't know what to do. We were surrounded by a mix of music and movie posters and surreal collages that combined old pornographic magazines with cutouts from Disney stories. There was the head of Belle on the naked body of a woman preparing herself to swallow the gargantuan penis of a fireman with the face of the Beast. This might seem incredibly wrong and offensive, but we always made sure the Disney couples we used stayed together, which we did almost without thinking. It's strange, but the fact was that none of us would have dared create a wild orgasm between Pocahontas and someone other than John Smith. Nothing was violated. Likewise, none of us dared to say out loud that the group was dissolving and not just taking a "break." That our academic future was just a pretext to avoid having to accept that we were a band without a future.

Beneath an enormous sticker of Claim's logo, the members of Alice in Chains could be seen, looking something between sullen and serious, peering out at Jonathan and me. As if they felt sorry for us. Like they were saying, "Your group was, is, and will be the last fuckup in rock history. Epic performances and success turned their backs on you the first day you played, and they won't be coming back today, to dance around you like Hawaiian dancers welcoming tourists as they land in Honolulu. We, however, have been on a break since 1996, Layne Staley died last year, and even then we'll reunite in a few years and it will be epic and successful. Assholes." Well, the bit about assholes and reuniting didn't come to me at the time, but the rest did. In fact, I felt that all those artists who were plastered over the walls in our rehearsal space looked a little sad that evening we decided to give it up.

Our last concert was in the knockout round of a battle of the bands held in Barcelona. With half a foot in the finals and the KGB club applauding our performance, the judges decided to let through a trio of posh kids who did watered-down, inoffensive punk and who had sold a bunch of tickets to their bourgeois friends. A bunch of filthy rich, wishy-washy, inoffensive punks. Money. Fucking money.

We'd put all our hopes into that competition. We'd imagined ourselves recording an album for free, which was why we'd entered. Until then, I'd been true to my clean-living philosophy. At the age of twenty-one I hadn't tried alcohol or tobacco, and, of course, my body was totally free of any kind of drug. My relationship with these substances was a passive one, through my friends and friends of my friends, but I'd never downed a beer. If you add to Claim's anticlimactic finish my breakup with my teenage sweetheart, you'll have an idea of the explosive cocktail that blew most of my moral fiber into oblivion. I left that last concert like a bank robber after his last heist. The least rock 'n' roll member of my group of friends, my nemesis until then, was waiting for me with the engine running at the doors to the club. After saying goodbye (badly) to my musician friends, I got in the back seat and shouted for him to drive off, to accelerate. "Let's get outta here," I shouted. I wanted to get away. I changed clothes and sprayed myself with deodorant right there in the car. By three in the morning I was completely out of it, swaying at the bar of a club, trying to drown my anguish with shots of tequila.

Stumbling around to the rhythm of the worst Latin tunes imaginable, I blurted out to some poor girl who happened to be dancing near me that earlier that evening I had almost seven hundred people wildly applauding me. Me, my friends, and our music. She looked me up and down in disbelief. She assumed that that was my pathetic attempt to chat her up. She took a swig of her cocktail, and this pale-faced redhead said something along the lines of, "Sure, and I'm Beyoncé."

I went off the rails for two years. I put my guitar away in a cupboard and stupidly sold my 110-watt Carvin amp. I got shit-faced every weekend during that time. I did all I could to punish my liver with gallons and gallons of vodka and tequila. I regurgitated my dignity and my convictions, served up with a healthy dose of bile every Sunday morning until well into 2004. My bitterness rasped my tongue, and my esophagus was burning the evening I got the call from Jonathan. He was phoning from Manchester. He'd moved there shortly after leaving Claim. He'd apparently talked to the other guys from the band, and they suggested I join them all on a trip to the north of England. After two whole years we were going to see each other again, catch up, and maybe even take in some music. We all fell in love with the city and laughed again like we used to. We smoothed things over and ended up talking about the group, about our music, and about how amazing it all was. Lost in countless pints of beer and bewildered by the early morning hours, we decided to rerecord our demo and turn it into the album we never released. We arranged to meet in Barcelona when the trip was over to breathe life back into the group that had given us so much energy. It was a few weeks before Jonathan came back from Manchester and dusted off the drums of his old Mapex Mars Pro. A beautiful green drum kit. We rented a sound-proofed space by the hour and plugged in our guitars. We improvised a few heavy riffs, reliving our passion for Black Sabbath and Faith No More. We tried to get back the freshness of the syncopated rhythms and pseudofunk that we'd mixed up with heavy metal and punk. It all sounded clumsy and embarrassing. One rehearsal was enough for us to realize we'd lost that spark, that special feeling. It was like spending two hours performing CPR on a body that's been dead for hours. We ended up pounding our fists into that musical corpse, trying desperately to hide our frustration and get back a heartbeat that was maybe never as intense as we'd thought. We gathered up our instruments and exchanged meaningless impressions. Banalities. We soaked our mustaches in a few beers and organized a second rehearsal, which was then repeatedly delayed until the whole idea dissolved into nothing. Like all the other hopes and dreams surrounding that inconsequential rock group.

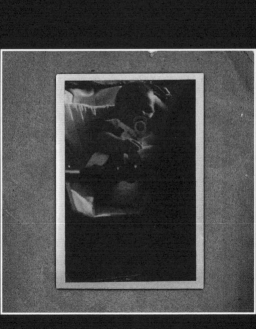

THE SUMMIT MEETING

WATCHING HIS FRIEND DISINTEGRATE LIKE AN ice cream melting beneath the spotlights of the Axiom spurred Daniel into action. He leapt onto the stage and held Ricardo in his arms, as if he were the Virgin Mary embracing Christ after the crucifixion. "Get me some water!" he shouted to one onlooker. "Call a fucking ambulance," he barked at another. Everyone seemed to burst into action at Daniel's orders. The drought that their relationship had been dragged through in recent years was softened that night. The old friendship between the two was the only thing that was revived by that show. Danny threw his friend a lifesaver in the middle of the immense emptiness in which Ricardo was starting to drown.

The ambulance workers treated him in the middle of the venue. They decided not to take him to hospital but did recommend that he rest and avoid making any unnecessary effort. They also advised him to see a doctor once he was back in El Paso. "I hope all this wasn't just to get out of unloading and loading the gear!" said Will with affectionate sarcasm. Ricardo's episode had given them all a scare. In fact, his fainting had eclipsed the feeling of having played such a catastrophic gig. The night was particularly bitter for Ricardo; with Teresa still recovering, he decided not to say anything to Lupe about the episode, not to burden her with concerns she didn't need right now. He quickly fell into a deep sleep. He couldn't help it, despite his irrational fear that he might never wake up again. He was sharing a room with Daniel and Annette. The couple found it difficult to get any sleep that night thanks to the feverish ravings of the ELPASO singer. He shouted and wailed in his sleep, as he had done so often as a child and teenager.

The next morning, Daniel woke up and sensed Ricardo was sitting next to the radiator beneath the window. It was early, and the light of the dawn just about traced his silhouette against the yellow curtains. You could say that what he saw that morning was a ghostly and unrecognizable version of his friend. Only that wouldn't be true. Danny recognized him in an instant. In a split second he knew that the person looking out the window was the same insecure, nervous, and reserved kid he'd sat next to in Mr. Milam's class ten years before. The person who collapsed at the Axiom may have been the optimistic Ricardo, father and musician, but that wasn't the Ricardo who had woken up the next day. Daniel could tell that the Ricardo who was going back to El Paso would be the oddball who was incapable of saying a single word to him during his first months at Ysleta High School.

※

Lupe threw the garbage bag to the floor. Pieces of cake, plastic spoons, and the remains of the confetti and decorations were strewn across the floor. "Talk to me, for God's sake," she cried. "What happened to you in Houston? What's going on?" Ricardo stopped sweeping for a moment, drew in a deep breath, and without raising his eyes said, "Nothing. Nothing happened . . . If you keep shouting like that, you'll wake her up," and he went on sweeping.

Teresa's birthday party had brought Lupe's family together with some of the couple's friends. Two days later, the little girl was feeling better and was starting to regain her energy and playfulness. Her vitality was in stark contrast to her father's apathy. Everyone who was there that day asked Ricardo over and over again if he was OK. In response, he simply forced a smile and assured them he was just tired after the long drive, that was all. His attitude became increasingly hard for Lupe to bear, until, finally, after the party, she exploded and shouted at Ricardo in an effort get some kind of reaction. Teresa's arrival in their lives had had its repercussions on them as a couple, but never to this extent. After seeing her daughter's father looking so miserable and distant during the celebrations of Teresa's first year of life, Lupe couldn't help but enter into what would be the couple's biggest fight to date.

There were no blows exchanged. It was nothing like Foreman against Ali in 1974. It wasn't an even fight that went to eight rounds. No, no. It was not remotely even. Ricardo simply took on the role of Lupe's sparring partner, allowing her to hit him as fiercely as she wanted. She vented everything she'd been feeling and cruelly accused him of putting more into "that damn concert in Houston" than into his daughter's birthday party. She reproached him for spending a year avoiding being a partner and father but still trying to be a "fucking rock star." She told him a bunch of things she didn't really feel but that were dragged up from the pit of her stomach by his apathy. Lupe loved Ricardo so much that she hurt him every bit as much as he wanted her to. She regretted everything she'd said before she'd even finished saying it. She was crying in desperation, hoping he would defend himself against all her bitter accusations. All she wanted to do was shout as loud as she could just to hear him fight back and reclaim his place as the backbone of the family. She didn't really mean half of what she said to him that evening. She begged him with her eyes first and her hands after. She finally told him straight up, "Just tell me it's not true,

Ricardo," she sobbed. He said nothing. He was just storing up all that pain she was inflicting on him in his heart, where it would slowly eat away at him from head to toe. And the agony reached right down to the tips of his fingers. That knot came back in his stomach. Lupe left without another word. She had no idea that the man she loved had fallen apart beneath the stage lights in front of a nonexistent audience. The layers that covered and protected the depressive and absent Ricardo had been torn apart on the other side of Texas. There was no trace of the uninhibited, lively person she had slept with for the first time the night that Black Flag set El Paso on fire. Ricardo went to bed and tried to get to sleep as quickly as possible to calm the volcano that was simmering inside and causing his depression. That was the word that Felipe used to describe his son's state of mind. *Depression.* He gave Lupe a big hug that evening. As well as being the mother of his granddaughter, Lupe had also become his confidante.

The following months were hard on the Salazar family, and especially on Ricardo. He put on weight because of his anxiety and spent long periods without playing the guitar and without so much as touching his record and cassette collection. Sex with Lupe was reduced almost to the vanishing point. He focused the little energy his uncared-for body could muster on Teresa. He poured everything into her, completely neglecting his father, his partner, and himself. This brought the mother and grandfather closer together, each becoming the emotional support the other desperately needed. They tried unsuccessfully to get Ricardo to talk with someone. His emotional instability was reflected in a series of job changes between January and September 1989. He got up early, worked, and came home. The routine was just enough to keep him, and his family, afloat.

At one of his most critical moments, Daniel reappeared in his role as Ricardo's savior. After the episode in Houston, his presence in Ricardo's life became more regular again, and they began to see each other once or twice a week. They talked of the good times and of Danny's many future projects. At that time, his ambitions seemed to be getting increasingly distant, and these meetings between the two old friends served to bring back the memories of their struggle as apprentice punks. Their old roles began to flourish once more. It was as if Ricardo's low moments put him in a position of submission, which made it easier to socialize with Daniel. Little by little, Danny regained the influence he used to have over Ricardo's opinions and future decisions. That was how the summer went. Danny managed to get it into Ricardo's head that ELPASO could self-finance the record-ing of an album. He could see clearly that his friend's band had a similar DNA to the groups that were beginning to emerge in the Northwest from *Sub Pop*. He was convinced that the owners of the Seattle-based label would love an alternative band that was originally punk and had the exotic touch of Spanish lyrics. He believed so strongly in this that he convinced Ricardo not only to get the band together again to, at last, record the ELPASO album, but also to foot the entire cost of the project. "If you get those guys together and record the album, I prom-ise you I'll make sure it gets to those bastards at Sub Pop." It was like in the early eighties when he'd convinced Ricardo to start a fanzine, set up a band, or buy that ugly Ford Econoline instead of the blue Chevrolet of his dreams. At the tail end of 1989, and for the first time in months, the sparkle seemed to be returning to Ritchie's eyes.

✳

The meeting to decide whether the band would get back together again and give it one last try took place in Juárez. That was where the instruments had stayed after the fiasco in January in Houston, left in

243

a corner and covered in dust after half a year of inactivity. Octavio had left the apartment he'd been sharing with the Davis brothers and they, in turn, had moved to a smaller and cheaper apartment on the outskirts of the city.

Despite not having played together again (unlike during their previous break) the guys had continued to see each other. As Will and DD were still burning up the hours in the kitchen of the Hamburger Hut, the restaurant became a logical meeting point. Octavio and Ricardo passed by there once a week, before closing time, and the four of them dined on hamburgers and reminisced about the band. That was where Ricardo proposed what you could call a more formal meeting. He'd taken the idea he'd forged together with Daniel so seriously that he wanted to give the meeting a certain air of solemnity. He was doubtful as to whether the Davis brothers would go along with the project. They were about to set off on their postponed return to East Texas and were working all the hours they could manage.

Ricardo's hands were sweating. He was nervous. Daniel sat down next to him and squeezed his thigh. The orange rays of evening sunlight slipped in through the two small windows above the white garage door, tracing a black line that split the room into two faintly lit spaces. Daniel and Ricardo were in one, and the rest of the group sat in the other. The deformed shadows of all five of them seemed to be trying to scale the wall that separated the garage from the house. Tiny specks of dust gravitated around the black line, like the glass that separates a prisoner from his family on visiting day. In a trembling voice, Ricardo began to outline what he'd spent days narrowing down as the best reasons for getting into the studio and recording an album of their own material. As he knew the biggest problem would be money, he was quick to tell them that he would pay all the recording costs. Daniel gave his support throughout, without interrupting him, backing him up for the arguments he thought would be easiest to counter. They were a team. If the black line projected by the evening sun had been a tennis net, they would have been the winning team. Firing hard, accurate serves at their opponents, which they had no hope of returning.

The silence that followed the proposition lasted all of a couple of seconds. "I'm in, man," said Will. Octavio and DD also accepted. Ricardo held back tears and let Daniel ruffle his hair, a satisfied smile spread across his face. Danny was so sure the answer would be "yes" that he already had a producer, date, and recording studio ready. "Nothing can go wrong," he said. "At the worst, our shitty lives will carry on just as they are today, but at least we'll have a goddamn album to play to our grandchildren."

GOLDUST STUDIOS

DECEMBER. 1989. THE GUYS SPENT A few days in Las Cruces, New Mexico, and made a few test recordings. They sounded amazing, and the group was starting to get excited. Even Ricardo. Daniel, who had committed himself to documenting the recording of the album, didn't let them down and was just like another member of the team. It was during those days that the camaraderie among the band reached its height. They laughed, hugged one another, and ended one another's sentences. It was like in the good old days. For Ricardo, those days of recording were his best days since his panic attack in Houston. Daniel was feeding him the oxygen he needed, just as he did when they first met. He had that feeling again that this guy could, at last, help him get his ass out of the pit of misery he'd fallen into. Riding on that wave of unbridled fraternity, they decided to call the album *Rock & Lovets*, after their old fanzines. The rest of the band thought it was a great idea. Danny used some of his most valued collages for the album's graphics, and they sat down to write out a list, something they hadn't done for a long time, that would define their strategy for the album's release.

Rock & Lovets **plan:**
- Design the covers with Daniel's collages
- Design the inside with family photos and song lyrics

- Record the best album of 1990
- Write a letter to Sub Pop Records asking them to release the album
- Come up with a plan to get the music media on board
- Shoot a video for "Caverns of Sonora"
- Conquer the goddamn world (at long fucking last!)

The norm in Goldust was that Emmit, the owner, would take charge of production of what was recorded there, but with them he made an exception and allowed another producer to take control. It was an excellent decision. ELPASO's songs shone like never before thanks to the musical wisdom of Jeff and his assistant, Harold. The two worked in a small studio they'd set up eight years before in Austin. They produced records for small bands in the area, although most of their money came from recording voice-overs for commercials. More than half of the ads you heard on local radio stations around Austin had been recorded by Jeff or Harold. Daniel had found out about them through his contacts at school, and they had both loved the band's demos. To work on the album, they accepted a substantially lower fee than what they were used to with the commercials and traveled to El Paso a few days before to oversee the rehearsals in the lead-up to the recording. One of the first things the producers suggested was a live recording. No metronome. At that time, it was normal to record all the instruments separately, to the time set by a so-called "click track." This way of working enabled the construction of perfect songs that were easily editable and, often, overproduced. During the rehearsals, Jeff realized that ELPASO had a special sound together. They were compact and powerful. He wanted to create a raw, hard-hitting, and fresh base of guitars, bass, and drums and then add the arrangements, vocals, and harmonies. Taking the time that was necessary. Was this a risky strategy? Yes. It was easy for one of the four to make a mistake during the recording, and that might mean having to do take after take. But placing the responsibility of the recording in the hands of the group was a gamble worth taking. During their time at Goldust Studios the four musicians didn't need to play the songs earmarked for the album more than five or six times. In most cases, the version they chose for each song was the first one. Despite the odd error in timing or tuning, they all oozed that feeling of freshness and power that Jeff was looking for.

In the course of ten days, including weekends, the band recorded a total of eight songs, including old songs, short songs written especially for the album, and those that best defined the essence of the band.

The definitive list was:

- Río Bravo
- Punk2
- John Wayne Gacy
- Abducción en Marfa
- Tierras Prometidas
- Luz
- Caverns of Sonora
- Folk Song

01. Río Bravo. 04:14
(music: Ricardo Salazar and Octavio Quintana · lyrics: Ricardo Salazar)

Harold was sitting at the mixing desk. The index finger and thumb of his right hand held a chin from which grew a small graying goatee, which, try as it might, would never link up with the hair from his sideburns. In fact, his cheeks were like the arid and cracked earth of the desert, and his beard gathered under his face in a tricolored bush in which white prevailed over gray and blond. A Fu Manchu mustache framed a mouth full of small graying teeth, which gave him an unkempt look. It was hard to imagine those dry lips producing succinct comments that were well-constructed and filled with masterly advice on musical production. The doubts he had about what to do with the harmonies made his nose twitch like a hamster's, and his eyes, which were already narrow, squinted further as if trying to focus on a solution that was hard to see among the vast array of buttons and lights of the 1968 ADM mixing desk. His eyebrows arched, sending waves of creases spreading across his forehead that broke on the shore of his hairline.

He wore a black shirt with a pocket stuffed with pens and a comb in different shades of brown that he used from time to time to tidy up his moustache. On the inside of his left arm he had a tattoo with the silhouette of Texas painted with the state flag, which read: "Son of the suburbs. Adopted Texan." Harold was born in New Jersey and moved to the suburbs of Dallas when he was just six years old. His Texan pride was such that he had forced a Southern slur, which was uncommon in El Paso and which Daniel imitated remarkably well. Everyone laughed about it and teased him, saying that he only spoke that way because of his complex about not being a real Texan. It didn't take much time for him to impress the band with his professionalism, effort, and guitar skills. Jeff, as the producer, was all charisma and someone everyone enjoyed working with, but Harold had turned up at the rehearsals with little in the way of leadership capacity and had to gain the band's respect in just over ten days.

In "Río Bravo," one of the band's more recent songs, he not only proposed a beautiful melodic solution for the verse harmonies but also composed the guitar arrangement that Octavio recorded at minute 3:03. The picking enters almost imperceptibly and progresses majestically to the final chorus. This is when the song grows to its full size and starts to accelerate. Will pounds on the drums to the rhythm of his brother's bass guitar. The insatiable guitar soloist takes over at the end of the chorus when Ricardo sings, *"grietas en las almas que supuran lava del volcán interno que transforma a otro rondador"* (cracking souls spit lava from the volcano inside, transforming another wanderer).

02. Punk2. 01:37
(music: Ricardo Salazar and DD · lyrics: Ricardo Salazar)

Will's left arm. What began as a light tingling became a numb hand, which lacked the sensitivity needed to play. As he couldn't hold onto the drumstick properly, he couldn't feel the beats on the snare and was unsure if he was drumming in time. In order not to waste any more takes, he decided to raise his stool a little. This allowed him to hit his thigh with his forearm each time the drumstick touched the drum. This was a masochistic solution that was ideal for ensuring that the timing was perfect for each song. The nerve endings in Will's left leg sent the information, in the form of pain, straight to his brain on every beat. That night he came out of the soundproof booth where his drum kit was set up in the recording room with his trousers around his knees and showing the rest of the band the enormous bruise that had spread across his thigh. The hematoma was the fruit of nonstop drumming during a session that had lasted over four hours. Jeff was so amazed that he immediately reached for his trusty Polaroid. He wanted to add that snapshot to his collection of "memorable moments during the recording of an album." He'd managed to put together more than eighty snapshots in a hilarious album composed of bizarre instruments, naked musicians, drunk musicians, and war wounds, like the coagulated blood of the ELPASO drummer.

Ricardo asks him to take a second photo to include in the design of the inside of the future LP. The producer brings his camera to his eye once again. He aims, shoots, and flash. The machine spits out the photo with its iconic white border. It takes a moment before the snapshot can be seen, Jeff shakes it and looks at the final result.

"Son of a bitch! You see it much better in yours," he says while he offers it to Ricardo and frowns in mild frustration.

"My band's drummer is about to have a fucking heart attack, let me keep the good photo, man!" Ricardo responds.

"Heart attacks make your right arm go numb, not your left, you asshole."

"I don't give a fuck, Jeff, this Polaroid is mine!"

"What a bastard!"

"Are we done for today, boss?"

"That's right. Let's go to the motel."

At the end of every day in the studio, they all went over to the nearby motel to spend the night. DD reread some old issues of *Mad* magazine that he found in Goldust, and Will and Octavio played poker with Jeff. Ricardo spent the time with Daniel scribbling down notes and going through the lyrics, and Harold went back every night to his house in El Paso. No matter how little he'd slept, the next day he got up at the crack of dawn, had breakfast with his daughter, and took her to school before coming back to Las Cruces and carrying on with the sessions. Harold's wife had also left him, and he had to play the role of a single father. He spoke with pride about his little Brit, about how he was going to give her every opportunity, whatever the cost.

Moved by this, the ELPASO singer changed the original lyrics of "Punk2" and decided to write something connected with the abandonment he suffered as a kid. And that's exactly what he did. It was succinct and in English. According to his own rules, he would do the vocals of the Spanish lyrics, and DD would take care of the "*gringo parts.*" The bass player had an unusual timbre and a fantastic range. When Ricardo passed him the paper with the lyrics for him to sing, there was no need for an explanation. He stood up, all six feet, two inches of him in front of the microphone, and howled out those two lines in English six times: "She suffered the biggest mental breakdown / My mother took a gun and shot me down."

No one had any doubt that Ricardo had to echo DD's vocals. He wrote something on a piece of paper and read it out to Harold:

"What do you think of this: *hizo diana en el centro de mi pecho, aún vomito sangre en mis pies.* (She drew a target in the middle of my chest, and I'm still throwing up blood onto my feet.)"

"Wow . . ."

"What's wrong? Don't you like it?"

"Ritchie, man, I can't think of a better way to sum up how it feels to be abandoned."

03. John Wayne Gacy. 01:36
(music: Ricardo Salazar and DD · lyrics: Ricardo Salazar)

"Glad to See You Go" was one of the Ramones songs that Daniel and Ricardo had listened to most when they met in the late seventies. The song appeals to the glory of Charles Manson as leader of the Family, the group that perpetrated the murder of Sharon Tate on August 9, 1969. When the two friends began writing ELPASO's first songs, they created a list of possible ideas for the lyrics. The influence of "Glad to See You Go" can clearly be seen in one of them, "John Wayne Gacy."

They both thought it an interesting idea to portray someone as horrifying as Manson. And Gacy certainly was that. In less than a decade, he ended the lives of thirty teenage boys and young men after torturing and sodomizing them, burying most of them in his garden. What was more, Gacy often attacked his victims while he was dressed up as a clown. Nobody ever suspected him.

Of the eight songs that ELPASO recorded at Goldust Studios, "John Wayne Gacy" is the oldest. Like in "Punk2," DD and Ricardo alternate as the lead vocals. The former sings in English and the latter in Spanish. Both songs are from the same era and share the same intensity and anger in little over ninety seconds of pure punk. Both feed off the early Rhythm Pigs, Minor Threat, and their beloved Black Flag. They are so compact that there isn't space for any frills on the guitar, which plays in time with the bass and the drums. The most notable arrangement in "John Wayne Gacy" undoubtedly comes from the hands of Octavio Quintana with a magnificent trumpet solo that bursts into the final seconds of the song, giving it a borderland feel and raising it to a higher level. In fact, the whole album is taken up a notch, as far as its quality is concerned, thanks to Octavio's participation. He transforms one song after another, going through each to make it infinitely better. Like a musical version of a serial killer, whose chosen weapon is his enormous talent.

04. Abducción en Marfa. 03:14
(music and lyrics: Ricardo Salazar)

Goldust was a studio with more than twenty years of history. It was built in the sixties inside a modest adobe house at 115 East Idaho Avenue in Las Cruces. Emmit Brooks, a native of New Mexico, began his career in music as a performer in the fifties. He was alternating between the guitar and his studies at NMSU when he created Goldust, first as a record label and later as a studio. The singer Steve Smith says he was one of the biggest recording icons in the Southwest. Good old Emmit wore a shirt and jeans and snakeskin cowboy boots. His only regret was not having produced or recorded an album for Bobby Fuller, one of the most charismatic musicians in El Paso and songwriter of one of the first albums that Ricardo listened to as a child. That night, the session went on longer than expected, and the ELPASO singer was humming "I Fought the Law," a Sonny Curtis song that the Bobby Fuller Four made popular in the sixties, while sharing a bag of Lay's Cheddar & Sour Cream chips with Daniel.

Both had gone out into the parking lot to take some air while Octavio finished fiddling with his parts in the song "Abducción en Marfa." It was late and the crunch of the chips sounded loud in the silence of the early morning. The moon was almost full and lit up the intersection of Idaho Avenue and Main Street, just at the point where Daniel was staring blankly. He'd been distracted all day. Absent and unsure. It comforted him to be sitting there in the early hours with his old friend Ritchie, shoulder to shoulder and without the need for conversation. They'd spent hours and hours sitting next to each other like this during the first years of their friendship. They had no need to speak. "My dad loved Bobby Fuller, man," said Ricardo suddenly. "Did you know his music was one of the reasons he moved to the US?" Daniel took that as a rhetorical question, he wasn't even sure his friend had directed it at him, and the words vanished into thin air with the next mouthful of Lay's. Danny recalled the story of his parents' first days in the US, he thought about his sisters, his brother, and the nephews and nieces he hardly knew. He conjured up the image of his father, old and wrinkled at Christmas the previous year, and a chill ran up his spine at the realization that his death was going to be sooner rather than later. Going back to Oxnard gave him mixed feelings of longing and terror. In a few weeks he would go there for New Year's, and he began to realize that once again his modern vision of life was going to monopolize his conversations with his family. December always made him melancholic. As did having to leave New Mexico and return to his routine in El Paso. The recording sessions were about to end, and their time in Las Cruces was beginning to take its toll on the guys.

Recording an album is not a particularly frenetic adventure; there are a lot of dead hours, and when you've repeated the same take ten times you often lose your perspective. Everything seems to sound bad, and you enter into a state of paranoia that makes you suspect your songs are not as good as you thought they were. The high of the first days comes back only at the end of the sessions, when the songs have all their instruments recorded and mixed and you start to get a definitive idea of what they're going to sound like.

Ricardo ate the last chip and crumpled the bag up into a ball. He got up and opened the side door that led inside the studio. He held it open so that his friend could go inside, but Danny remained sitting with his back against the adobe. "You staying here a while longer?" he asked. Daniel nodded his head and closed his eyes as the door shut. His gaze followed the faint shadow cast by the utility pole on the pavement, which then dissolved in the fence that delineated the Goldust premises. He looked at the moon angrily and cursed himself for having missed the perfect opportunity to tell Ricardo what was eating away at his insides.

05. Tierras Prometidas. 03:59
(music: Ricardo Salazar · lyrics: Tino Villanueva)

Octavio's falsetto creeps along beneath Ricardo's deep voice. The adapted verses of poet Tino Villanueva slip from the mixing desk's speakers. Jeff and Harold have their eyes closed and are nodding as the song progresses. DD's bass guitar takes hold of the Spanish guitar and together they weave a kind of small, soft, and fluffy mattress on which the sound of Octavio's nylon strings bounces around freely. The studio is filled with Mexico. Lights, *calaveritas,* and color. For Ricardo the song smells of his grandfather's cooking, whom he met when he was already grown up. Tino Villanueva's poem seems to be talking about his grandfather. About Daniel's parents and the man who raised Felipe Salazar. They all taste of the borderlands and he feels like this song represents them. Octavio speeds up as the bars progress. First based on improvised melodies with the trumpet and then with electric riffs that crisscross and snake around each other, rising to a tense finale that would become one of the darkest and most beautiful moments on the album.

Everyone is pleased with the first completed song of the recording sessions. Will looks at Ricardo with his small eyes, which are beaming a sense of pride in the band. DD covers Octavio's shoulders with the immensity of his right arm and winks when Octavio looks at him sideways. They laugh. The two producers break the silence with a small applause and congratulate the band. "That's great, guys. Really great," says Jeff. Daniel, who is deeply moved, tries to contain his emotion. He knows that the beauty of this powerful song is, in part, thanks to Octavio, who was supposed to be his enemy. The Mexican guitarist is still a hostile figure to him, still the number one contender for the position of Ricardo's best friend. During the ten days that

257

ELPASO has been shut away in Goldust Studios, the only black mark on the daily dynamics was the relationship between the pair. Or the lack of one. Danny, who was about to congratulate Octavio on three occasions, considers putting an end to this stupid, divisive tension after listening to "Tierras Prometidas." But he doesn't. A mix of pride and shame gets the better of him. "When we finish with the album," he says to himself. He bumps fists with Ricardo and they look at each other knowingly, realizing that this could be the step that begins the career they've always dreamed about.

"Partners, we got two days left, and we've still got quite a lot of work to do. What are we working on now?" Harold asks.

"I've got a few guitar overdubs," Octavio replies. "If it's OK with Ricardo I'll do them this afternoon."

"No problem for me. I can do the vocals tomorrow."

"Perfect!" Jeff exclaims. "Harold, prepare the amp, let's do it."

06. Luz. 03:44
**(music: Ricardo Salazar and Octavio Quintana ·
lyrics: Ricardo Salazar)**

Answering machine at the Salazar home in El Paso. Message 1:

Hey, girls, how are you? How's my little Teresita? Who loves you? Daddy loves you! Lots and lots! I got you some presents! Yeah? Let's see you clap. Bravoooo! (. . .) Lupe, honey, how are things at home? I wanted to call you this morning, but the takes of the main vocals went on for longer than expected and I haven't had time till now . . . I hate catching you when you're out and having to talk to the answering machine. Today we finished "Luz." I think it's

258

our best song . . . well, I mean our best song that I wrote
. . . (. . .) I was just about to change Luba for Lupe, but I
remembered your threat and opted for the cool factor of
dedicating a love song to a comic-book character. Harold
asked me if the woman from the song was my mother and,
of course, I told him it wasn't . . . but you know what? I'm
not sure. At the end of the day it's a song I wrote for Teresa,
like a lullaby. The lyrics talk about when we began and my
fears that you'd leave me, you know? Maybe I am unconsciously talking about my mother. I'm starting to doubt
whether I've gotten over all that bullshit . . . Goddamn sub-
conscious!! (. . .) I miss you, you know? I'm so grateful
that you made it so easy for me to be here, shut away and
focused on the album. You're incredible, and you always
have been. Little Teresa is like you, you know? She's nat-
urally good and trusting. I love her . . . I love you both
deeply, Lupe (. . .)

Answering machine at the Salazar home in El Paso. Message 2:

Being here has made me think a lot about the last few
months, and I know I've been absent, drowning in all my
shit . . . I'm sure my dad would have explained this to you,
but that's my natural state . . . I was a pathetic kid, totally
isolated and shy. In fact, I didn't stop being that asshole
until I met you . . . I thought that music . . . having my own
band, you know . . . I always thought that all that punk bullshit would make me a better person, but I realize now that
it's you and Teresa that have done that. You're my lifesav-
ers. Oh my God I can't believe I'm hitting you with all this

in a phone message! You'll have to erase the tape! (. . .)
Really, the only thing I wanted to tell you with this call is
that I'm sorry, darling. I'm really sorry . . . I want you to
know that I really believe in this album, and I'm sure that
1990's gonna be a great year. My year . . . our year! (. . .) I
wanna put an end to this depressive shit and take back the
controls of my life, you know? Stop blaming others for my
failures and all that crap (. . .)

Answering machine at the Salazar home in El Paso. Message 3:

I've been thinking . . . I want to know what you think
about . . . Well, I'll tell you, Danny thinks we should
definitely send the album to Sub Pop. He thinks they'll
release it for sure. The fact is it's a label that is at its peak
right now and it'd be incredible if they included us in
their catalogue. We've finished and mixed six songs and,
Lupe, they sound really good. You know I'm not normally the optimist, but I'm sure that we've got something
really big here. *Gimme These Songs!* was well-played, but
it's funny, they were still other people's songs. Our songs
really sound fantastic; they're so powerful and moving . . .
And we still have to master them! (. . .) Sorry, I digress.
My doubt is whether or not we should release the album
ourselves, you know? There's something that tells me this
is the perfect time to set up our own label and release our
album along with albums by other young bands in the city.
What d'ya think? (. . .) I don't know, maybe that's just stupid! At this stage in the recording my head's whirling . . .
I'm gonna have to leave you, honey. I'll call tomorrow at

the same time as always. Give the little one a kiss for me.
I love you.

07. Caverns of Sonora. 03:54
(music and lyrics: Ricardo Salazar)

Imagine a beagle walking. Its stiff tail traces a curve that points back toward its three-colored back. Black. Brown. White. Its snout is stuck to the pavement and its ears hang down, despite its repeated efforts to lift them. They flop down and drag along the floor like the bell-bottom jeans of the girl who is taking it for a walk. Its sense of smell is strong, making the dog swerve this way and that as it follows an invisible trail. Its hind legs move lightly, its furry butt swinging from side to side with almost exactly the same rhythm as the backside tightly wrapped in its owner's jeans, which has Daniel mesmerized. He's driving slowly because the traffic on Alameda Avenue is keeping his speed to a minimum.

He and Octavio have left Las Cruces because they both have things to see to in El Paso, and Ricardo has let them take the van. Their relationship is still tense, and they only exchange the odd word about the traffic, the music from the cassette, or the rear ends of the beagle and its owner. When they arrive at the intersection with Delta Drive, the tide of vehicles comes to a standstill, and the lights of a squad car reflect off the bodywork of the cars around the Adelitas restaurant. An ambulance with its doors wide-open swallows up a stretcher with what looks like the most seriously injured casualty. The girl with the beagle stops with the group of curious onlookers huddled around the cordoned-off area. Her butt joins a line of other butts. Just one figure is ignoring the commotion, standing away from it stiffly, looking directly at the band's Ford Econoline.

Daniel and Octavio look at the figure, and the former recognizes this odd observer. Standing in front of them, unblinking, is the homeless guy who had intimidated Daniel on the day of Debbie's funeral and who has been making ghostly appearances at random moments of Daniel's life over the last four years. "You can see him, can't you?" he asks Octavio. "Holy shit. That's one scary old bastard!" The response eases Daniel's tension somewhat. It's the first time anyone has confirmed the existence of the homeless man, and he laughs nervously as he gently presses his foot down on the accelerator. Daniel holds the man's stare from a distance and watches as he drops away from them, along with everything else, as the van presses forward. His eyes fall on the beagle, and he sees him barking soundlessly at the homeless guy, while in the Econoline all that can be heard is one of the songs from Metallica's . . . And Justice for All album. It looks like the animal is the only one paying any attention to this guy, who is slowly slipping out of the frame of the passenger window. Daniel then looks straight around at Octavio, who is shouting at him. But he doesn't hear him. He tries to read what his lips are saying, but it's too late. They're moving in slow motion like everything else. They're in the middle of the intersection, and a black Aston Martin smashes violently into the passenger door. Everything explodes into a foggy gray, which quickly fades to black.

※

Daniel half opens his eyes and manages to focus his gaze slowly on the faces of a young man wearing a stripy T-shirt and a blonde woman who is covering her face with her hands, apparently in horror. "Don't move. You've just had an accident," says the young man. Daniel can scarcely hear a word. He's confused, and the last Metallica song that had been playing in the van is pounding at his brain in an endless, macabre loop. His back hurts. A lot. He screams and passes out. The black curtain falls again and everything is silent.

He wakes up a second time and recognizes the stripes of the guy's T-shirt in the background of the scene that his moistened eyes are trying to take in. In the foreground is a stretcher. The horrified lady has disappeared from his line of vision. The stretcher-bearer asks him what his name is, but he can't think with the din of that music jammed in his mind. "I . . . I . . . can't remember . . ." he murmurs, feeling afraid now. In actual fact, he does remember, but his head isn't working properly, and the drawer that's concealing his identity is shut tight. He complains about his back again, hears the word *morphine* and soon begins to relax. He even smiles and, suddenly, boom! The drawer opens and "Daniel Álvarez" leaps above the screaming guitars. He hurriedly responds to the man holding the stretcher, "My name's Daniel!"

"OK, Daniel, do you remember where you were going?" The question falls like a concrete slab on Danny's brain. His neurons are hopelessly flapping about in search of information, but nothing comes. This time they don't even know where the goddamn drawer with the answer is. "Don't worry, kid, we're taking you to the hospital." Daniel recognizes a friendly gesture but no actual facial features. The stretcher-bearer is faceless. He can hear him talking and knows he is looking at him, but there is no sign of any eyes or mouth. He thinks for a moment and realizes he can't remember the faces of the young guy and the horrified woman.

Since returning from the first fade to black, no one has a face, and that scares him. He thinks, for the first time, that perhaps he's dead. Maybe these faceless people are the ones who manage the transition from life to death. Maybe it's not something that just happens straightaway. Maybe something has to happen in between. This part of death is too much for him, and he starts gasping for air. Suddenly he's picked up and put on a stretcher. The inside of the ambulance looms into view, and then two lights, red and blue, flash through the window, coloring the white sheet covering his legs. The lights remind him of the police, which makes him think of the people huddling around the scene on Alameda Avenue. From here his mind wanders to the girl with the beagle and suddenly the satanic loop relentlessly turning inside his head comes to a standstill and disappears. He remembers saying goodbye to the others in Las Cruces just before getting into the van. He remembers Octavio putting on the Metallica cassette. He remembers hating him a little. He remembers Octavio shouting at him in slow motion, and that's where, with that muted scream, the film comes to an end. A girl in a doctor's uniform and holding some scissors tells him she's going to cut his clothes to be able to carry out some test or another. The morphine is taking effect, and Daniel jokingly tells the doctor she should have dinner with him before taking his clothes off. The girl looks at him pitifully, and he gets scared again. "Am I gonna die, Doctor?" The reply is a confusing list of technical medical terms he doesn't understand, so he closes his eyes and entrusts himself to a higher being, begging to let him live.

✳

The kidney. The kidney is what's worrying the doctors. The catheter they've stuck down his penis is filling with blood, which, apparently, is coming from his kidney. Perirenal hematoma. He's dazed and immobilized, and his eyes can take in only the white ceiling of his hospital room. From time to time, a wide-angle shot of the nurse comes into view, and Daniel tries to cling to the polite smile she gives him—it's all he has since the faces came back. And for the first time he understands the importance of a friendly gesture at the right moment. He can feel his heartbeat accelerate, like a child who's been given a sweet and decides to keep it instead of eating it. Danny saves the smile for if things get any worse. He might need it later. He can't seem to work out how much time has passed since the accident. The bedroom is dimly lit, and all he can hear are the machines giving anyone within earshot the lowdown on his vital signs. He assumes it's been a matter of hours, but it feels like weeks. He can't sleep. He's afraid he won't wake up the third time around. He feels as if he's come back to life after two practice runs at dying and doesn't want the next time to be the real thing.

Unexpectedly, the body invading his field of vision is now that of Ricardo, who looks shaken, tears welling up in his eyes. His body puffs up with joy and relief. His friend is back. The morphine, which is still prowling around his blood, making everything seem more bearable, decides to give the encounter a touch of humor and moves Danny's mouth like a ventriloquist operating his doll: "Ritchie, call Harold and tell him that tomorrow I won't be able to sing the harmonies for 'Caverns of Sonora.' I don't think they'll let me out in time" (he laughs). It's an encouraging comment, he thinks, one that is sure to ease the tension. But far from finding it funny, Ricardo's smile fades and he looks at the doctor, who tells him not to worry; it's perfectly normal. "What the fuck's going on, Ritchie?" asks Daniel nervously. Ricardo takes a deep breath and replies, "Man, that's the third time you've told me that."

Shit, something's not right. How could he have said the same thing three times without realizing it? What if his brain's all mashed up? Could these be his final ravings before he is thrown into the arms of the Grim Reaper? He feels like his body is being swallowed up by the hospital bed, as if it were quicksand. A mini tornado whirls through his stomach, while the anxiety works his heart rate from a steady jog into a frantic sprint. The morphine is following orders; just keeping the pain at bay. All that can be heard for a while are the noises from the machines he's plugged into. No one says anything. There are questions he wants to ask Ricardo, but it terrifies him to think that he's repeating himself without realizing.

"Ritchie . . ."

"Yeah, man."

"How did you find out?"

"The police got my phone number through the insurance company and called home. They spoke to my dad. To start with he thought it was me that had been driving. He went to the recording studio, and that's when we found out it was you. I was outside with Will and DD."

"Do my parents know?"

"I don't know. If you want, I'll talk to them."

"And Annette?"

"She's on her way. Don't worry."

Daniel thinks and breathes deeply.

"Am I going to die, Ritchie?"

"Relax, brother, the doctors say you'll get better."

The sense of relief causes the conversation to pause momentarily, allowing a small space for silence and reflection. It doesn't last long.

"How's Octavio?"

Ricardo lowers his eyes, and his lower lip begins to tremble. "Is he bad?" asks Daniel. Ricardo can't talk, he's holding back tears and looks away. Daniel's ears and face begin to burn up. "What happened, man?" Their eyes meet. There's no need to say anything. The unspoken information is transmitted straight down the invisible line that's connecting their pupils. Daniel emits a sob, which brings Ricardo crashing down. They both cry. Octavio's dead.

08. Folk Song. 03:18
(music: Octavio Quintana · lyrics: Ricardo Salazar)

Daniel spent two days in intensive care until they moved him to a bedroom with Marb, an old guy whose chest had just been stapled back together. The rest of the band went back to Las Cruces to finish off the songs. There was just one day left and three songs to finish off. Will suggested to Ricardo that he rewrite the lyrics to "Folk Song" and turn it into a small homage to his dead friend. Hence, the song became known as "Octavio." The lyrics are dotted with some of his recurring idiosyncrasies and phrases. Ricardo recorded the vocals in a single take brimming with emotion. He held back the tears until the last verse, when the others noticed two teardrops streaming at full speed down his cheeks, as if in a hurry to get away. They hung from Ritchie's swollen eyes, eventually falling into the emptiness.

The atmosphere in Goldust Studios for the last three days made the place feel more like a funeral home than a recording studio. The continuous jokes and fooling around of the previous days became long silences and bowed heads. Jeff did nothing but press buttons, taking it for granted that everyone was happy with the last vocals that had been recorded. The last day had been saved for photo and video sessions, which they would use to promote the album, but Daniel had to stay in the hospital a while longer, and Lupe was looking after Teresa in El Paso. No one could get behind the lens. The only visual record they could put together were the two Polaroids that Jeff had taken a few days before. They put the songs on an Ampex 456 tape and said a heartfelt goodbye to the producers. Despite the bitter end to their stay in Las Cruces, they knew that the ELPASO magic had flourished once again during the sessions prior to the accident. Now they had to rest, digest the roller coaster of emotions they'd been dragged through, and face the heartache of burying their friend.

For the second time in their short history as a band, they put a cassette containing their music on someone's coffin. One of the copies of *Mountain* accompanied Debbie on the day of her farewell, and Octavio Quintana would lie forever with the first tape of *Rock & Lovets* in one of the pockets of the suit he was dressed in for the funeral. They met at the cemetery in Ciudad Juárez with Octavio's mother and the rest of his family. He had a heap of little cousins who queued up to kiss his forehead, including Joel, who lived in El Paso and who had dazzled them with his innate gift for drumming. Will hugged him delicately. The great man crouched down and gently wrapped his arms around the boy's comparatively tiny body. He got back to his feet with a look of heartbroken sorrow on his face and hugged DD in a demonstration of brotherly love his friends had never seen before. Ricardo was there with Lupe, Teresa, and Felipe. Jeff and Harold were there, too. Everyone, without exception, was moved at the sight of the Davis brothers holding each other tight and murmuring words of affection.

Daniel cried in his hospital room while Marb talked to him about the shoddy job they'd done on his heart. Wrapped up in his sobbing was a mix of guilt, pity, and anger. Guilt for having stopped the van in the middle of the intersection and, above all, for coming away from the accident almost unharmed. The driver of the Aston Martin was driving at twice the speed limit and with too much alcohol flowing through his veins. Like Octavio, he was killed instantly.

Pity for Ricardo, Will, and DD. He knew that this was a hard blow to the band's aspirations and guessed that the space left by the guitarist's death would be hard to fill. He also felt anger. A whole lot of anger. Anger for having let his jealousy toward Octavio get such a hold on their relationship. Anger for never having told him what a great musician he was, when he had thought as much so many times. Anger for never having congratulated him for his contribution to the band, which was, in a way, both of theirs. Anger, anger, anger.

Dante once described anger as a love of justice perverted to revenge and spite. It arises at a nonspecific point between your stomach and your lungs and twists your innards while at the same time raising the temperature inside your head. It often reddens your cheeks and ears and soaks your eyes with tears that refuse to fall. It destroys your appetite and clouds your thinking. Anger tenses your jaw and grips your muscles. Any object is at risk of being hit because your perception of material value plunges into the bottomless pit of obstinacy. The instinct for self-preservation is ripped apart, allowing you to destroy your hand by smashing it through the most expensive glass doors in your home, and you're capable of pulverizing your toes by kicking a steel post with all your might. Anger invites you into a tunnel of self-destruction. And it's not just physical, but emotional self-destruction, too. You might put an end to a fantastic friendship, leave a stable job, or abandon a project you've been working on for years, because every decision you make has been infected by anger. And do you know what the worst of it is? Anger is impossible to kill. You can try to channel it, but you can't kill it. It's inside of you and has no intention of leaving. And it'll stay there, standing the test of time, its foot on the accelerator of your rage and taking you to the edge of God only knows where. The evil son of a bitch lies in wait ready to pounce at your neck when you're least expecting it. Save for suicide, your only option is to learn to live with your anger, as it pummels away at your stomach and lungs, and try to settle on some kind of arrangement to share your life with it. That's what Daniel did. But its mere existence is the mother of all omens.

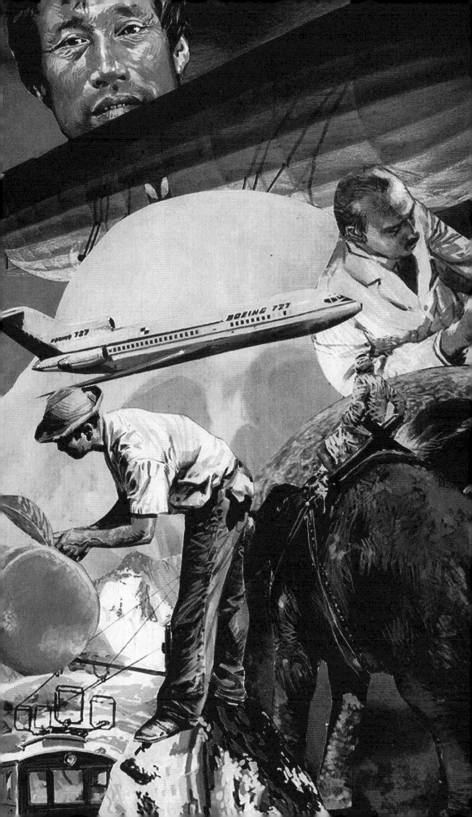

THE SUMMIT MEETING (Vol. 2)

ON APRIL 2, 1990, IN MADISON, Wisconsin, Nirvana recorded the first versions of what would be their second album, *Nevermind*. Sub Pop, despite their financial hardships, gave them their full backing and sent them to Smart Studios with Butch Vig as their producer. For five days they recorded demos of songs like "Breed," "In Bloom," "Lithium," and "Polly." Kurt Cobain and company used that tape, financed by the Seattle-based independent label, to look for a multinational record label that would want to sign them up and release their future album, with all the guarantees that a major could offer them. It was DGC, which Sonic Youth had already signed with, that ended up taking on Nirvana and recording their second album. The album turned the American alternative scene on its head and the market, shortly afterward, used it with its own interests at heart.

The path that Cobain's band trod on its rise to stardom was not unlike what Daniel had had in mind for ELPASO. Seattle had previously been a city with a scene similar to El Paso's. Both cities were a long way from the musical epicenters of New York and Los Angeles, but they had veteran groups that had gone out to tour the sewers of the underground in the eighties. The Rhythm Pigs and the Melvins shared the bill for several shows, and the two bands chose San Francisco as an alternative to the land they were born in. Furthermore, Sub Pop had a lot to do with Nirvana's meteoric rise. As Daniel had predicted, the label of Jonathan Poneman and Bruce Pavitt became a benchmark for the alternative world in the new decade. Releasing an album with them was a big step up the ladder for unknown bands at the time, like Mudhoney and Tad.

For the guys, April began with another meeting called by Ricardo. On April 4, the Davis brothers and Daniel sat down again to listen to the ELPASO leader, this time at his place. He, Lupe, and Teresa were still living with Felipe. The magnitude of the tragedy that had befallen them didn't seem to have sunk in, and Ritchie was obsessed with the album. Losing Octavio was a hard blow for him, but he was convinced that getting *Rock & Lovets* out there was the best way of honoring the memory of his friend. He often gave the impression that he was hoping he'd come back, as if the ELPASO guitarist had just taken a short break and would be back at the end of the summer. Only this summer was not one of those that toasts your skin and leaves the smell of salt in your hair. For Lupe and Felipe, the first months of 1990 were anything but ideal. They watched as the depressive version of Ricardo that had returned from Houston a year ago fell into his own personal hell, becoming a kind of intolerable, self-effacing version of himself. A Ricardo who could not even find consolation in playing with his daughter. The little girl was growing up and bringing at least some light into the darkness her father emanated. Although it was no easy task to illuminate the murky corners of the pit the ELPASO leader was trapped inside. He'd trampled all over his own beliefs concerning tobacco and alcohol consumption and spent hours shut away in the garage with Felipe's tools. With a bare light bulb glaring down at him from the ceiling, he would rattle out disconnected and inharmonious chords on his acoustic guitar. He alternated scribbling ideas for the album release and song lyrics with long swigs from a bottle of Jack Daniel's.

His phone conversations with Daniel were filled with worrying comments about depression, abandonment, and death. He pressured Danny into gathering together all the audio and graphic material they had created since the band began. He managed to find photos, flyers, cassettes, and videos, as well as the master copy of *Rock & Lovets*, the Ampex tape that came out of the sessions at Goldust. By the end of January he'd made a full recovery from the injuries he'd suffered in the accident. He was spared the journey to California to visit his family at Christmas, but it couldn't stop his mom from coming to El Paso to look after him. She was there a few weeks with Annette, who hit it off with her boyfriend's mother, so much so that she went back to Oxnard, reassured that her son was in good hands.

In February he started to design the graphics for the LP with collages that he'd chosen especially for it. He spoke with this brother, Gustavo, who had good friends in Portland and Seattle, in his efforts to figure out the best way to get the album to Sub Pop and wrote as many as seven versions of the letter he would eventually send to the record label. But in March things took a turn for the worse. Once he'd recovered physically and was able to lead a normal life, he collapsed emotionally. He was haunted by the ghosts of that fateful day, which invaded his head and hacked at his state of mind. He hardly ate, looked awful, and lost a lot of weight. Just at that moment, Ricardo stepped up his calls, and the pressure began to take its toll.

"We need the graphics as soon as possible, Danny."

"I know. . ."

"I thought we could have it mastered in New York. What do you think?"

"It's a lot of money, man."

"Yeah . . . I'll think of something. Let's talk tomorrow."

"But, Ritchie. . ."

The ELPASO singer thought finishing with the group meant giving in to a fate they didn't deserve. He wanted to make it, and that's why he organized a meeting with the other band members. So they could give him their support. In the hope they had handled their loss as badly as he had, that Danny and the Davis brothers were also stuck in denial. But they weren't. Daniel had surfed the wave of his anger and had now sunk completely into depression.

Will and DD, however, seemed to have left behind their worst weeks. They were still dispirited and downcast but had come to terms with their loss. As they sat in the Salazars' living room, they listened in grim silence to Ricardo's optimistic vision. It was absurd to them, not to mention a little worrying, to hear their friend base his entire discourse on a lie. They didn't want to be hard on him and simply declined the invitation to carry on with ELPASO as delicately as they could. "It doesn't make sense to keep going with the band, Ritchie," said Will. "None of this makes any sense without Octavio, man. I can't do it, honestly. You gotta understand that."

Ricardo received the drummer's response like a dagger straight to the heart. He was tongue-tied and felt an infernal heat running through his body. Right from his ears down to the tips of his toes. His jaw tensed, and he shook his head in dismay. He tried to seek out Daniel's support, but his old friend's head remained bowed and unmoving in the beige chaise longue that dominated the room. The intense light of the two white lamps cast impossible figures on the walls, as the silhouettes of the group fused with those of the objects in the room, creating a haunting theater of shadow puppets auguring a cruel end to the play. "You can't do this to me, Will!" shouted Ricardo. His eyes were glued to the photograph of him and his father on the little table that separated him from the Davis brothers. Will wanted to answer but felt pity for the ELPASO singer. The drummer wanted to let fly with all the venomous sarcasm he was capable of in a situation such as this one, but he couldn't. He covered his head with his hands and started to weep. Frustrated. Pissed. Hurt.

At that moment DD joined in and squeezed his brother's leg with his huge right hand. "Listen, you asshole!" he exclaimed, his blue eyes fixed on Ricardo, "We haven't done anything to you, OK? We could have torn you to pieces the day you found us in there," DD gestured toward the garage where he and Will had broken in to play ELPASO's instruments five years before. "We said we were sorry, and we left. We agreed to be in your band when you asked us. We believed in this as much as you did. We didn't go back to East Texas because we knew the band had something special. We went through all that for you, and we ignored the signs that were telling us this project was going down the tube, you know? You gotta get it into your head that what happened to Octavio meant the end for this fucking project, Ritchie. We lived with that guy, he was family to us, and ELPASO makes absolutely no fucking sense to us without him. You do what you want with the album. It's yours. You paid for it, and you have every right to it. We left our souls in those goddamn songs. This leg-acy is all of ours, so don't ask us to do anything else. We just wanna go home, and that's fucking that."

An awkward silence filled the room. The bass player sat back down on the sofa. He was trembling slightly when he crossed his arms. They'd never heard him say so much and with so much clarity. DD, who was so frugal with his words. Until that moment he'd always left it to his brother to speak for the two of them, and in all those years he'd never felt the need to speak up for himself. Daniel and Ricardo couldn't hide their amazement at the little Davis's outburst and, at last, their eyes met.

"Danny, man. Let's do it together."

"Ritchie . . ."

"Fuck! Come on! We owe it to ourselves. We've done it before, haven't we?"

"Ritchie, I . . . I'm not good, man . . ."

"I know, brother! I'm also fucked. Will and DD are, too. But we started this ten years ago, man. Remember our agreement? I've got it upstairs, Danny! You gave me your word!"

Ricardo began to sense a certain tension in the air. As if the other three knew something that he didn't. "What the fuck's going on? You're not fucking off to Houston, too, are you?!"

"No, man . . . I'm going to Europe with Annette."

"What?"

"I'm getting out of here, Ritchie . . . I tried telling you that night in Las Cruces during the recording sessions, when we were eating chips in the parking lot, remember? Before the accident and all that . . ."

"Seriously? You're leaving? You're a goddamn selfish bastard, you know that? You promised me you'd help me with this! That you'd get me out of here!"

"Ritchie, man, you've got a daughter now, and I need to disconnect."

"Fuck you, Danny! Don't bring Teresa into this, you bastard! What about the album? What about Sub Pop and all that bullshit about managing the release of our fucking album?"

"I'm sorry, really. All this shit is too much for me."

"Get outta here, you asshole!"

"Ritchie . . ."

"Get the fuck out of here, I said! And you, too, get the fuck away from me."

DD and Will got up and hugged Daniel, who was still sitting

downcast on the chaise longue. He'd been broken inside. The drummer got up and went over to Ricardo. He grabbed him by the back of the neck and thrust his face into his chest. They wept. DD came over and also put his arms around them, like when they were about to go out onstage. Daniel looked at the three of them from the sofa, his cheeks reddening with emotion. The headlights of a car came in through the window that looked onto the street, lighting up Ricardo's face as he muttered his final reproach at Daniel. "Go to hell," he sobbed. And he stormed off into the kitchen. From the living room they heard chairs being slammed against the floor. Plates and glasses shattering. Danny and the Davis brothers left the house, fleeing the noise and Ricardo's internal earthquake. The door closing behind them marked the final end to the band. The rehearsals. The songs. The hours in the van. Everything. ELPASO disintegrated forever in that instant.

When I think about that scene I can't help doing so with a kind of split screen, in which Nirvana can be seen 1,500 miles away in the studio in Wisconsin, at the same instant, recording the first demos of the album that would bring to life what Ricardo had predicted in "Caverns of Sonora." It's impossible for me to forget the day that, at nineteen, I stopped my car and Raúl got out without saying goodbye. In my twenty years as the most amateur of musicians, I've played in a fair number of bands. Out of all those different projects, it was only the first one that really felt fluid and natural. At times, I'm surprised at how easy it was. Raúl and I had been in school together from the time we were three years old, and we met Jonathan when we were five, when the three of us played together on our neighborhood's youth basketball team. We grew up side by side, seeing one another on a regular basis thanks to school and basketball. Raúl and I saw each other every school day for thirteen years. Every single one. He was just a day older than me, and we often shared birthday parties. We were born in a small, sleepy town on the outskirts of Barcelona. Our families, like most of the families of kids like us, had migrated from other parts of Spain in the sixties, fleeing the miseries and wounds inflicted by the fascist dictatorship. At that time, the big city promised something along the lines of the American dream: work, stability, and progress. The population of our neighborhood had grown exponentially, which is why most people like us lived crammed into immense, gray, and impersonal housing blocks. The little space the city had to expand into meant that it grew upward. Apartments, apartments, and more apartments. Our parents broke their backs doing low-paid and unskilled jobs. Your family and humble and nomadic beginnings set the pace for your life, never mind how much television and movies tried to drum into you that "you can achieve anything if you want it enough." Bullshit. In my neighborhood it was basically about surviving. We were all survivors. People trying to stay on their feet in a reality that was shaking like an earthquake.

If you consider the social reality of our surroundings in the nineties, the most normal thing would have been for the three of us to have quit school at fourteen. In all likelihood we would soon have gotten into drinking, smoking, and drugs. We could easily have ended up in one of the violent gangs that persecuted, humiliated, and beat up people like us. So why was it we were like we were? Well, Raúl, Jonathan, and I were teetotaling, culturally active teenagers who discovered alternative rock at just the right time. While kids like us were falling apart because they had no future, we built ourselves one. We each thought we would be someone, thanks to music. We identified with that guy from Seattle and began to wear flannel shirts. What I find fascinating about our first wild adventure into music is that it developed and took shape in its own time, unpressured. The circumstances were such that everything flowed and fitted into place, despite the adversity of the context we lived in. We all chose different instruments, for example. Jonathan got hold of a crappy drum kit, and Raúl and I worked one summer to buy ourselves a guitar and bass, respectively. I know people whose first groups consisted of three Spanish guitars and a guy who played the tambourine. We, however, were able to put together the minimum lineup of a rock group, like Nirvana or the Rhythm Pigs. We recorded seven songs, gave seven concerts, and split up in July 2001. The seventh month. To say we split up is a romanticism. The drummer and I felt we were trapped in Nameless and gave the guitarist and lead singer an ultimatum. We wanted to keep growing and put pressure on him to write more songs. He, however, felt increasingly uneasy, to the point that he refused outright to write another song. He said that for him the band was just a hobby and that his aspirations were more than satisfied by playing a few covers every once in a while. I felt that my wings had been clipped and decided to leave. Jonathan did the same and we ended up setting up a new band. Claim. We were nineteen years old the day we had that argument. When he got out of the car, I hadn't bargained for losing sight of someone who had formed a part of my life since kindergarten. That decision tore apart more than a band. It took fifteen years for us to talk about it. It was during the summer of 2016. We had chatted together on virtual platforms, but Raúl, Jonathan, and I had not sat down together since that evening in July. I had just gotten back from my second adventure in El Paso, and I decided to suggest we get coffee together, with the idea of tempting them into bringing those seven songs back to life. "We could rerecord and edit them, couldn't we?" I told them. "It'd be fun to play together again!"

Jonathan liked the idea, although he had the good mind and

responsibility to remain prudent. He and I had failed in our attempt to salvage Claim's music, so he was waiting to see what Raúl had to say. It was hard to hear him dismiss my suggestion. To see how he felt no excitement whatsoever about the prospect. He tried to cover up his discomfort and asked me to leave it all as it was. "I know you'd like to do something with our music, but for me it is just too painful. You have to remember that, for me, all that doesn't just take me back to the day that Nameless ended. Our music reminds me of the day I lost my best friends. I'm sorry, but no," was his response.

It was like we were having the same disagreement as fifteen years ago. Only this time we respected and understood each other's decision. We all apologized for the hurt we may have caused one another and carried on chatting about work and fatherhood and recalling anecdotes. I left with a bittersweet taste in my mouth, but at least Jonathan and I had had the chance to speak to someone we had once been so close to.

CODA

DANIEL IS WALKING THROUGH A DISTORTED version of downtown El Paso. It's something that happens often in his dreams and nightmares, in which he mixes up architectural features that, for him, are somehow connected, creating impossible, sordid scenarios. In this case he is coming out of UTEP which, oddly, is opposite the Plaza Hotel. In reality, they are more than a mile apart. There's an uneasy calm in the air as he walks past the intersection of San Antonio Avenue and El Paso Street. The sun is shining, and the sky is steeped in a deep blue, providing the perfect backdrop to the city's architecture. Suddenly, he sees Octavio coming toward him. His blood freezes. He's dead. He shouldn't be here. He can't be here. Danny begins to tremble and feels a chill run down his spine, like a bolt of lightning traveling through him all the way down to his fingers and toes.

Octavio looks at him, smiles, and approaches. Daniel looks around him and sees that they are alone. There is no one who can confirm whether what he is seeing is real. He's standing in front of a fucking ghost. Or a zombie. Maybe he's going to feast on his brains. "What's up, Daniel?" says Octavio. Daniel is incapable of speaking. He opens his eyes as wide as he can in a desperate attempt to tell him that this is not good. "You're dead, Octavio. You can't be here," he thinks. The ghost nods and puts his hands on his shoulders. "I know,

I know," he fires back. Despite being terrified at the thought of conversing with a dead person, he feels a certain sense of peace. Octavio's gestures and the warmth of his words are comforting. "Bu—but you . . ." he whispers. Octavio smiles, hugs him, and says to him something like, "Everything's OK, Daniel, don't worry. Take care of yourself!" And he leaves. Daniel wants to cry, but instead he smiles. Or is it the other way around? With his unusual gait, Octavio's silhouette vanishes down El Paso Street, heading toward the border, and Daniel wakes up.

That essentially sums up the recurring dream that haunted Daniel Álvarez during his first nights in Europe. The dream that somehow allowed him to make his peace with Octavio Quintana.

When the left the United States in the spring of 1990 he had no idea that he was saying goodbye to his country forever. He would be back in California a few years later for his father's funeral, and from then on he would distance himself further and further from his family. He and Annette left Texas and traveled around Eastern Europe before going to France and meeting her family. Octavio appeared in his dreams for the first time at Annette's family home. That's where their relationship began to crumble. They broke up once and for all a few months later, on another adventure around the Old Continent. They were to leave Spain and settle definitively in Paris, but he refused. Their two-year relationship evaporated under the heat of the Andalusian sun. Daniel decided to settle in Cordoba and teamed up with a group of artists and activists, rekindling his love for performance. In no time at all, his life in America was just a distant memory. Octavio stopped visiting at night, and his Spanish improved. His speech even took on something of an Andalusian accent.

Twenty years had flown past before Daniel heard anything about the friends he left behind in El Paso. It was between 2008 and 2009.

Everyone was talking about Facebook, a social network that was taking the world by storm and which, among other things, was allowing people who hadn't seen each other for a long time to reestablish contact. In the first months of its journey toward world domination, dozens of reunions began springing up among the people in Daniel's life: former students, ex-colleagues, and old friends. To start with, Daniel was staunchly against giving information to a company that seemed to be sharing data with the CIA and God only knows who else. But, in the end, he gave in and registered with the internet giant. His online friends began to grow in number. The first friend requests from the US were quick to arrive. His nieces and nephews were uploading content that he would see when he woke up. A digitally harmonious, fictitious relationship began with his siblings and all his Californian family. Once he had fully delved into the madness of social media, his curiosity got the better of him, and he made contact with old friends from UTEP and even spoke with Annette Leduc for the first time in many years. He also found out that the Davis brothers had enjoyed some success in the nineties with one of the bands they set up in Houston. He was happy for them but didn't delve too deeply into their digital profiles. He typed in Ricardo's name and surname countless times, but his friend never figured in the social network's databases. He liked the idea that Ricardo had refused to form part of a phenomenon as banal and massive as Facebook. But that wasn't the case. Ricardo had been missing for fifteen years. Nobody knew if he'd died or if he'd simply decided to leave El Paso without telling anyone and was now living a different life in Mexico under a different name. Whatever the real story, Daniel felt a deep sense of sorrow when he read Lupe's words during a brief chat they began through her daughter's profile. Teresa was the closest person to Ricardo whom Daniel was able to find. He saw that little girl grow up in the blink of an eye.

She was barely two when he left, and suddenly he was looking at a woman who'd just turned twenty. In the photos she looked happy with her friends. Traveling. On the beach. Having dinner. Somewhere that could have been her home, with her mother or with her grandfather. Seeing Felipe was what most moved Daniel, before he found out about the disappearance of his friend. There was the man who had treated him like another member of the family. The guy who used to smoke, leaning up against the wall, while they hammered away at their instruments in the garage. A faded version of Pheel, as he called himself. With his hair dyed white by the passing years and his mustache, which was smaller but just as dark as ever. He wept as he stared at this man on the screen, standing next to Teresa on her nineteenth birthday. He looked happy, too. He sent the girl a friend request, along with a short text that he thought would help the family remember who he was. But there was no need. Lupe replied effusively and with a generous helping of affection. This woman, who had retained her beauty and insightfulness, detected a note of guilt in Daniel's first message. And so she was careful how she trod when it came to Ricardo. Daniel was amazed at Lupe's composure. He admired how she had rebuilt her life so well after her daughter's father had abandoned them. It was true, of course, that Daniel had only just found out and was still reeling from the news, which she had had sixteen years to digest. "He did to us what he had so often reproached his mother for doing, Danny. He'd promised never to leave Teresa, and, in the end, he did. It's not worth our tears still today. Teresa has been enormously happy without him."

After recording the album and the fateful meeting at his home, Ricardo fell into a spiral, increasingly isolating himself from the world. He tried to set up a record label in the city to help emerging bands record albums while at the same time releasing *Rock & Lovets,* but his

attempt ended in abject failure. The local kids had no interest in playing with him and didn't need a mentor to guide them anyway. He felt
vilified by the next generation and the alternative scene in the US in
general. In an attack of absurd rebellion, he decided never to speak
English again. He reproached his father for having left Mexico and
settled in the United States. He threatened to go to Cuernavaca to live
with his grandparents and disowned the place where he was born. El
Paso, the city, could only remind him of ELPASO, the band that had
so disappointed him. He'd shelved his idea of heading to Boston or
San Francisco to set something up so that he could develop his project in El Paso, but he felt betrayed by the borderlands. He thought
that maybe he should cross that line and never come back.

Lupe, Teresa, and Felipe began to feel the violence of living with
someone who was self-destructive, depressive, and detached. They
allowed a prudent distance to grow between them and Ricardo. A
space of tension that, if it wasn't penetrated, kept Ritchie's bouts of
rage at bay. Lupe began to communicate with him through the cameras they had at home. They no longer spoke. They didn't laugh.
They didn't have sex. She merely took photographs of and filmed
her partner as he smoked Marlboro after Marlboro in the garage.
Accompanied only by his acoustic guitar. With the dim light of the
bare light bulb hiding the features of his face behind the shadows of
his long, straight hair. The slow, clumsy zoom of the VHS video camera was the only thing that allowed Lupe to get close to Ricardo's lips
and face during those months.

The family was hit hard, but little Teresa was lucky enough to
enjoy the paternal figure that Felipe had become. A grandfather act-
ing as father to the girl and friend to the mother. This man had had
his heart half ripped apart seeing his son crumble like that but had
the strength to double the intensity of the other half and poured all

the love he had left in it into his granddaughter and her mother. The little girl forced him to rise from his weakened state and, despite his physical deterioration, he was able to get through it and stay strong. As he did the day Lupe told him that his son had left. After weeks of threatening to leave, Ricardo packed his suitcase with some clothes and the money from the top drawer of the dresser. He gave no reason. He didn't leave a note explaining why, just his guitar, leaning up against the bed. The sorrow that Felipe felt, living for the first time in that house without his son, turned his hair white in record time. He grew old during the summer of 1992.

It was the summer that Daniel traveled to Barcelona to watch the Dream Team play in the Olympics. Watching Magic reminded him of when he and Ritchie went to Phoenix Suns Arena to watch Magic Johnson play with the Lakers. What he couldn't have imagined then was that at that very moment, on the other side of the Atlantic, his old friend was plummeting into the very depths of hell.

LIST OF CONCERTS

September 19, 1979
Talking Heads + Teenage Popeye
at the Corbett Center Ballroom.
Las Cruces (NM)

November 9, 1979
Ramones + Teenage Popeye at
the Old Buffalo. El Paso (TX)

July 2, 1980
Black Sabbath + Riot at the El
Paso County Coliseum. El Paso
(TX)

March 11, 1983
Victims and Civilians +
Aftermath at the Sancho Bros.
Ballroom. El Paso (TX)

June 24, 1983
No Trend at the Koke House. El
Paso (TX)

May 19, 1984
Big Boys at the On Broadway
Theatre. San Francisco (CA)

July 24, 1984
The Dickies at the Koke House.
El Paso (TX)

August 13, 1984
Dead Kennedys + Rhythm Pigs +
Red Zone + Kor-Phu at the Sancho
Bros. Ballroom. El Paso (TX)

August 20, 1984
Minutemen at the Koke House.
El Paso (TX)

November 12, 1984
Black Flag + Rhythm Pigs at the
Sancho Bros. Ballroom. El Paso
(TX)

November 22, 1985
ELPASO in the art gallery.
Ciudad Juárez (MX)

February 10, 1986
ELPASO at Rob's house.
Denison (TX)

February 12, 1986
Dislexyc Jow Blobs + ELPASO +
Jumpers. Fort Worth (TX)

February 14, 1986
ELPASO at Circle Ranch. Dallas
(TX)

February 15, 1986
Scratch Acid + Killdozer +
ELPASO at Liberty Lunch.
Austin (TX)

February 16, 1986
The Crunchy Golden Nuggets
+ ELPASO at Tacoland. San
Antonio (TX)

February 17, 1986
ELPASO at the Railroad Blues.
Alpine (TX)

May 14, 1986
Meat Puppets + Hernia Briefs +
Moral Crips + Abandon Ship at
Sound Seas. El Paso (TX)

July 27, 1986
Rhythm Pigs + ELPASO at
Sound Seas. El Paso (TX)

November 28, 1986
Bad Brains + Afflicted + D.R.I.
+ Rhythm Pigs at The Farm. San
Francisco (CA)

December 5, 1986
Jane's Addiction + the Miracle
Workers + Doggy Rock at
Scream. Los Angeles (CA)

February 23, 1987
ELPASO + Uglor at Sound Seas.
El Paso (TX)

May 23, 1987
Suicidal Tendencies + Short
Dogs Grow + ELPASO at Sound
Seas. El Paso (TX)

May 31, 1987
Descendents + ELPASO at
Sound Seas. El Paso (TX)

May 17, 1988
MDC + Uglor + Phantasmagoria
at the Mesa Inn. El Paso (TX)

December 26, 1988
ELPASO + Phantasmagoria at
Coronado High School.
El Paso (TX)

February 20, 1989
ELPASO at the Axiom.
Houston (TX)

PHOTOGRAPHIC
RECORD

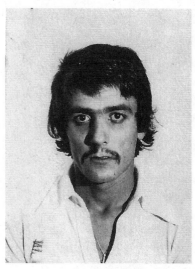

Portrait of Daniel Álvarez

DD reading *Mad* magazine

Self-portrait of Daniel Álvarez

The group's Ford Econoline after the accident.

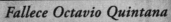

Fallece Octavio Quintana

EL PASO — Un músico juarense falleció la tarde ayer, víctima de un accidente de tráfico en el cruce de la Alameda y Delta en la vecina ciudad de El Paso. La furgoneta Ford Econoline en la que viajaba el joven, impactó con un Aston Martin costándole la vida. Los conductores de ambos vehículos se encuentran hospitalizados y presentan heridas de diversa consideración.

El músico regresaba de Las Cruces donde estaba registrando un disco con el grupo de rock del que formaba parte.

Octavio Quintana

ELPASO promotional photo

ELPASO in front of the AIDS mural. Promotional photo

Photo in the Caverns of Sonora made by
Lupe

Felipe Salazar. Ricardo's father

ELPASO
THE AXIOM, HOUSTON (TX)
PHOTO: DALVARES

Ricardo in concert at the Axiom (Houston)

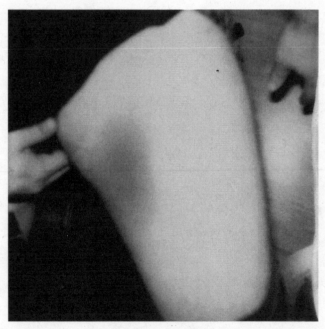

Hematoma on Will's leg

Octavio in concert at the Axiom (Houston)

ELPASO in front of the SEGUNDO BARRIO mural. Promotional photo

ELPASO✪
THE AXIOM, HOUSTON (TX)
PHOTO: DALVARES

Ricardo in concert at the Axiom (Houston)

Teenage Popeye – The Hollow Men

Mike Nosenzo

The Victims – One Second Zero

Clutch Cardon (One Second Zero), Robb Rebb (Red Zone), and
Charlie Wendell

Kathy Smith with her One Second Zero single

Rhythm Pigs – Wisconsin, 1985

George Hurley from Minutemen wearing Daniel's Red Zone T-shirt

Michelle and Billbo in Sound Seas – 1980s

Uglor live at Sound Seas 1986

Uglor

Steve'O'cide and
the Uglor van

Steve'O'cide Flyer

Piggy Bank (Rhythm Pigs and Teenage Popeye crossover – 1989).
GC Adams, Mike Nosenzo, Ed Ivey, Benzuda, John Evans.

Arlo singing in a Stinging Fish show

Twisted Thought – 1988

Foss single cover (Beto O'Rourke and Arlo Klahr)

Mike Nosenzo. Teenage Popeye reunion at Tricky Falls

Benjamin Villegas was born in Spain. He was named after *Fantastic Four*'s the Thing, and grew up in a household full of comics, music, and movies that shaped his taste for American pop culture. He is a musician, illustrator, audiovisual producer, and graphic designer. He is also the author of *Huele como a espíritu posadolescente* (*Smells like Postadolescent Spirit*).

Jay Noden lives in Catalonia, Spain, where he has worked as a translator for the last twenty years. His portfolio encompasses a wide range of subjects including children's and adult literature, books on art and design, scripts for films, documentaries, and TV series, art critiques, and journalistic articles. Aside from *ELPASO*, his translated works notably include *Tiny Creatures* by Dos Ilustrados, *Inspiration Dormant* by Play Attitude, *Process Design* by Alejandro Masferrer, and the *European Institute of the Mediterranean Yearbook*.

PARTNERS

pixel ||| texel

ADDITIONAL DONORS, CONT'D

Mark Haber
Mary Cline
Maynard Thomson
Michael Reklis
Mike Soto
Mokhtar Ramadan
Nikki & Dennis Gibson
Patrick Kukucka
Patrick Kutcher
Rev. Elizabeth & Neil Moseley
Richard Meyer

Scott & Katy Nimmons
Sherry Perry
Sydneyann Binion
Stephen Harding
Stephen Williamson
Susan Carp
Susan Ernst
Theater Jones
Tim Perttula
Tony Thomson

SUBSCRIBERS

Ned Russin
Michael Binkley
Michael Schneiderman
Aviya Kushner
Kenneth McClain
Eugenie Cha
Lance Salins
Stephen Fuller
Joseph Rebella
Brian Matthew Kim
Andreea Pritcher
Anthony Brown
Michael Lighty
Kasia Bartoszynska

Erin Kubatzky
Shelby Vincent
Margaret Terwey
Ben Fountain
Caroline West
Ryan Todd
Gina Rios
Caitlin Jans
Ian Robinson
Elena Rush
Courtney Sheedy
Matthew Eatough
Elif Ağanoğlu

AVAILABLE NOW FROM DEEP VELLUM

MICHÈLE AUDIN · *One Hundred Twenty-One Days*
translated by Christiana Hills · FRANCE

BAE SUAH · *Recitation*
translated by Deborah Smith · SOUTH KOREA

MARIO BELLATIN · *Mrs. Murakami's Garden*
translated by Heather Cleary · MEXICO

EDUARDO BERTI · *The Imagined Land*
translated by Charlotte Coombe · ARGENTINA

CARMEN BOULLOSA · *Texas: The Great Theft* · *Before* · *Heavens on Earth*
translated by Samantha Schnee · Peter Bush · Shelby Vincent · MEXICO

MAGDA CARNECI · *FEM*
translated by Sean Cotter · ROMANIA

LEILA S. CHUDORI · *Home*
translated by John H. McGlynn · INDONESIA

SARAH CLEAVE, ed. · *Banthology: Stories from Banned Nations* ·
IRAN, IRAQ, LIBYA, SOMALIA, SUDAN, SYRIA & YEMEN

ANANDA DEVI · *Eve Out of Her Ruins*
translated by Jeffrey Zuckerman · MAURITIUS

PETER DIMOCK · *Daybook from Sheep Meadow* · USA

ROSS FARRAR · *Ross Sings Cheree & the Animated Dark: Poems* · USA

ALISA GANIEVA · *Bride and Groom* · *The Mountain and the Wall*
translated by Carol Apollonio · RUSSIA

ANNE GARRÉTA · *Sphinx* · *Not One Day*
translated by Emma Ramadan · FRANCE

JÓN GNARR · *The Indian* · *The Pirate* · *The Outlaw*
translated by Lytton Smith · ICELAND

GOETHE · *The Golden Goblet: Selected Poems* · *Faust, Part One*
translated by Zsuzsanna Ozsváth and Frederick Turner · GERMANY

NOEMI JAFFE · *What are the Blind Men Dreaming?*
translated by Julia Sanches & Ellen Elias-Bursac · BRAZIL

CLAUDIA SALAZAR JIMÉNEZ · *Blood of the Dawn*
translated by Elizabeth Bryer · PERU

JUNG YOUNG MOON · *Seven Samurai Swept Away in a River* · *Vaseline Buddha*
translated by Yewon Jung · SOUTH KOREA

KIM YIDEUM · *Blood Sisters*
translated by Ji yoon Lee · SOUTH KOREA

JOSEFINE KLOUGART · *Of Darkness*
translated by Martin Aitken · DENMARK

YANICK LAHENS · *Moonbath*
translated by Emily Gogolak · HAITI

FORTHCOMING FROM DEEP VELLUM

MIRCEA CĂRTĂRESCU · *Solenoid*
translated by Sean Cotter · ROMANIA

MATHILDE CLARK · *Lone Star*
translated by Martin Aitken · DENMARK

LOGEN CURE · *Welcome to Midland: Poems* · USA

CLAUDIA ULLOA DONOSO · *Little Bird*, translated by Lily Meyer · PERU/NORWAY

LEYLÂ ERBIL · *A Strange Woman*
translated by Nermin Menemencioğlu · TURKEY

FERNANDA GARCIA LAU · *Out of the Cage*
translated by Will Vanderhyden · ARGENTINA

ANNE GARRÉTA · *In/concrete*
translated by Emma Ramadan · FRANCE

JUNG YOUNG MOON · *Arriving in a Thick Fog*
translated by Mah Eunji and Jeffrey Karvonen · SOUTH KOREA

FISTON MWANZA MUJILA · *The Villain's Dance*, translated by Roland Glasser · *The River in the Belly: Selected Poems*, translated by Bret Maney · DEMOCRATIC REPUBLIC OF CONGO

LUDMILLA PETRUSHEVSKAYA · *Kidnapped: A Crime Story*, translated by Marian Schwartz · *The New Adventures of Helen: Magical Tales*, translated by Jane Bugaeva · RUSSIA

JULIE POOLE · *Bright Specimen: Poems from the Texas Herbarium* · USA

MANON STEFAN ROS · *The Blue Book of Nebo* · WALES

ETHAN RUTHERFORD · *Farthest South & Other Stories* · USA

BOB TRAMMELL · *The Origins of the Avant-Garde in Dallas & Other Stories* · USA